Dedications

*To my angels: My mother, Andrea L. Randolph, My Grams, Sandra Young-
White, Grandma Lorean, and Grandmother, Thank you all. For surrounding
me and holding me up in times when it seemed like I wouldn't be able to
stand on my own two feet again. Thank you for the love that I continue to feel,
even from heaven. Thank you for the nights you came to me in my dreams and
wrapped your arms around me and held me throughout the night. Thank you
for all of the words of wisdom while you were still with me. I love each one of
you and miss you all terribly. This is for you.*

*To my #1 fan: You are the reason I am the woman that I am. You shaped me,
molded me, nurtured me, loved me and believed in me. You are everything.
You gave me what I otherwise never would have had and words will never be
enough to express what you mean to me. It is because of you that I have been
able to stand tall amidst the wreckage of my life. You taught me how to be a
lady, all class and nothing less. You've loved me even when I was unlovable.
And I know that I'll never be able to repay you for all that you have done for
me but I will strive for the rest of my days to make you proud. I love you with
my whole heart. You are my very best friend. All I can say is that "Having you
there made the difference"*

*To my Children: The two of you have been my sole purpose for living. I wanted
to be able to show you by example that it was possible to watch your dreams
become realities. It hasn't always been easy and I know that there were times
when you both probably thought I was losing my mind but thank you for
putting up with me, with my ranting and my raving. Thank you both for giving me joy, laughter and lots of smiles. You two remain my motivation. If I do
nothing else in the world correctly, I will always be able to say that you two*

were the best things I've ever done. Thank you for the lessons and for making me a better person.

To my Pastor & First Lady: The two of you are part of the reason that I am still here. Outside of God's grace and his mercy, it was your love that lifted me. I will forever remember that it was at my lowest point that God sent the two of you into my life. A million thank you's will never be enough. Please know that I understand that you could have looked at me like so many others have and judged me because of my past, because of my pain, but you chose to see the good in me. Like the song says "You saw the best in me, when everyone else around me could only see the worst in me." Even as I write this, I get emotional because I will never be able to adequately express or explain what your presence, your love and your guidance in my life has meant and continues to mean to me. I know that you still see something in me that I've only just begun to see in myself. Thank you for recognizing the halo, even though it's been tilted. I love you!

To Dana: Ahhh, what do I say to the person that knows me almost as well as I know myself? You know how sometimes, you meet that one person and you can't even remember when you met or when you became friends? That's us. It seems like you've always been here. Thank you for knowing me well enough to know when things aren't right. Thank you for knowing me well enough to see that even though, I wear a smile and joke around, that sometimes things are just not right. Thank you for paying enough attention to me that you can read me like a well-worn dog eared book. Thank you for being my ear, my shoulder, my sister. Our sisterhood and friendship will always mean the world to me. I appreciate you in ways that words can't begin to describe. Thank you for loving me enough to put me in my place and tell me when I'm wrong. Most people wouldn't do that. It just goes to show how close we really are. You are the best big sister a girl could have.

To Robyn: Six long and sometimes frustrating years. What can I say? You've been my best friend and at the same time my worst enemy, but we're still here.

You've played a part in this dream becoming reality that no one else played and for that I say Thank you. Thank you for putting up with me, with my attitude and my disappearances. Thank you for understanding that sometimes, I defy logic in ways that other's just wouldn't understand. Thank you for the days full of tears that sometimes dragged into night and into the next day. Thank you for the long nights, the edits, the chats, the text... Simply put, Thank you for being a friend. They say that it's in the hardest times that you find out who really has your back and we've had some pretty hard times. You will always have a special place in my heart. I love you.

GENESIS

I sat down on the edge of the bed. My legs felt as if they were going to give out on me at any minute. I looked around the room; nothing looked familiar. I closed my eyes, and inhaled a very deep breath, so deep my chest hurt. I wanted this to be a dream. I was trying to wake myself up. When I opened my eyes, he was still standing there, in the same spot between the closet and the bathroom doors.

I felt sick. I ran into the bathroom just in time to release my lunch back into the toilet. I flushed, brushed my teeth, and washed my face with cold water. But I didn't speak. I just stood there waiting for him to say something. Anything. I'd asked him a question. He had yet to answer.

I spoke again first. "I said, I need to be tested for what?" There it was. The anger that I'd been looking for instead of the explosive pain that was my first reaction to his announcement. One of his lovers had been diagnosed with HIV six months ago and he had just found out. Not only was he sleeping around on me, he was doing it unprotected. *Bastard*.

"Answer me Kenyon. Now."

I was no longer in the mood to play games. This affected my health. It affected more than his selfish behind. I never thought I could feel hatred for the man that I'd pledged my love, my life, my all . And then I remembered. I looked at the calendar that I kept on my nightstand. I'd circled today's date, actually put a heart around it. It was our fifth wedding anniversary. Some gift. This was what he chose to do on the day we'd made vows to one another. Tell me not only was he being unfaithful, and not only did he want a divorce, but that it was possible he'd contracted and given me HIV. I wasn't a praying woman, but before it was all over, God would be the only one I could lean on.

I walked away from him then spun on my heels facing him. "You still haven't answered me. You were man enough to cheat on me, not with one female but with two. You were man enough to tell me that you want a divorce but you can't tell me which one of your mistresses could have killed us both? I hate you!"

"Oh and Happy Anniversary Kenyon," I reached into the armoire where I'd kept the gift hidden for the past month and threw the box at him.. I'd made it to the bottom of the stairs and was getting ready to enter my charcoal gray and black living room when he grabbed my elbow. I looked at him with such contempt that he immediately released me.

"Can we just sit down and talk about this like two adults. Genesis, please. I never meant to hurt you. Really." He wanted to sit down and talk about this?. Okay. I sat down on the couch.

"I'm listening,". He walked around to the love seat that was facing the sofa and sat down.

"Addison isn't a woman." He looked at me to gauge my reaction. I gave him none. Inside I was trembling. Had he just told me that one of his lovers was a man? *God is this really happening to me?*

"What do you mean, Addison isn't a woman? If she isn't a woman, that means she's a he and he's a man and you're, oh God, are you telling me, I know you're not telling me that you're, are you? Oh my God, how could you do this to me?"

The tears were back. I didn't like this emotional roller coaster that I was on. I was always in control of my emotions. Always. Right now, I wasn't in control of anything. *My husband is gay*. I jumped up and looked around. I ran to the front door and snatched it open. There was no one there. I ran to the back of the house. Still no one was there.

I was looking for cameras. This had to be an episode of candid camera or that new show everyone watched with Ashton What's-his-face. Punked? Yes, clearly, someone was punking me.

"Genesis, what are you doing?"

"Shut up! Just shut up! Why are you doing this to me? What did I ever do for you to do this to me?"

Today was supposed to be a good day. Not the day my whole life got turned upside down. I collapsed onto the couch and just stared at him. So far he hadn't said much. Other than to admit that he was a bisexual married man who was having an affair with a man named Addison and some other woman.

"So, he's the one who could have given us the disease? How long have you known?"

He didn't say anything, just sat there like I wasn't talking to him. He chose now to be silent. For the longest time, he just sat there with this silly look on his face. You know the kind of look you get from a child who is trying to think of what to say to stay out of trouble instead of just telling the truth? It was that same look.

"I know you hear me talking to you," I said through clenched teeth.

I walked over to him and slapped him as hard as I could. "Say something. You don't get to come in here and disrupt my life and then sit there looking stupid. Not today. I deserve more than this, so say something."

"Why did you hit me?"

He wasn't serious. He couldn't possibly be serious. Not after the things he'd just told me. I slapped him again and again. He grabbed my wrist and held them.

"Stop hitting me, Genesis."

"Let me go, Kenyon." I was afraid. He had this crazed look in his eyes, like he wanted to hurt me. When he let me go, I picked up the phone and started to dial 9-1-1. He took the phone out of my hand and clicked it off. Now he wanted to explain.

"I'm not sure what you want me to say. I'm in love with him. He makes me feel. I can't explain it. He gives me something that I've never gotten with you." He was right about that. I didn't have a, well you know I wasn't a man so yes, he was right about that.

"Ya think? He gives you something that I can't because I don't have a penis. Fool."

"Genesis, it's not about the sex. Although-" I stopped him with a look. He knew better than to go there. "He has AIDS and you're leaving me for him. This is unreal. Have you told your other mistress that you're leaving her too?"

"No, because I don't plan on leaving her. You're the only one I no longer want to be with. They complete me, each in different ways. I love them, him more but I love them both." I felt sick again. I stood up and got really dizzy. He stood up to catch me. I looked down and saw blood. I panicked. .

"Call an ambulance, Kenyon!"

I knew what was happening. He had no idea. I had planned to tell him at dinner tonight that we were expecting our first child. With just a few words, he'd managed to take this away from me too.

KENYON

"She's having a what?"

I knew that I'd misheard the doctor. What he'd just said to me couldn't be possible. What had I done? All I wanted was to tell her that I wanted a divorce. I didn't mean for things to go this far. I hadn't even told her everything yet. She stood up to walk away from me again and she started to sway. I caught her and noticed blood. I thought she had just started her cycle. It was more than that. She'd just lost our child. I wasn't sure how to feel about that. I had no idea that she was pregnant. *How? When?* I tried to think back to the last time she and I were together. I couldn't remember. The doctor said that she was exactly twelve weeks along and that something had put Genesis and the fetus in severe distress. He was right. I was that something.

I felt horrible. I sat down in the chair that was in the corner of her hospital room. She looked so fragile lying in that bed unconscious. I started to rethink this whole thing. I could have done things differently. I hadn't realized today was our anniversary. I was too caught up in my own world to care anything about what was going on with her.

My phone vibrated in my pocket. I took it out to look at it. It was Addison. He was probably calling to see how things went; I told him that I was going to tell her I wanted a divorce today, but I wasn't so sure I'd done the right thing. I was positive before. I clicked the button for ignore and closed the phone.

It vibrated again. It was a text from Justice: "I can't wait until tonight. I miss you. I have a surprise for you. See you soon."

I didn't bother to respond. Just closed the phone and continued to watch my wife.. I knew Genesis well enough to know that since I put it out there, our marriage was over. The only thing that she ever really expected of me was to be faithful. I knew that she was. She loved me. That much I never doubted. She was a good wife. She was educated, brilliant, beautiful, vivacious, and rambunctious, in the beginning.

When her career as a writer took off she became serious. Always traveling, always busy. I should have just told her that I felt neglected. I should have told her that all her time on the road was making me feel like I wasn't important to her. Instead I chose to look for what I was missing in other places. Her celebrity was too much for me. It was like she became a best seller overnight, an instant sensation. I never expected for her books to ever sell. I guess I never believed in her dreams like she believed in mine. When I told her that I wanted to go into marketing, she stood by me. Whatever I needed her to do she did it.

She didn't know that I'd never really been faithful. I mean, we had been together for a long time. We met when we were seniors in high school on a college tour. I bumped into her and knocked all her things out of her hands not paying attention to where I was going. I'd been watching her all that day and wondered if I'd get the chance to actually talk to her. She was a PYT. About 5'7, thicker than a snicker and hazel eyed. She had the prettiest hair I'd seen on a girl, jet black and down her back. After we bumped into each other we spent some time talking before we had to get back to our groups. When we got back home, we spent all of our free time together. Her father didn't like me, but it was her mother that I was most afraid of. Something about that woman let me know she wasn't the one to play with.

The doctor came back in and stopped my stroll down memory lane, looked at her, and then turned to me, and said, "There doesn't appear to be any significant damage to her reproductive organs, so conceiving again shouldn't be an issue for the two of you. We are still running tests to be sure , but if you're a praying man, I'd say a prayer that what we are seeing is all there is. .She has no idea what's happened so if she wakes up, she's going to really need your support." He shook his head and walked out of the room.

She was going to need my support. She'd lost that when she chose her career. . I guess maybe I couldn't handle the fact that I was married to the all-famous Genesis Swan. I should have been proud, but I was jealous. I'd ruined her life and killed our child all because I was selfish and insecure. Then I remembered. I went to find the doctor and told him that she needed to be tested for HIV without giving him complete details about the situation. He guaranteed me that he would order the test to be performed while she was still out. I went out into the waiting room. I couldn't stand to sit there and continue watching her like that knowing I was the reason she was here. I couldn't recall the last time I'd felt guilty about anything that I'd done but I was feeling guilty now. I needed to call her parents, but what would I tell them? I dialed the number I had for her mother. She answered on the first ring

"Genesis darling, is that you?"

"No, Mrs. Maicott. This is Kenyon." I could feel the shift.

"What do you want? Why are *you* calling me?

Her mother wasn't my biggest fan; in fact she had insisted that Genesis not marry me. It was only within the last few years that she and Genesis began speaking again.

"I'm sorry to be the one to call you, but Genesis is in the hospital. She's had a--"

"She's had a what?!? What did you do to my daughter, young man?"

I took a deep breath before I finished. "She's had a miscarriage. She is at Harmony Center on the thirteenth floor, room 1322. It's a private room. Please come as soon as you can." I hung up before she could question me further. I knew that I'd have hell to pay when her mother and her father arrived. Her mother had already made it very clear that if I hurt her daughter she would have someone hurt me and I'd not only broken their daughter's heart, but I'd just caused her to lose their grandchild. I went back into the room to check on Genesis. I wanted to see if she was still asleep. I stuck my head in the door and checked. She wasn't awake but she looked as if she was having a bad dream. I walked into the room and over to the bed and noticed that tears were falling from her eyes. I'd never seen a person cry in their sleep so it freaked me out. I backed out of the room and closed the door. I decided to go outside. I needed some fresh air. I stepped outside and as soon as I did, my phone vibrated again. It was Addison, but this time I answered.

"Hello." I said nothing more. I really wasn't in the mood to talk to him. Today went totally wrong. It wasn't supposed to be tragic, but that's exactly what it was.

"How did things go?' he asked.

I knew that's what he was calling to find out. I slipped out of his bed a little more than sixteen hours ago and told him that I'd call him as soon as things were done. I hadn't called so he should have assumed that things weren't done. I'm a man of my word.

"They didn't go as expected. I'm at the hospital. She."

He cut me off. I was getting tired of being cut off today. I was ready to smash something.

"She did what?" he asked, full of attitude. If anyone had the right to be angry right now, it wasn't him. Another deep breath.

"She's had a miscarriage." He was silent for a minute. I was lost in a million thoughts.

"Well good. That makes things simple, doesn't it? At least now when you leave there won't be any children to keep you attached to her."

I pulled the phone away from my ear and stared at it. I knew that he hadn't just said what I thought he said. *How in the hell?*

"That was my child too, Addison." I said to him, putting emphasis on the word my. "I'm not happy about this; it puts things into a new light. Maybe I'd acted rashly. Perhaps I don't want the divorce after all. My wife is laid up in a hospital bed, unconscious, because I told her that I was sleeping with you, that I wanted a divorce, and that you have HIV. I informed her that she needed to be tested. It didn't go over well. I was tripping to think that it would. I should have rethought it before going in there with that kind of announcement. I didn't know. I didn't know. Today is our anniversary. I'd been so caught up in you that I'd selfishly chosen to tell my wife all of this devastating news on the day that I'd pledged to love and honor her."

I thought back to my wedding day. She was the most beautiful bride I'd ever seen, my only bride. We had both just turned twenty-five She was a recent college graduate, and I'd made it out of college in three years, so I'd graduated a year before she had. She was still a virgin. Can you believe that? We got married in 2005 and she was still a virgin; it was unheard of. She had done it. Managed to be beautiful and intelligent and still remain pure. Her parents raised her right. The Bishop and Lady Maicott.

That was part of the reason they hated me, because I wasn't into the church. I wasn't even sure I believed that God existed and it was no secret. Genesis had stopped attending church after she met me. Her father said that if I really loved her I'd convince her that walking away from God was the wrong thing to do. How could I do that though? God had never done anything for me. They had no idea the kind of life I'd lived. I'd only gone to college because I refused to be like my father or my brother. I didn't want to be a product of the streets so I worked my way out of the hood. I didn't have a relationship with anyone in my family. Once I finished high school and moved away, I put them out of my mind. I'd told Genesis that my family died in a fire. No one knew that they were very much alive and I would keep it that way. So when her father asked me to convince his daughter not to turn her back on God, I told him that I couldn't do that because as far as I was concerned God had turned his back on me.

She took my breath away when she walked down the aisle of the

Christ Is Life COGIC. Complete with the white dress, she was an angel. Literally, it seemed as if she were floating toward me.. She glowed. She was about to be mine. Love and Honor. I'd done nothing but mistreat and disrespect her. I felt regret begin to take root.

"So what you're telling me is that you regret telling her you were leaving her for me? Are you fu--?" This time it was me who cut him off.

"I wish you would. Say it and this conversation is over." I knew that I was wrong, but I hated for him to use profanity, even when he was angry. And I felt he had no right to be.

"I'm sorry Ken, really, but are you seriously telling me that you're having second thoughts about leaving her." I knew that now, it was too late for second thoughts. My marriage was over. There would be no more Mr. & Mrs. Swan. I wondered if she would keep my name or go back to hers.

"Yes, that's what I'm telling you. I regret doing this the way I did it. Do I regret doing it at all? I'm still not sure about that. However I know her well enough to know that she will never stay married to me after this so if you're wondering will I be a free man, the answer to the question is yes. I will still be getting a divorce." Unless God saw fit to bless me in a way I didn't deserve by touching her heart. I didn't say that to Addison. I didn't need any more drama.

"Well good. I didn't work this hard to lose you at the eleventh hour. Not without a fight." That sounded like a threat. I chose to leave it alone.

"Addison, I'll call you back later. I've got to go."

I heard him sigh. "I know you're not planning on staying there with her. You just told her it was over."

Did he not realize that I'd, that we had just lost a child? Albeit, one that never made it to see the light of day, but a child nonetheless. He was part of the reason my child was gone. I was starting to get angry at his heartlessness. "I said I'd call you back Addison. Goodbye." I closed my phone and sat down on the bench in the hospital's garden. I put my head between my hands as I began to do something I don't think I'd ever really done. I prayed. I didn't think God was listening but I needed something that would take the pain away.

When I first met Genesis, her relationship with God was solid. Unshakeable. As she fell in love with me, that relationship began to take a backseat. Now I wondered if I should have been proud of leading her to the dark side.. I sat here thinking about everything that had happened. I thought that telling her I was leaving would make me happy. I should have felt free, but instead I felt like cement blocks had been attached to my feet, heavy. Maybe I hadn't really given this enough thought. I mean, I thought that being unhappy was good enough reason to cheat, good enough reason to leave, but could I have been wrong? Yes I felt neglected but I traveled almost as much as she did. I wondered if she'd ever felt like I'd neglected her. If she had, she didn't make it known. I was beginning to see that tragedy had a way of sneaking up on you and making you rethink things that you should have already thought about. I was mad at myself. I wished that there was some trick I could perfom that would give me the chance to go back and right my wrongs but there wasn't. I'd have to deal with the fallout. I had no idea at the time just how bad things would get.

AURELIA

I knew that before it was all said and done, he was going to hurt my daughter. I tried with everything that I was to keep her from marrying that boy. Something about him had never sat right with my spirit. I still don't know what that was, but before it was all said and done, I was going to find out. I called my husband at the church and told him that he needed to come home right away. Our daughter needed us. We were scheduled to leave that morning, but God had a way of working things out. There was a change in the revival plans and we were now leaving the following Friday. That was my God. Oh how I loved Him. After I hung up the phone with Kenyon, immediately I fell to my knees and asked God to look out for and dispatch His angels to my daughter's bedside. I asked Him to protect her heart and her mind but most of all, I asked Him to protect her health, and to allow her, even after this loss to be able to have children just as He'd done me. Even if it was just one child as He'd given me. I was thankful for my miracle. Genesis deserved to have one of her own. I sat on the edge of the sofa waiting for my husband to arrive so that I could go see about my little girl. Yes, I realized that she was now a 29-year-old woman, but to me, Genesis Sophia Maicott Swan would always be my little girl. You see, Genesis would have been my third child. However, for some reason, each time I became pregnant in my fourth month, my body would spontaneously rid itself of my children. It killed me inside to think that I'd never be able to have children, especially since I wasn't exactly a "young" woman anymore. Thank God I was married to a praying man, who believed that if God could do it for Sarah and Abraham, He could do it for us. I was skeptical, but I trusted my husband's prayers, and so I prayed with him, that just as God had saw fit to bless Sarah with a child in her old age, He'd see fit to bestow upon me that same blessing. Five years after the second miscarriage, at age 35, I discovered I was pregnant again. As soon as I got the results of the test, my heart sank. I knew that I couldn't survive another loss. I prayed with all that I was that God please allow my child to live and for the rest of my days I'd serve Him in any way He told me to. I meant that. God told me that He would.

I'll never forget the day. It was a Sunday morning and I was preparing to go to church, I'd heard someone call my name, thinking it was my husband. I called down the stairs to him, "Yes Judah?"

"I didn't call you 'Relia," Judah had said.

I'd heard it again, but this time it sounded closer and I knew that this wasn't my husbands' voice. No one else was in the house but the two of us; I knew that it had to be the Lord. "Yes Lord. Here I am," I said skeptically. I felt silly speaking to the Lord, like I'd just really audibly heard the Lord call my name.

"I will grant your request." I was confused.

"My, my req…Request?" I was not at exactly twelve weeks and was very fearful that within the next few weeks I'd be back in the hospital suffering another loss. But I felt the presence of God so strongly in that room at that very moment that I knew everything would be alright. I sat down in the chair that was next to the window and the tears just flowed. I thanked God in earnest. With all that I was, I thanked Him. It was then that I'd made that promise to God that I would live for Him until He called me home. I'd done that. Now I feared that maybe, I was going to lose the only child I had. I stood up and walked over to the window to see if my husband was pulling around our circular drive. He wasn't. What was taking him so long? I loved Judah Maicott but I swear that man could be slow as molasses. Didn't he realize that this was an emergency? Knowing my husband, he'd stopped to pray before leaving the church. That was his motto: Pray now, never worry, trust God. He would make it alright. Send the Lord before you and everything will be fine. So far, he'd been right. Whenever I left somewhere in an emergency and I failed to pray things seemed to be hectic and out of control when I arrived, but every single time I sent the Lord before me, there was a calm, even in the most tragic situations. This time, I'd sent the Lord before me. Why was I worried? My baby would be fine. Her husband may not be so lucky. Finally, I heard the horn. We had a little over a two-hour drive ahead of us. I grabbed our bags that I'd packed and rushed out to the car making sure that the doors were locked and secured before leaving. I got into the car and grabbed my husband's hand. Just his touch was reassuring. Yes. Genesis would be just fine. "Hurry up, Judah. My baby needs me." I couldn't help it. I was still a mother. I was still *her* mother.

JUDAH

When Aurelia called me to tell me that my baby girl was in the hospital, my mind went into fifty different directions. I wondered what was wrong. It was a good thing I was already seated behind my large mahogany desk in the comfortable wingback leather chair that I'd recently purchased for my office; otherwise, I would have passed out. I felt my knees go weak although I was already sitting down. I felt the tension begin to form at my temples. Then I stopped myself. I knew better than to allow worry to creep in. I went into the sanctuary and knelt at the altar. This was praying time. I was a man of faith and a strong belief that as long as you sent God before you in a situation, he would turn things around.

"Lord, my baby girl is in need. I don't know all the details at the moment but Lord, you know. Please dispatch angels to her bedside right now, Father. I ask that you keep her cradled in your loving arms, God. I know that she's strayed away from you Lord, but please don't take her without giving her the opportunity to make things right with you. I know that she loves you, Lord. You know her heart. I feel in my spirit that right now, she's broken, God. Please just protect my baby, Lord. I trust you to keep your word to me and to Aurelia. Even if you see fit to answer this prayer in a way that I am not expecting, God, I thank you in advance for the victory. I love and praise your name. In the mighty name of Jesus. Amen" I rose from my knees, poured a small amount of blessed oil into the bottle that I carried with me at all times, and notified my secretary that I had an emergency and would be leaving unsure of when I would return. I saved the file that I was work-ing on when Aurelia called, shut down my pc, turned off the lights and closed the door to my office. I walked the long distance from the door to my car, which I'd parked in the shade. Today was one of the hotter days, but I liked to park father away from the door so that I could get some form of exercise on a daily basis. It worked out pretty well usu-ally. I reached the car and placed my briefcase into the trunk. I could imagine that by now my wife was looking out the window wondering what had taken me so long. Forty-five minutes had passed since she'd called to tell me that we needed to leave right away. I knew she'd have a fit once I arrived at the house. To my surprise, I was wrong. Instead, whenshe got in the car, she squeezed my hand. That gesture alone let me know just how worried my wife was. One of the things I'd loved about Aurelia from the moment we'd met was her quiet strength. I re-alized that this had to be hard for her. She'd said that Kenyon had told her that Genesis had just suffered a miscarriage. I could only imagine what Aurelia was thinking. We suffered two miscarriages before God decided to bless us with Genesis. That was something that we rarely discussed after Genesis was born. We were blessed. The doctors had told us that we should all but adopt if we ever wanted to be parents. Instead, we chose to trust God and He'd proved himself faithful then. I had no doubt that He would prove himself faithful now. I squeezed my wife's hand back. "I love you, Aurelia Mae Maicott." I knew that she hated for me to use her middle name. She often referred to it as backwoods and country as if that's not where the both of us had come from. We were born in Okolona, Arkansas, a place most people never even knew existed. Yes, we were indeed backwoods and country. But it wasn't obvious by speaking with either of us. We both decided at early ages that as soon as we were old enough, we were leaving the backwoods. We both longed for sophistication and worked hard for it. We'd come a long way from the poor kids that we were. I remember walking up the dirt road on the way to school the first time I laid eyes on her. She had these long sandy-brown ponytails that swung in the wind. I couldn't look at her without blushing. I knew at the age of eleven-years-old that she would be my wife.

"Judah, I know you love me, and I love you too, but if you call me Mae one more time, I'm going to pop you a good one."

It was good that we could laugh now. I knew that it was just to keep each of us from drifting off into our own thoughts about what had caused our only child to lose her first child. We didn't even know that she was expecting. We'd soon find out that no one but Genesis had known.

GENESIS

I thought I was dreaming. My parents were in the room when I woke up. I tried to sit up but couldn't move. Everything hurt. I wasn't sure where I was. "Where am I? What happened?" I looked from my father to my mother, and then to my husband. Everyone had looks of pity on their faces, but no one spoke. I tried to get out of bed, but my mother advised me not to move. I could tell by the tone in her voice that something was seriously wrong. "Mama? Why are you here? Someone please tell me what happened?" I was getting scared. I didn't recall coming to the hospital. Kenyon had tears in his eyes. He never showed any emotion. Now I was really scared. "Daddy, tell me why I'm here." It wasn't a question. It was a statement. A request. He looked at me lovingly, took my hand and told me that everything was going to be alright. That wasn't an answer but it was more than I'd gotten from my mother or my husband. "Can one of you please get the doctor since no one wants to tell me what's going on? Why am I here?" Everyone just stood there. I was beginning to get upset. I felt the tears well in my eyes. I hated to not be in control. I took three deep breaths to try to calm myself. It wasn't working. "Kenyon, why am I here?" I looked at him. He looked at the floor.

"I'm sorry. I'm so sorry" he said.

Nothing more. What was he sorry for? "You're sorry? What did you do to me? Did you hit me or something? I don't remember. I have no idea why I'm lying in this bed and you're all standing here looking at me like I'm some poor, pathetic invalid. What is going on? Someone please tell me something. Don't I deserve to know what's happened to me? I'm the one laying in this bed."

The tears were streaming full force now, I didn't reach up to wipe them away. I looked at my mother and she was crying too. She wouldn't look me in the eyes. "Mama, look at me, please." I knew that the pleading tone in my voice would crack her; she was always a sucker for it. I was her only child, their miracle child.

"Genesis, baby, just rest," she said.

How was I supposed to do that? Really? "How am I supposed to rest and I don't know what's going on? I don't even know what day it is. Today is Thursday, right?"

"No, baby. Today is Monday." That was Daddy.

"Monday? What do you mean it's Monday? No, today is Thursday." I lay back on the pillows. Something was definitely wrong. I had no recollection of things. The last thing I remembered it was Thursday. "Monday? Daddy, are you sure? How long have I been here?" They all looked at each other.

My father looked at Kenyon and said, "Son, I think you'd better talk to her. You caused this; you should be man enough to tell her what's going on." He leaned forward and kissed me on the forehead. To my mother he said, "Aurelia let's get something to eat so that he can tell her what's going on."

My mother looked at Kenyon and started to protest. My father held up his hand to let her know that it would be wasted on him. She was leaving. He had spoken. She kissed me and assured me that she would be back. She looked at Kenyon and said, "You have no more than forty-five minutes to tell her what you've done. When I return, I want you to leave." He didn't speak, just watched them leave the room. He came over to the right side of the bed and tried to take my hand.

"Don't touch me. Just talk. Tell me why my parents are here. What did you do to me?" He looked at me, walked over to the window, looked out, blew a deep breath and turned back to me. "Do you remember anything?"

If I'd remembered would I be sitting here crying because I had no idea why I was lying in a hospital bed, in the most excruciating pain I'd ever felt before in my life.

"No, what should I remember? Stop beating around the bush and just tell me what's going on." I had a thought but I shook it off. I knew that what I was thinking was far-fetched, must have been a dream or something. We were happy. I was expecting a baby. Things were good.

"I… I… Genesis, on Thursday I told you that I…" He blew another deep breath. He came back over to the bed, but didn't get close enough to touch me.

"You told me what on Thursday?" I was running out of patience. He looked up to the sky and said, "God please help me." God? This man wasn't a praying man. When had he ever met God? I braced myself. I knew this had to be bad. Was I sick? Was something wrong with the baby? Oh God, the baby, he didn't know. But, if I'd been here since Thursday I'm sure that by now they'd figured things out. "The baby, Kenyon? Is the baby alright?" It felt like something tightened around my heart when I said the words. He looked away. When he looked back he was crying. "What happened? What happened?" I was yelling now. The nurse came into the room.

"Is everything okay in here?" She asked. I was shaking so hard I couldn't respond. I just needed him to tell me that my baby was okay.

With tears I asked, "Is my baby okay" The nurse looked at me, then at my husband.

"She doesn't know," he said to the nurse.

"I'm so sorry to be the one to tell you this Mrs. Swan but you suffered a miscarriage on Thursday. We tried all that we could to save the fetus, but there was nothing more that could be done. You were under a severe amount of stress; you've been unconscious since you got here."

I couldn't speak. There it was again, that feeling. I couldn't quite explain it. I laid there unsure of what to say. I couldn't look at my husband, but I asked the nurse if she would please leave us alone. "My baby? You did this to me, to us?"

"I didn't know. I had no idea that you were, that we were going to have a baby. I didn't intend to cause you to lose the baby, Genesis. Really." He reached out to touch me and I snatched my hand back. I felt like I'd been burned.

"I. Want. You. To. Get. Out," I said so calmly that I scared myself. I was still crying but I was calm.

"Please just let me explain." He was pathetic. Now he wanted to explain. My parents came back into the room. My father looked at me.

"Did he tell you?" I looked at Kenyon.

"No. He didn't. The nurse told me. I still don't understand what caused this. I still have no idea exactly what he did." My father walked over to Kenyon and stood in his face. It took a lot to anger my father. He was both slow to speak and slow to anger.

"Did I not tell you that you needed to tell her before we got back here son?" Kenyon looked up at my father. He was a big man, intimidating. My father stood 6'6, about 300 lbs., solid, salt and pepper gray hair, mocha brown skin, gray eyes. He was a very handsome man.

"Yes. Yes, sir, you did." Kenyon sounded small standing there with my father in his face. Kenyon, in comparison with my father, was small. He only stood 5'11 and weighed about 185 lbs. He was a thin man. My father could easily take him out and he knew it.

"Then why haven't you told her what you said to her to cause all of this. This is your fault. You will not shirk giving her an explanation. I suggest you begin speaking and don't stop until you have reached the end." I noticed that Kenyon had stepped back a few steps. Yes, my father was scaring the hell out of him. Good.

"I... Thursday I'd come home to tell you that I wanted a divorce. Not only that, but that you needed to be tested for HIV, and that I was having an affair with not one but two people. One of which is a man named Addison. You were walking away from me when you began to sway like you were going to pass out. I caught you and noticed that you were bleeding. The last thing you said to me was to call an ambulance."

I was holding my mother's hand. It hadn't been a dream after all. It was all true. I felt the pain all over again. And the nausea. There it was. Now I remembered bits and pieces.

"Now, you can leave." My father said to Kenyon while holding the door open for him to go. "I suggest you think twice about coming back here while she's in this hospital. I will call you when she is released so that you can have your things removed from her home by the time she gets there." He had officially been dismissed. He knew better than to say another word. He just walked out the room.

He turned around once he'd reached the hall, "Genesis, I really am sorry. I love you." My father closed the door in his face.

KENYON

I had been dismissed. I wasn't fool enough to go against her father. That man was huge. He'd basically told me that since I'd hurt his daughter, he would spare me because he was a man of God, but that I needed to get my things and vacate the premises. That was our house. Who did he think he was to put me out of it? I called Addison on my way to the house. I hadn't spoken with him since Friday. I knew that he was mad, and I knew that if I couldn't stay with him, I could stay with Justice. Oh sh… Justice. I'd forgotten all about her. I laid my head on the steering wheel. Addison didn't answer. He was still upset.

I called Justice. She answered on the second ring. "Where have you been?" She wasted no time on pleasantries.

"I had something I had to take care of." That was all she needed to know. She wasn't aware that I'd planned on leaving Genesis and she knew nothing of Addison. "I was called out of town on an emergency. My sister is very sick. They didn't think she was going to make it at first, but thankfully, she's going to pull through. I'm sorry that I'm just now getting back to you."

"Oh, I had no idea. I'm so sorry to hear that. I guess you had to handle that. So how are you? We need to talk. When are you coming to see me?" That's just what I needed her to say.

"Well that's what I was calling for. I've just gotten back in town and was hoping to spend a few days with you. You know I miss you girl."

She laughed. "I miss you too. You can come straight here from the airport if you'd like. I'll make you dinner and we can catch up."

I wondered what was so important that she wanted to talk to me about. "Okay. I have a few stops to make and then I'll see you, let's say around 7:45 or so."

"Okay that's fine. I love you."

I hadn't spoken those words to Justice yet. I didn't see any reason too. "Me too. See you in a while."

I clicked off before she could continue. I started to call Addison again but thought better of it. I didn't feel like his drama. I loved him, but I still couldn't believe how selfish he'd been. I had no idea that he was that way. I'd lost my child and granted it was a child that I'd never laid eyes on or touched, but it was still mine. I was hurting. He should have been there for me. Instead, he just wanted me to abandon Genesis. Leave her at the hospital to be with him. Especially after Bishop and Lady Maicott arrived. That had been hell. I didn't expect to have to tell the Bishop what had caused it, but as I said I knew better than to go against him like that. I wasn't crazy. So when he walked in to the room and asked me what happened, one look at his face told me not even to try to tell him any lies. I knew that this man could read people. That was the main reason he didn't care for me because he could see things about me that weren't obvious to the eye. I was aware that he wasn't looking at me through his natural eyes, but, like everything else, he was reading my spirit. So I told him. Against my better judgment, of course. He looked like he wanted to hurt me. I knew that because of who he was that he wouldn't. Aurelia Maicott, however, was another story altogether. She just may have someone take me out when it came to her child. She loved Genesis with all that she was. This I'd known since the first time I'd met them and it was her, and not Mr. Maicott, that told me in no uncertain terms, "If you hurt my child, I won't hesitate to have you disposed of." It wasn't the threat that bothered me; it was the look in her eyes and the tone in her voice that let me know that this woman, all 5'2, 125 lbs. of her meant just what she'd said. Thursday when they had arrived was no different.

She gave me that same bone-chilling look after I'd recounted the argument, not leaving out any details.

Mr. Maicott said, "So I've been correct about you all these years. Son, I told you what's done in the dark will always come to the light. The truth will always make its way to the surface no matter how much you try to deny it or hide it. Now you've put my child in danger because of your lies and your selfishness." I didn't respond. Mrs. Maicott just looked at me, and if looks could kill. That's why I knew that it would be best for me to just get my things and not stay in the house because there they knew where I was and they could easily have someone come and find me. I was afraid for my life. I walked into the house, pressed four buttons on the alarm panel, and closed the front door behind me. It felt surreal to be back in this house. I hadn't been here since Thursday. I walked up the stairs to our bedroom and took a suitcase out of my closet. I started placing my items in the suitcase, things I thought I'd need right away. Business suits, toothpaste, toothbrush, that kind of thing when I came across the box that Genesis had thrown at me before she'd walked out the room. I picked the box up, sat down on the edge of our bed, and removed the top. It was the pocket watch I'd been admiring the last time she and I were shopping together. I loved this watch but it was $1700 and I wasn't going to pay that for it.

I took the watch out of the box and flipped it open. On the inside it read: For the man I've promised to spend the rest of my life with, love in spite of his flaws & imperfections, the father of our child, Happy 5th Anniversary. I love you with all that I am.

I just stared at it. This was her way of telling me that she was pregnant. The weight of the situation began to set in and I realized that I'd made a very big mistake. It was too late to go back now. Time couldn't be rewound. Words couldn't be unspoken.

ADDISON

So he thought he was going to just tell me that he thought he made a mistake? I don't think so. Addison Limón is not someone whose feelings you can just play with. If you tell me that you're going to be with me, then you're going to be with me, or you're going to pay. I loved this man. I hadn't planned it that way. I never planned to fall in love with a married man. It just happened. We met on business. He was the marketing director for a PR firm that I'd hired to do some promoting for me. One look at him and I knew that I had to have that man. He was F-I-N-E- FINE! This man, paper bag brown, 5'11, about 185 lbs., locs down his back, pulled into a ponytail, hazel brown eyes, manicured nails. And a wedding ring.

You would have thought seeing that would have halted me in my tracks but it didn't. I was determined to see if Mr. Man was switch-hitting. He didn't come across as one of us, but as soon as I made eye contact, I winked at him. He smiled. One dimple. Left side. Dang this man was FINE! I had to figure out a plan to get him alone so I could ask him to dinner.

It was a brilliant plan. Marketing director. He needed to meet with me. I could tell him that the only time I had available was in the evening. There was no way that he could turn me down. I walked over to the desk where the secretary was seated and asked her what his name was. She told me it was Kenyon Swan. I liked the sound of that. She was flirting. I wasn't interested. Poor thing. She was trying really hard to get my attention but someone else had beaten her to the punch.

"Mr. Swan." I called out to him. "A word when you have a chance please." He looked surprised that I was addressing him.

"Uh, excuse me for just a moment," I heard him say to the woman he was talking to. "Yes, sir. How can I be of assistance?" Professional. I liked that. A lot.

"I need to schedule a meeting with you. I know that you're busy working around here during the day, what with your many projects and things. So let's make it a dinner. Next Friday. 7:30. Be there. I will have my secretary give you all the details."

I walked off leaving him with a dumbfounded look on his face. I knew that he'd show. He knew how much money was at stake. He was a smart man, I could tell. If there was anything I found sexy, it was intelligence and a tight butt and this man had both. My goodness. I'd like to shake hands with his mama and tell her thank you for giving birth to that paper bag brown beauty.

I'd just gotten in the car and started it when my cell vibrated. It was Jeremiah. He obviously didn't get that we were over. I was moving on. And if luck was a lady, then it would be with Kenyon Swan. I pulled my midnight blue Lexus sedan out of the space it had been parked in, turned up my Kenny G and sped off with the windows down and the breeze blowing my thoughts down the high way.

This was the way our romance began.

JUSTICE

I was cleaning and waiting for Kenyon to show up. He should have been here hours ago. I called again but this time I didn't get any answer. I wondered what was keeping him. I decided to cook dinner while I waited. I figured he'd be hungry. Plus, I thought maybe feeding him would make giving him the news easier. I was sure that he was going to try to kill me when he found out but I wasn't really afraid. It would be no one's fault but my own if it came to that. I lied to him from the beginning. My mama always said that, sooner or later, every lie you tell catches up with you and you reap what you sow. She sounded so sure. Poor Mama. Rest her soul. I missed her some days. Other days I was glad that she'd finally closed her eyes and went home to be with the Lord. It left me free to live my life the way I wanted to live it without always having to hear Mama talking about Jesus, repenting, salvation. You know all that Christian stuff. My mama was the epitome of SAVED. I swear, I never heard her cuss, gossip, lie, steal, nothing. Everyone who knew her had something nice and sweet to say about her and I believed that they all meant the things they said. Anyway, Mama was gone now and if she had been alive to see the mess that I'd made of my life. Well I think it probably would have been enough to kill her.

It was dark. It had been almost 3:00 in the afternoon when we had talked. I walked to the window and glanced out. I saw headlights coming down the street and then they pulled into the driveway. He was here. He had a key and would let himself in. I ran into the bathroom to make sure that I still looked good and to add a bit more body oil to those hot spots. You know, wrist, cleavage, behind the ear. What did they call them… err… erro…erogenous zones or something like that. Yeah, that was it, erogenous zones.

I heard the front door open. Footsteps in the foyer. Still no sound of his voice. He was tired. I could feel it. I wondered if I should let him rest before telling him what I needed to tell him. Would it be best to wait? That had now become the question. Once I saw him, I knew that waiting would be my best bet. I'd feed him, sex him, and then we'd talk tomorrow. He'd be here a while. It could wait for a while longer. I walked out of the bathroom and into the living room where he was seated on the couch.

"Is everything okay? You look stressed."

He looked up like he'd been lost in his thoughts. I wondered where his mind was. It certainly wasn't in this room with me. That was one of the things I hated about this relationship. Even when I had his attention, I didn't have his attention. He always seemed to be in another location mentally. I wanted all of him. He had all of me. Was that too much to ask for in return? It seemed so. I sighed deeply and walked into the kitchen when it became painfully obvious that he wasn't going to answer me.

"I made dinner. Are you hungry?" I said while making his plate of shrimp linguini alfredo, his favorite. I wanted him to be happy. He should have been here hours ago. I wondered what he had been doing all this time. Had he been with his wife? I looked toward the foyer. A suitcase. He hadn't been home. I walked out of the kitchen and handed him the plate.

"Thank you," was all he'd said to me. I wondered if his thoughts were still on his sister

"Have you talked to anyone about your sister since you've been back? Is that why you seem so distant?" Still no answer. I stood in front of him and he sat there looking, as if he could see through me. I knew then that tonight wasn't the right time for the conversation that we needed to have. I leaned in, kissed his forehead and went into the bathroom. I closed the door and I cried.

When my tears dried, I told him I was going to bed. Still nothing. I slammed the door, climbed up in my king size bed, and fell asleep. I wanted to hate him, but my secret only made me love him more.

GENESIS

I never realized that I had this much water in my body. You know that old Ray Charles song "Drown in My Own Tears?" That's how I was feeling. I had never known pain this explosive. It was like someone set off a bomb in my heart and it just kept going off. I didn't know what I was going to do when I got out of the hospital. I was sure, however, that life would never be the same. I was afraid, but there was no one for me to express my fears to. I couldn't tell my mother. I couldn't tell my father. There was no one. This time, I was alone. I didn't think that I could bounce back from this crisis. Usually when I was in pain, I'd go to Kenyon. He was my best friend. Or so I thought. I never thought he'd hurt me like this. Betrayal was definitely the word for what he'd done to me. I'd been betrayed. Broken. Beaten. Bruised. But I was still alive. For that alone, I was thankful.

I wiped the tears from my eyes. I was tired of crying. Tired of trying to figure things out. I just needed peace. My peace had been shattered like a vase thrown across a room in the middle of an argument. A million pieces were all over the place. I had to try to figure out how to put those pieces back together. I loved him with everything I was I never would have done to him what he did to me. Not even in my imagination. I could never be unfaithful to Kenyon. He had my heart lock and key. I belonged to him. Maybe that was the problem. I'd made him my world when he'd only made me his wife. Even that had no meaning. A woman *and* a man. How could he do that to me? Really? Was I really that bad as a wife? As a woman?

I guess I had been lost in my own thoughts because I didn't hear the doctor come in the room. I wondered how long he'd been standing there. "Mrs. Swan, how are you feeling?"

I hated the way that name sounded. I used to love it. Now it just made me sick. Literally. "I feel okay. Physically."

"I just came in to tell you that we have the results of your tests back."

I felt like someone sucked all the air out of the room. I didn't know what to think and I was scared. I didn't want to be alone when he gave me the results. "Can we do this when my parents come back?" He looked at me and I couldn't tell if the look he was giving was a look of pity or concern. Either way, I didn't like the way it felt.

"Yes, that was the reason I came in. I wanted to know if you wanted them now. Some patients prefer to have them in private. I will do as you requested. When your parents return, have the nurse page me and we can do it then."

"Thank you." That was all I had to say. He walked toward the door. Turned around and looked at me, and then walked out of the door. As soon as the door closed, the tears began to fall again. How did I end up here? And how did I get out of this place? *Lord, if you can still hear me and you remember my name, please, help me?*

AURELIA

Seeing my baby lie there for days had taken its toll on me. I was so thankful to God when she finally opened her eyes. In the same instant, my heart was broken all over again when I realized that she didn't know why she was in the hospital in the first place. I was the First Lady of a prominent church. I knew better, but a part of me wanted to have that little boy hurt for what he'd done to my child. I'd never speak those words out loud but I'm sure he knew that I was the wrong one to play with. Truth is I am a powerful woman. I know people who know people. One false move and well, the world would be short one cheating, lying male.

My phone rang but it was in my purse and by the time I got to it, it had already stopped. I dug down in my bag for the purse. That was the trouble with these big ol' purses, I thought to myself. I finally pulled the phone out of my purse. I scrolled to the missed calls and it was a number that I didn't recognize. When I pressed the talk button to redial the number, I got a recording for the hospital. Genesis. I wondered if something was wrong. I called her back on her cell and told her to call me from the hospital phone. She didn't sound good. My cell rang again and I pushed the green button for talk. Stupid contraptions.

"Yes, baby. What's wrong?" She was quiet for a few moments. "Genesis, what's the matter?" Still she didn't speak. She sniffed as if she were crying. It hurt my heart to know that my child was in pain and I couldn't fix it.

"Mama, I need you." In those four words, I heard a multitude of things.

Maybe it was my mind playing tricks on me, I didn't know, but I said, "Baby, I'm on my way." She hung up. She knew that there were no more words needed. I was glad that we stayed at her house instead of going home like we had started to do after she'd regained consciousness. Judah had wanted to go home. I told him that I understood if he needed to go back to handle business at the church but I wasn't leaving my baby until I knew that she was going to be alright. However long that took, that's how long I planned to be here.

I planned to head up to the hospital after taking care of some business but since Genesis called, I immediately walked out of the door. I grabbed my purse off the table in the living room, and searched for the keys to the rental car on my way out the door. By the time I'd reached the car at the end of the drive I'd gotten the keys out of my purse. Judah always asked why I insisted on parking at the end of the driveway when I could simply pull closer to the door, but I needed the walk so I parked at the end of the drive and walked to and from the door whenever I drove. I got in the car and was at the hospital in less than twenty minutes. It was usually a forty-five minute drive to the hospital but today I was in a hurry. My daughter needed me. Mama was to the rescue. I did ninety-five miles per hour all the way over praying the cops would stay away long enough for me to make it to Genesis.

When I found a parking space, I put the car in park, didn't bother to lock the doors and was in the hospital headed to Genesis's room in a matter of minutes. I walked to the nurse's station when I got close to her room and asked the nurse if everything was okay. She told me that as far as she knew everything was fine. I walked down the hall and stopped at the door outside of the room. It was quiet. No television noise, no nothing. Something was definitely wrong. I pushed open the door and walked in the room. Genesis was staring at the wall with tears falling from her eyes. I felt my heart break all over again. I walked over to the bed and wiped the tears from her eyes.

"Baby, what's wrong? What happened?" She looked up at the sound of my voice, like she was just realizing I was in the room.

"How long have you been here?" I guess she hadn't heard me come in.

"I haven't been here that long, baby. I just walked in the door actually."

She took a deep breath and said, "Mama, my results are back. I'm scared. There's something wrong. I can feel it. I told the doctor not to give me the results until you came back. But I need to know. That's why I called you."

I'd forgotten that she was tested for HIV. My heart began to beat faster. "Well, where's the doctor now?"

"He said to have him paged when you made it here and he'd come back in."

I walked out of the room and back to the nurse's station. "I need to have the doctor for Genesis Swan paged, please."

The nurse assured me that she'd page him right away. I walked back to the room but wasn't sure what to say to Genesis when I got back, so I just sat down in the chair and turned on the television. It was way too quiet in the room. I could tell that she was afraid. She appeared so small. She was lying in the bed shaking so, even though she was fully covered. I was getting ready to say something to Genesis when the doctor walked into the room. I stood up and walked over to the bed.

"Do you feel well enough to get out of bed and take a walk with me, Mrs. Swan?"

I knew at that exact moment that her results were positive. I heard the Lord speak clearly to me, "Be strong." That was it.

"Yes. That's fine." There was a tremble in her voice. I wanted to hold her like I used to when she was younger and had fallen off her bike. I wanted to do what mothers did, kiss it and make it better. I couldn't. We waited for her to climb out of bed. Once she was finally up and had her robe on, we followed the doctor out of the room and down two halls and into an office that was decorated with all kinds of plaques and degrees. The man was obviously good at his job. That gave me comfort. We sat down in two very comfortable overstuffed leather chairs. He began shuffling papers in a folder, then he pulled out a sheet of paper and looked up.

"Before I give you the results of your test, do you have any questions? Is there anything that you want to know?"

"What are the chances that I'll be able to have children after this?"

I wasn't expecting her to ask that question. I could understand why she'd want to know though; Genesis had always wanted to have children.

"Well, to be perfectly honest, Mrs. Swan, there shouldn't be any problem with you conceiving after this miscarriage. There wasn't much physical or internal damage so that was good." He offered a smile.

"Okay." She said nothing more.

"Do you have any other questions?"

She shook her head no. I could tell that she was holding her breath now. I took her hand and whispered to her. "Breathe. It's going to be okay."

Tears were falling already and he hadn't even said anything yet. He took a deep breath and said, "Mrs. Swan, I'm very sorry to have to be the one to tell you this, but the results of the test you took were positive. You have HIV."

A sob escaped her and I held her. This was the hardest thing I'd ever had to do. I wanted to call Judah. I needed him. She needed us. The doctor sat there quietly until Genesis seemed to calm down.

"I know how hard this news is to receive. Going from being perfectly fine one day to having your whole world flipped upside down overnight or so it seems. The good news is that you know."

She screamed at him, "How is that good news? I'm going to die and I didn't do anything wrong."

His voice was calm, gentle. "I know. It doesn't seem good. It doesn't seem fair. I get that. Really. But it's not a death sentence. Twenty years ago, yes, maybe that was true, but today you can still live a long, healthy and productive life. Yes, it's going to take careful management and there are so many things that you will have to do differently, but it can be done. That's what matters."

Neither of us spoke. I appreciated the fact that he was very caring. It wasn't just a "You have HIV and there's nothing we can do about it." He was actually offering her hope.

"I don't want to die. Why is this happening to me?"

I held her tighter. "You're not going to die. We know the Lord. Honey, all things work together for the good of them that love Him. Do you want me to call your father?"

She didn't respond.

"Of course we'll have to do some more blood work and start you on a plan of treatment but I don't see any reason that you can't live a full life. Not only that, you will still be able to have children. Just keep praying, Genesis."

So the doctor was a praying man. That was even more good news. In spite of the way things seemed, God was going to work this out for her good. I knew it. Maybe He was just trying to draw her back to Him. The doctor excused himself and told us that when she had calmed down we could go back to the room and he would check in with her later.

KENYON

I knew that Justice wanted to talk but I couldn't bring myself to say one word to her. My thoughts were on Genesis. I still couldn't believe the way things had turned out. I didn't think that she would be in a semi-coma for four days. I never intended to cause this amount of damage. I wasn't sure what I thought would happen. I had no idea she was pregnant. I basically killed my own child. Genesis had wanted children ever since we'd said, "I do." I didn't think I would ever want children, but now that I knew that we were pregnant, my feelings had changed. I was supposed to be a father and it was my fault that it would never happen.

Right now I wished I'd never met Justice. I knew that it was wrong for me to feel this way because she had never asked me to leave Genesis. It was just that, even though she never asked, I knew that she always hoped I would. I hadn't told her upfront that I was married but why would I? I met her in a club one night I was out with the boys. She was wearing an all-black mini-dress and stiletto heels. The first thing I noticed about her in the dark was her figure. I eased behind her on the dance floor and couldn't help thinking just from the way she moved that she would be good in bed. I bought her a few drinks and told her she should spend a few hours with me. She agreed. We ended up getting a room. The things that she did to me I only wished Genesis would consider doing. I knew she was young. I made it clear to her that I wasn't looking for a relationship and at first we just kicked it from time to time. I started spending more time with her whenever Genesis was out of town on business. I can't even pin point when I began to have feelings for her. She just became a permanent part of my life. So it was only natural for me to call her when I figured I couldn't go home but I didn't want to be around her for real. Everybody wanted to talk or at least that's how it seemed and I just wanted to be alone for a little while to sort through my thoughts.

Justice went to bed. I knew that she was upset, but I really didn't care. Whatever it was that she had to tell me would have to wait. There were more pressing matters. I knew that before this was all said and done, everything that Genesis and I had worked for would be split. At least I hoped I wouldn't come out of this with nothing.

Yes, I realized that I was the cause of this. I took responsibility for that. I was supposed to be relieved. I was no longer carrying the secret. My wife knew about my two lovers. She knew about the possibility of being HIV positive. I put my head in my hands. It had been pounding since I'd left the hospital yesterday. Luckily for me, Justice thought I was still asleep. My cell had been ringing off the hook all night. Addison. I needed space. I needed time to gather my thoughts.

I sat up. I'd opted to sleep on the couch last night. I didn't have it in me to make love to Justice with all that was on my mind. I was starting to realize that I still loved my wife. A day late and a dollar short, I could hear her saying clearly. I'd ruined things and there was no way that I could go back and make this right. I thought about praying but I knew that God wasn't even trying to hear me. I heard the door to the bedroom open. It was too late to lie back down so I just sat there.

"Good morning. Still no words for me?"

I was hoping that she wouldn't start with me right now.

"Good morning, Justice. I'm sorry for last night. I was just really stressed about things with my wi… with my sister." I really hoped that she didn't catch that. I almost slipped up and said wife instead of sister. I really needed to be more careful. The last thing I needed was for her to trip out over Genesis. I had nowhere else to go at this point. I mean I could move in with Addison; he'd be pleased to have me there. That's what had started this whole ball rolling. He forced my hand. Either leave Genesis or he was going to tell her that we were sleeping together. I couldn't take that chance.

"Ahem." I must have gotten lost in thought. I stood up and walked over to Justice. I kissed her. I knew that all she wanted was my attention. I needed coffee.

"We need to talk Kenyon. This can't wait. I've been trying to get you to talk to me for a very long time now, at least a month. Each time I've seen you, it's been wham, bam, and thank you ma'am. Well, not today. You need to have a seat because I have something to tell you."

I didn't like the tone in her voice. I looked at her and did as she instructed. "What's up, Justice? What's so urgent that it can't wait until I've had my coffee?"

She was not moved. "If you wanted coffee, you should have gotten up and made it while you were out here pretending to be asleep. See, you think I'm stupid but I'm not. I've let you push me off and put me off for a month. Not anymore. Now it's my turn to do the talking."

She was pissed. She had never spoken to me like this in all the time that we'd been together. She always went out of her way to make me happy. She was a good woman. I was sorry that I was going to have to end it with her. I really did love her. She took care of me.

"That bad, huh? All I wanted was a cup of coffee. I'm tired and no one was pretending to be asleep."

At this rate, all the lies I was telling were becoming enough to build a house.

"Look, Kenyon, I'm tired too. I've been good to you. I've accepted the fact that you won't leave your stuck up little wife to be with me and I love you anyway. Sue me. This time though, you can't put me off. You walk out of here once I tell you what I have to tell you, you will regret it. I promise you that."

"Oh now we're making threats, huh? My mind started going

down a list of things that she could possibly have to tell me. I couldn't think of one. We'd always used protection and she was on the pill so I knew that she couldn't be pregnant. She got tested regularly so I knew that she was clean. She didn't do drugs. She was faithful. So what could it be?

"Are you seeing another man, Justice?"

She looked at me and laughed hard like I'd said something funny.

"If I were, what could you do about it, Mr. Married to the Infamous Genesis Swan? No. I'm not seeing another man."

I breathed a sigh of relief. I was beginning to get jealous. I wondered what it was.

"Well? I think you need to get to the point and stop wasting time. I'm sitting here now, with nowhere to go. You have my undivided attention."

I wasn't ready for what she said next.

"I'm pregnant, Kenyon. Four months. With twins."

She never took her eyes off of me. I guess she wanted to see my reaction. I felt like I'd been sucker punched. I rubbed my locs. "You're? No, that's not possible. How can you be? You're on the pill. We always use condoms. I've never. Why? That ain't my baby."

I could tell I'd struck a nerve. I didn't believe the words when I said them. I knew that she was telling the truth. She was carrying my child.

"Why are you yelling at me and what do you mean it's not your baby? You've got a lot of nerve sitting there talking to me like I'm some common whore. You know I'm not sleeping with anyone else. I haven't been with anyone but you in over a year and not only that, there were plenty of times that we didn't use protection. Maybe if you stopped drinking every time you made love to me, you'd remember that."

I wanted to slap her. "But you're on the pill. What about the pill, Genesis?"

She went into a rage. "Genesis. Really, Kenyon? No, I'm the one you're screwing outside of your marriage, remember me? Justice, not your precious Mrs. Perfect. I was on the pill. I've been off for six months. It was making my hair fall out."

She was crying the whole time. I knew that she was trying to hold it together and that it was hard for her.

"What are we going to do with children? I told you I didn't want no babies. Now you're carrying two? The hell, Justice? The hell? I can't do this. My wife is…"

She slapped me. "Your wife is what? You keep standing in my face talking about your wife as if I care anything about her. I don't owe your wife anything. I didn't know anything about her until recently, so stop. If you're trying to make me feel guilty, it's not working. You are married to her. Not me."

Everything she said was true. "Justice, get rid of them."

She looked at me and turned to walk away. I grabbed her by the back of her neck and spun her around to face me. "Get rid of them or I'll do it for you." I knew that I was hurting her. I was trying to.

"Let me go you sorry son of a…" I slapped her before she could finish her sentence then slung her to the floor. I felt sick right now. This had to be some kind of joke.

"GET OUT OF MY HOUSE. Get the hell out of my house. NOW."

I looked at her but didn't speak. I noticed she'd had the phone in her hand when I heard her speaking, "Yes, I need an ambulance and the police to 21612 Crescent View Crest. I'm pregnant and the father of my children just assaulted m…"

I knocked the phone out of her hand. "How dare you call the police on me? What the hell is wrong with you? You made me hit you and you called the police on me?"

She got up off the floor, looked me in the eye and said, "I'm too far along to get rid of the babies. But you just made a very big mistake putting your hands on me. Get out of my house."

She turned and walked away. I knew that the police would be here any minute. She lived in a predominately-white, influential neighborhood. I grabbed my suitcase and walked toward the door. As soon as I opened it, I heard the sirens and saw the cars pulling into the drive. I just stood there.

What else was I going to do?

JUSTICE

This negro actually had the nerve to put his hands on me. Just as he was about to walk out the door, the police showed up. Thank God. I was pressing charges. I loved him but I'd never been one to let a man hit me and get away with it. I came out of the bedroom when I heard the sirens. I walked to the front door and met the officer in the yard. My nosy neighbors were gathered on their lawns, peeking out of curtains. I wanted to holler at them to take their nosy behinds on somewhere; this did not concern them.

"Ma'am you called for an officer and an ambulance?" an officer named Garcia asked.

"Yes, Officer. I'm four months pregnant. I was giving the father of my children the news and he snapped out, hit me, and told me to get rid of the babies. Then he threw me on the floor. I asked for the ambulance because I didn't think it would be safe for me to drive myself to the hospital. I'm not in too much pain other than where he slapped me."

"Is this him over here?" Garcia asked again.

"Yes sir. That's him."

He walked over to where Kenyon was standing. I stayed where I was. I didn't want to be anywhere near him.

"Sir is there a problem here?"

"No officer. There's no problem. My girlfriend and I were just having a conversation that got a tad bit out of control."

"You call slapping a pregnant woman and throwing her to the

ground a bit out of control?"

He looked at Kenyon like he wanted to slap him and see how he liked it. "Ma'am, do you mind stepping over here for a moment?"

I walked over to where Officer Garcia was standing. His partner an officer name Alejandro had joined us. I shook his hand when he introduced himself. He was going to take my formal statement. Officer Garcia asked if I wanted to press charges. I informed him that I very well intended to do so. Since they'd come in separate cars, he said that one of them could take me to the hospital as long as someone would be able to pick me up. I agreed, made my statement and had Kenyon arrested. I bet he'd think twice before putting his hands on anyone else ever again. I wondered right then if he had abused his wife. He never struck me as the abusive type but as I was quickly finding out, things weren't always what they seemed.

I walked into the emergency room just as a pain struck my side. I bent over. I prayed to God that nothing was wrong with my babies. One of the nurses came rushing to my side.

"Are you okay?"

"I don't know. Please help me. I'm pregnant. I--" I screamed as a pain ripped through me. Tears were falling down my face. "Please help me."

While the nurse got a wheelchair, I stood against the counter. And that's when I saw her. Genesis Swan. It was like seeing a ghost. The nurse helped me into a wheelchair and rushed me back into a room. Once I was up on the table, she began her exam. I felt like I was going to pass out from the pain..

I couldn't believe how much my life had changed since I met Kenyon. When I met him, I was modeling, attending church on a regular basis. As a matter of fact, when I met him I was an aspiring Missionary. I couldn't even remember the last time I'd talked to God. I met him the day I'd brought my initial message entitled,

"Tricks, Traps, and Distractions: Recognizing Signs from Satan to Throw You off Course from Your Destiny." You'd think that having just brought a word like that I would have recognized him for who and what he was. I guess I was lonely and stupid. I had no idea that he was a married man. We'd been seeing each other for about nine months when I saw him on the cover of an Essence Magazine with his famous novelist wife, Genesis Swan. I confronted him.

I'd never forget that day. He'd come by because we were supposed to be going to lunch. He came in the house and I was sitting on the end of the couch, legs crossed, attitude on one hundred.

"You have a wife?" He wasn't expecting that but how exactly did he think it would stay a secret with his face all of the cover of a magazine sold in every store known to man? He stood there looking like the cat had his tongue. It was almost like he was trying to decide whether he should answer me or if he should just walk out.

"What are you talking about, Justice?" So he wanted to play stupid? Okay.

"What am I talking about, Kenyon? For real? This is how you want to do this?" I got up and went to the kitchen. When I came back I hit him in the chest with the magazine. "Are you sure you still want to play dumb?"

"Oh." That was all he had to say. I guess there was no way to get out of this lie. "Yes, Justice. I'm married but I'm not happy. If I was do you think I'd be here with you?" He walked over to me and I pushed away from him.

"I think you should leave." I didn't want to be around him right now. I couldn't explain what I was feeling but I knew it was too late. I was in too deep. I was in love. I knew better. I should have walked then. I'd allowed myself to believe his marriage was just a technicality, that we were destined to be together.

I wanted to ask the nurse was everything okay, but I couldn't speak.

They had me hooked up to every machine known to man.

"No bleeding," I heard someone say. I felt like I was only half-conscious.

"God, please don't let me lose my babies. I know I was wrong but please."

I wasn't sure what happened. When I opened my eyes, the room was quiet, except for the beeping of the monitors. I tried to sit up and couldn't move. I must have passed out. I reached for the remote on the side of the bed that had the nurse call button on it. I pressed the button.

"Yes," came back a voice through the speaker.

"Can you please send a nurse in?" I asked the voice.

"I'll be there in just a moment."

I put my hand on my stomach. It was still swollen. I hoped that was good news. The nurse opened the door and came into the room.

"My babies?" was all I said. I couldn't say much more because tears had my throat constricted. I wanted to cry.

"We were able to save the babies. They are fine. However, there is a problem with your cervix. The doctor performed what's called a cerclage to prevent any further problems. It seems that there was just some fetal stress, which is what your pain was from. The babies are well. You have nothing to worry about. The doctor wants to keep you for a few days for observation just to be on the safe side."

I breathed a sigh of relief. God had granted me that one prayer. My babies were going to be okay. *Thank you, Jesus.*

"Thank you very much, Nurse, for everything."

"Call me Claudia. I'll be your nurse until time for shift change. If you need anything else, don't hesitate to page me. Get some rest."

I felt like I could do just that now that I knew my babies would be fine. I picked up the phone on the bedside table and called my sister to let her know what was going on, where I was and that I'd need her to come and get me whenever I was released. I hung up from her and started thinking. I'd always wanted children but not this way. I guess I made the bed, so now it was time to lie in it. Things, I'd soon find out, were going to get a whole lot worse very quickly.

ADDISON

I'd been trying to reach Kenyon since Thursday afternoon. He told me that he would call me back. Tuesday came and I still hadn't heard from him. He had me confused with someone else because I was the wrong one for this mess. I'd make his life a living hell if he forced me to. That was a promise I planned to keep. I needed to talk to him. Immediately. I tried his cell again. There was still no answer. I was ready to go to his house and confront his wife myself. I figured she was making this hard for him. Maybe that's why he wasn't answering the phone.

We'd been together for almost two years. I knew that he was the one for me. I'd never had an issue with him answering the phone, even when he was with her. I gave him an ultimatum a few days ago. I basically told him that I wasn't going to keep being his piece on the side. Yes, I deserved better. I wouldn't settle for less than being with him permanently.

I was just admitted to the hospital. I hadn't been fully honest with Kenyon. I finally told him that I was tested for HIV and that the test was positive. Truth was I now had full-blown AIDS. I took my medication faithfully and things were well until two days ago when I started having fever and diarrhea that wouldn't go away. Every symptom I had was suspect. That was my life, so I called the doctor and he told me that I needed to come in so that he could run tests. When he called me, all he said was that I needed to come into the hospital as soon as possible. So, I cleared my calendar because I wasn't sure what was going on. I knew that going directly to the hospital wasn't a sign of good news. When I got there, I met him at the desk. He immediately had me admitted. Once we were in my room, he sat down and I knew that the name of this game had drastically changed. That's why I was trying to get in touch with Kenyon. He needed to know.

"Addison, we knew this day would come eventually. Well, you've developed an infection that we refer to as an opportunistic infection; specifically what you have is called mycobacterium avium complex or MAC. Only people who have developed the AIDS virus present with this virus. So, that means you are no longer HIV-positive. Addison, I'm sorry to tell you this, but you have AIDS."

I knew that this day would come. I just didn't realize that it would feel like this. When I first found out that I was positive, it felt like a death sentence. Now this was déjà vu. I felt like he'd just told me to get my house in order because I didn't have much longer to be alive. I wanted to cry but not in front of him.

"Okay. So what do we do now? How do we treat this?"

He looked at me like he didn't want to tell me that I'd have to add yet another medication or two or three to the already long list of things I was taking on a daily basis.

"We'll have to start you on medication right away. This is going to take a very long time to treat, so you'll be on this medication for at least a year at minimum. Your fever should begin to improve in a few weeks."

Weeks? I didn't have weeks to be laid up in the hospital. "So, I guess I need to schedule some time off work."

It wasn't a question; it was more of a statement. I knew how this went. I'd take another leave from work. It was a good thing I owned the company and had many competent people working for me.

"It's a good thing you're the boss." It was almost like he was reading my mind. "I'll give you some time to adjust to what I've just told you and I'll come back in later. In the meantime, I'll send the nurse in with the first round of meds. If there's anyone you need to inform, now would be the time to do it because once the nurse's start coming in, you'll be in and out for tests."

He shook my hand and headed out of the room. I sat on the bed. My heart hurt. Literally. I wasn't expecting this news. I thought I was fine. Thought the medication was working. I guess I thought wrong. I've been sick for seven years. I still wasn't sure who'd I'd contracted the virus from, although I notified all of my past lovers when I'd found out. None of them ever told me whether they'd gotten tested or not. None of it mattered now. I had AIDS. I felt sick just thinking the words.

My cell rang. I picked it up and answered without looking at the caller ID. I thought that maybe it was Kenyon calling back. I was wrong. When I heard his voice, I cringed inside. I should have checked.

"Jeremiah, what do you want?" It was my crazy ex. I knew I should have changed my number. He didn't get that we were over.

"Well hello to you, too, lover boy. How are you?"

I dared not tell him that I'd just been admitted to the hospital. The last thing I wanted was for him to be anywhere near me.

"I'm fine. What do you want? I told you we were over. I'm seeing someone else now. When are you going to get that? We've been over for two years. Move on."

I was getting ready to hang up when he said, "No, sweetheart, you are the one who doesn't get it. We ain't over until I say we're over. And I'm not ready to be done with you yet. See, I know all about your lover man; I've seen him. I've seen the two of you together, smiling, laughing, hugging, and kissing. Yeah, I've seen it all. I'm about sick of being disrespected. You know that we were meant for each other. Then you decided you wanted to leave 'cause you got a new piece. I didn't care about you getting with him once or twice as long as you came home, but when you started talking about loving him and falling out of love with me, then, we had a problem. I told you I will make your life miserable. Now you're going to make me do something I don't want to do. I'm giving you one last chance to make this right, Addison. I love you. You are my man. Don't ever forget that."

Was he threatening me? I didn't say a word just held the phone.

"Addison, I'm serious. Don't make me make you regret playing with my heart."

I sighed hard. "Jeremiah, I'm done. I told you. I love Kenyon. I'm in love with Kenyon. We are together. You can't change that. Take your threats and go somewhere with that. I don't take kindly to being threatened. For real."

He was beginning to piss me off. "Oh, so it's like that, huh? Pour salt in my open wound. Well just remember you've been warned."

He laughed. I didn't like the sound of that but before I could say another word my phone rang again which meant that he'd hung up. This time I looked at the caller ID before I picked it up. It was an unknown number. I thought about not answering but something told me I needed to pick up.

"Addison Limón speaking."

It was Kenyon. He was in jail. Too bad for him there was nothing I could do about it from where I was sitting.

JUDAH

Ileft Aurelia with Genesis and went back to handle business at the church. Being in ministry full time was both a blessing and a curse. It called me away from my family in times when they needed me. I didn't leave until I knew that Genesis was going to be alright for the most part. I prayed that God would not take away her ability to have children. I knew how much that meant to her. I'd just gotten off the phone with Aurelia. She called to tell me that something was wrong but she didn't think it was news I needed to hear over the phone. I thought that maybe the doctor had informed Genesis that she'd never be able to have a child. I told my wife that as soon as I finished in this ministers board meeting I was in, I'd be on the road back to them. My family needed me and this time, I would be there for them.

I excused myself from the meeting. The other ministers were aware that I was in the middle of a family emergency, minus any details. I went into the sanctuary and knelt in front of the illuminated white cross that was behind the pulpit. I looked up as tears fell from my eyes. Seeing your child in pain was something no parent ever wanted to endure, especially when you knew that you couldn't make it better.

"God, right now, my heart is heavy. I need You to give me a peace that surpasses all understanding because right now, I don't have it. I don't understand how or why this has happened to my daughter, but God, I trust You. I know that all things work together for the good. So, I'm trusting that You are going to show up and show out even in the midst of this impossible situation. Lord, I know that You are in control and that You're holding Genesis in the palm of Your hands. I ask You dispatch angels of protection to be around her, God, shield her heart from the pain of this situation, God. Keep her close to You, God. I don't know if You're using this as a tool to draw her back to You, God, but whatever You're doing, God, I submit and surrender to Your will. As her father, I want to step in and make it right. I want to cause harm to the one that harmed her, so Father I ask that You remove these feelings of anger and hatred from my heart, keep them from taking root. I'm placing the whole situation in Your hands, and I praise You in advance for the victory in this situation. I may not see it now but I know that she will come out a conqueror because Your Word tells me that she will. In Jesus' name, I pray. Thank you, God. Amen."

I opened my eyes, wiped the tears and stood up. God had her. He had me. I felt his peace. I was thankful. I glanced up at the cross again, said, "Thank you, Jesus," and headed back to my meeting. I hoped that this meeting didn't turn frivolous like some of our recent meetings had done. I didn't have time for it today, and if it got to be that way, I was leaving.

"Have your way, God," I said as I walked back into the meeting.

JEREMIAH

So, he thought he was going to be able to just leave me like that? Not after everything I'd invested. I wasn't going out like some chump sucker. I tried to give him chance after chance to come back. He obviously thought this was a game. It wasn't. I wasn't going to be played. I loved this man. I gave him years of my life—fifteen years to be exact and he really thought I was going to let go that easily? Please. Just goes to show that he really didn't know me.

I rescued him. I took care of him. I gave him some place to call home when he had no place else to go and he made me promises of forever, said that we would always be together. I had no reason not to believe him. After all we'd been through together. I stood by him even when I found out that he was HIV-positive. I stayed when I found out that he'd given me the disease or so he thought he had. As far as I was concerned, for that reason alone we needed to stay together. Then he met this Kenyon person and decided that he was in love. *In love.* For two years, I tried to figure out when he'd fallen out of love with me. I wasn't out of love with him. He had my heart. I gave it to him freely, then he chose to break it and he chose to make me his enemy.

I was done being nice. I was done buying roses. I was done writing love songs. I was done penning poems. I was done. Now he'd see a side of me that he never knew existed because he'd never given me a real reason to show it to him. Since he refused to listen to reason, I'd be his worst nightmare. He thought that being HIV-positive was the worst thing that had ever happened to him. I was getting ready to flip his pretty little world upside down. For some reason, light-skinned men thought they could do whatever they wanted to people and we would just take it lying down. I'd been writing in my journal when I called him. I really just wanted to hear his voice. I missed him. The way he smelled, the way he held me, the way his lips felt against mine. I missed us. The way we were. I just wanted to hear him say he was sorry for hurting me. That he still loved me. That he realized he'd made a mistake. Instead, he'd told me that it was over and that I needed to move on once and for all. When I was done with him, he'd wish that he never met Kenyon. I'd make sure of that. I was seeing flames I was so mad. I knew that he had insurance on his business and his house. My only decision was which to burn to the ground first. He thought it was a game.

Well, let the games begin.

JUSTICE

The nurse had been in several times since I called her in to find out about the babies. She took so much blood it was ridiculous. I was starting to feel like a pincushion. She came back in again and said, "Have you been tested for HIV/AIDS Ms..." She looked down on the chart for my last name.

"Denson. Justice Denson."

She nodded and wrote it on the chart. "Okay, Ms. Denson. Have you been tested for HIV? I'm asking because there was a law that was passed recently that requires all patients admitted to the hospital to be tested."

"No. I've never had a reason to be tested." She looked shocked, like I was operating in ignorance or something. "Even if you only have one partner there is a need to be tested, especially if you don't know what your partner is doing when you are not around. It's always best to know."

I guess she had a point but there was no way that I was HIV-positive. The only person I'd been with was Kenyon and the guy I'd lost my virginity to. Kenyon didn't look like he had HIV. What harm could it do to prove this nurse wrong?

"I've only been with two people so I'm not worried about that, but if it's a requirement I'll have the test done. I guess you're right; it's always best to know."

I had nothing to worry about. Kenyon was faithful to me. I knew that he was. Well, as faithful as a married man could be. I signed the consent forms and she told me that she'd be back to perform the test in a while. I laid my head back against the pillows. I felt so lonely. I didn't know what was going to happen but I wished that I could rewind the hands of time and go back to before when my life was simple. Back to before I knew what real heartache was, to when the only thing that mattered to me was pleasing God. I was hurting. I knew that it was wrong to pray only when you needed God for something, but I felt like prayer was my only option. Tears started to fall and I was upset with myself for allowing this man to lead me to a place that I really didn't want to be. I wasn't cut out to be the other woman. I knew it but loneliness will make you do things that you otherwise would not do. I learned my lesson the hard way and I told myself that I was done with Kenyon Swan; he wasn't worth the heartache or the pain. My mama used to say that hindsight is 20/20. I was beginning to see exactly what she meant.

"Are you okay?"

I could tell that she genuinely cared. "I'm fine. Just thinking about some things. Are you ready to do the test?"

I wasn't ready have the test done, but once this was over, it would be something I could put behind me. "Yes, I'm ready if you are."

She laughed "I'm ready even if you aren't. Let's get this done. We can do one of two tests. Both that will have your results in at least thirty minutes. There is a blood rapid test that requires a finger stick and there's an oral test that tests your saliva. I'd recommend going with the blood. It usually gives more accurate results."

"Okay, whichever you suggest is what I'll do. It's just a finger stick?" I stuck out my left hand so that she could stick it and get what she needed to perform the test. Since I was right handed, I never allowed them to give I.V.'s in that arm or stick that hand in case I decided that I wanted to write something.

"All done."

That was the quickest, most non-painful thing I'd experienced.

"I should have the results in about 30-45 minutes. In the meantime, would you like for me to send in a counselor to speak with you about any questions or anything that you have?"

I didn't need a counselor. That test would come back negative.

"No thank you. I don't have any questions. I told you before I've only been with two men in my life so there's nothing to worry about. I'm only doing this because it's a requirement of the hospital. Thank you. I just want to get some rest now. Can I have something for pain please when you get a chance?"

She reached into her pocket and took out a cup with two pills in it. "As a matter of fact it's time for pain meds so I bought them with me. Here ya go."

She handed me the cup. I took the pills and reached for the cup of water. I swallowed the pills and then it hit me. Genesis was here.

"I do have a question. Not about the test or anything but about another patient in the hospital. I saw Genesis Swan here yesterday. She's one of my favorite authors. Would you possibly be able to tell me which room she's in?" I lied. I'd never read a book the woman wrote. I felt like I needed to talk to her. Find out if she knew about me.

"That's against hospital policy, Ms. Denson I can't give out information on another patient. I'm sorry."

"It's fine. I just thought I'd ask. I know she must be in a private room. I thought maybe I'd be able to get her autograph or something. Thank you any way."

She told me I was welcome and then she left. I lay down. I had to figure out a way to find out what room she was in. Then it came to me. Call patient information. Hey, it was worth a try. I reached for my purse and dug out my cell, dialed the main number for the hospital and asked for patient information. I was transferred with no problem.

"Patient information," the voice on the other end of the phone said.

"Yes, I'm trying to get some information on one of your

patients. Can you please tell me what room Genesis Swan is in? This is her sister."

"Give me just one moment to check and see if that information is listed. Do you mind holding?"

I told the attendant that I didn't mind. Then I heard that cheesy music they play when they put you on hold. "Ma'am? Thank you very much for holding. Mrs. Swan's room number is 1322. Would you like to be transferred to her room?"

Oh my God. I didn't think I'd actually be able to get that information. "No. Thank you. I appreciate the information."

I hung up before she could say anything else. 1322, huh? I needed to decide if I wanted to call her or if I wanted to just go up to the room. I was thinking call first. I didn't want to go to her room and have someone else be there, besides I was bedridden for the moment. I'd call her before the night was over. I thought about calling Kenyon but he was in jail. I put the phone back in my purse and lay down. I closed my eyes. All I wanted to do for now was sleep.

KENYON

I could not believe that she actually had me arrested. I was sitting up in jail all because she let herself get pregnant? Really? How did this happen? I never meant to hit her; something just came over me. I still couldn't believe that this was happening to me. I made my wife lose our child and then found out that one of my lovers was pregnant, not just pregnant but carrying twins. I prayed to God that Genesis would never find out about those babies because that would be a major slap in the face.

I'd started doing a lot of praying over the past few days but I knew that God wasn't trying to hear me. I wasn't stupid. I was a man who didn't even believe in God until I saw Genesis pass out. Then I called on God like calling on God was going out of style. But I knew it was a waste. I'd give anything to go back six days and keep my confessions to myself. I broke her heart all because I thought I didn't love her anymore. Truth was, I loved her; I was just jealous of her. I never imagined that I'd be married to someone famous. Everyone knew her name and I was fading into the background. I couldn't deal with it. I wasn't a background type of man. I always thought that it would be me who had fans, me who was sought after. I was wrong. Most days I resented Genesis, especially after the Essence shoot. It was like people started walking up to me talking about, "Aren't you Genesis Swan's husband?" I'd just walk in the opposite direction. Granted I'd been cheating long before that, but that was my main reason; I couldn't deal with her ever increasing fame.

I waited for them to tell me that I could make my one phone call. I decided that when I could I was going to call Addison. I knew that he would come and get me. He was pissed beyond measure by now because I hadn't returned his calls but I knew that he wouldn't leave me sitting in jail. I'd just tell him that Genesis had me arrested.

Finally, they called me to make my phone call. I called Addison and he answered on the third ring. For a minute, I was worried that he wouldn't answer since I'd been avoiding his calls.

"Addison Limón."

I'd never been happier and more relieved than I was then.

"Babe, I'm sorry I haven't returned your phone calls; I've just been extremely busy. I've had a lot going on. Had to fly out of town on a business emergency, and when I got back, I got into it with Genesis. She's still not taking the news too well. She had me arrested. I need you to come get me. Addison, I can't stay in jail overnight."

I wasn't expecting him to tell me that he wasn't able to get me out, but that's exactly what he said.

"I'm not in a position to come get you right now, Kenyon. Even if I were, I'm not sure that I would. You've been ignoring me for six days. Don't call me pretending like all is well. When you clearly know that it's not."

More lies. "Babe, I know and I'm sorry. I didn't have my personal cell with me. I forgot it, so all I had was the business phone and you never called that one. I wouldn't ignore you for six days. Don't you know that?" I had to use my best "I'm sorry" voice. "Please, Addison. Just get me out of here. I'll owe you forever." I was laying it on thick but I was not staying in jail. That was just not an option. If he wasn't coming, I'd contact my attorney and have him post my bail. Either way I was getting out of here by the time night fell. It was already five o'clock.

"I'm in the hospital, Kenyon. I can't come. Find someone to get you out. I'm sorry. If you get out tonight, come directly to Blessed

Trinity room 2122. We have to talk."

There were those words again. We have to talk. I was coming to despise those four words. I didn't want to talk but I figured that if he was saying them, then something was very wrong.

"You're in the hospital? How long have you been there and what's wrong?"

He was silent for a long while like he was contemplating telling me or not. Then he said, "Just come as soon as you get out. We have to talk. It's important. And if you haven't already, you need to be tested immediately. Please."

Then he hung up. I sat there staring at the phone in my hand as the dial tone blared from the other end. I put the phone back on the cradle, picked it up again and dialed my attorney, told him where I was and to come as soon as possible. He assured me that he would have me out of here no later than 7:30. I hung up with him and went back into the cell. I wondered why he was urging me to get tested now. What made it so important? I hadn't told him that I'd already been tested and that I knew I was HIV positive. I had been being treated for it for almost a year now. That was the reason I told Genesis to get tested. Otherwise I don't think I should have. I probably should have told her sooner but I was only thinking about myself, especially since it was very rare lately that she and I were intimate. I remembered then that they had done a test on Genesis. I wondered what her results were. I wanted to talk to her, to hold her. I wanted-- No I needed to make things right. I could only hope it wasn't too late to stop the damage. .

I heard the guard call my name. My lawyer was here and I was being released. That's why it was good to have a lawyer on retainer. You never knew when you'd need one. I got my belongings, thanked Attorney Reese, got my court dates, and asked him for a ride back to my car, which was still parked in Justice's driveway. I could only hope that she wasn't home. I just wanted to get my car and leave. I needed to find out what Addison had to tell me. I didn't like the way he sounded.

I got to my car. To my fortune, Justice didn't appear to be home. At least she didn't come out and start with me. I was thankful. I threw my things into the back seat glad that I'd already placed my luggage in my car before the police arrived. I got in the car and headed toward the hospital. Something was wrong. I could feel it. I just had no idea what it was.

I pulled up to the hospital and found a parking space that was located as far from the hospital as I could find. I needed to walk before I saw Addison. Needed to clear my head, so I walked slowly. Once I reached the entrance to the hospital, I hesitated. Was I sure that I wanted to do this? I stopped at the information desk, got his room number again, and headed to the room. Once I reached the door to the room, I stopped outside, took a deep breath and knocked before pushing the door open. When I walked in the room, I was shocked to see Addison lying in the bed with IV's all around the bed. I wasn't sure what was going on but whatever it was obviously wasn't good.

"I didn't think you were going to come," he said when he looked up and saw me standing in the doorway. There was a look of sadness in his eyes. There was something else too; I couldn't figure out if it was regret or anger.

"Why wouldn't I come?" I was struggling to keep my composure. I couldn't stand seeing him this way. In all the time that I'd known him, he hadn't really been sick. I wasn't sure I could handle this.

"I've been calling you since last week and I haven't gotten any calls in return until today. Why were you avoiding my calls, Kenyon? And before you let a lie slip past your lips, save us both the trouble of finding out the truth later and just be honest."

He was upset. He had every right to be. I did tell him that I'd call when I left Genesis and that was last Thursday. I studied him. Something was definitely wrong. "What's the matter, Addison? Why are you here?" I asked.

"Don't try to change the subject. Answer my question. You owe me an explanation. What happened?"

He wasn't letting me off the hook. I had to explain and he was right, I did owe him that much. "I told her. She didn't take the news too well. I'm not sure why I even expected her to. I didn't realize that it was our fifth wedding anniversary until she reminded me, that I was leaving her on the day we'd pledged our lives to each other. Ironic. Anyway, she gave me this."

I handed him the watch and said, "Read the inscription." He read it and when he finished he looked up at me with a look that I couldn't read.

"Are you staying with her because of the baby? Is that why you didn't call? Guilt got the best of you?"

"Actually, she lost the baby. I didn't read that until the other day. I had no idea that she was pregnant but that was her way of telling me. And I caused her to lose our baby. Yes, I feel guilty, but I'm not staying with her. After all that's happened, that wouldn't even be possible."

"So what's going to happen between the two of us, Kenyon? Where do we go from here?"

I walked over to the bed, took his hand, looked him in the eye and said, "Addison, I love you. I'm prepared to spend the rest of my life with you if that's what you really want."

"Jeremiah's back."

I wasn't expecting those words. I said "Back? What do you mean back? Back as in your life? Or back as in town?"

I hated his ex-Jeremiah. I'd never met him but he'd been trying to get Addison back ever since he found out that we were together. He was jealous. He didn't realize that it was over. I thought of Justice and Genesis, but quickly shook the thought off.

"He's back in town, said that he can't let me go. He loves me too much to let you just have me without a fight. And I believe him. I think that we're getting ready to have a battle on our hands. Are you prepared for that?"

Was I prepared for that? I wasn't sure. I knew that I was in for a battle myself. I just wasn't sure exactly how bad the battle for me was about to get.

"I don't know if I can handle it or not, but we both have to be realistic. We are in for more than one battle. Genesis is going to make my life hell. I can feel it. She hasn't said it, but I know her. I hurt her."

He rolled his eyes. I knew that he hated it when I talked about Genesis but he had to realize that she was my wife still. I dropped it though.

"So tell me why you're here. What was so urgent that we needed to talk about?"

"Sit down." His voice now carried a note of seriousness that I hadn't picked up on before.

I sat down in the chair next to the bed and sat back. "I'm sitting."

I noted that his eyes were now filled with tears. I hadn't seen him cry before. Whatever he was about to tell me must have been really bad. My mind went through a catalogue of all the possible reasons he could be here when he started talking. I stopped mentally cataloguing reasons and began to listen.

"I have AIDS." I looked at him. I must have heard him wrong.

"No, you have HIV. It hasn't progressed to AIDS yet."

"Kenyon, look at me. I have AIDS; that's why I'm here. I have an infection that only AIDS patients get. The doctor told me today. I wanted you to know right away. If you haven't been tested, please get tested. We need to know how to progress from this point on. I need you by my side. I'm afraid. I don't think I've ever admitted fear to anyone, but right now, I'm afraid and I need you."

He had dropped a bomb and I had no words for him so I just nodded. The reality of the situation hit me like a ton of bricks. AIDS? How long had he been sick? Something wasn't adding up and I wasn't quite sure what, but I'd soon find out.

GENESIS

I got the results of my test when my mother came back to the hospital. I called her right after the doctor left the room. I wanted to get that out of the way and she was there in no time. It didn't take very long to get into the office with the doctor. When he said, "Mrs. Swan, I'm sorry to tell you this," I knew what he was going to say. I was HIV-positive. I felt like I'd been hit by a train. I couldn't deal with this. All I could think about was how long I had left to live. All the things I wanted to do with my life that I'd never get to do. I'd been handed a death sentence. That's all I could think about when I returned to my room. My mother wanted to stick around but I told her I wanted to be alone. It was amazing to me how one minute everything was fine, or so I thought, and the next minute my world had shattered like broken glass. There were a million pieces that I had to figure out a way to put back together. Thing was, I wasn't sure if I could.

The Dr. said that with the proper medication, I could still live a full life. I wondered how anyone led a full life with a disease like this ravaging their bodies. I felt numb all over. I wanted Kenyon to pay for what he'd done to me. This wasn't fair. I'd done nothing but be a good wife to him and this was how he repaid me for my years of loyalty and faithfulness? By killing our child and handing me a death sentence. Tears were falling again. I felt them but I didn't bother to wipe them away. Mama used to say tears were healing, cleansing. I wasn't sure if there was any truth to that but I wanted to trust what she said so I let the tears fall.

I kept trying to figure out where things went wrong. Was I that busy that I didn't notice the ever increasing distance between us? I mean, yes I'd been gone a lot, but so had he. We both traveled for work. We were each usually gone for a few weeks out of every month. I always asked if he wanted to travel with me. He always turned me down. Should that have been an indication that something was wrong? If it should have been, it wasn't. Maybe I was naïve to believe that he was being faithful but I'd put my full trust in him. When I was home, he was away on business. When I called, he answered. I didn't think anything was wrong. Now that I'd thought about it, I realized that we hadn't been intimate much in the past few years. I'd been so busy that I was rarely in the mood so we'd maybe been together once or twice a month, if that. The day I'd gotten pregnant was the last time. That was three months ago. Maybe I'd opened the door for his infidelity by being more focused on my work than on my marriage. I wasn't sure. Even if that was the case, this wasn't fair. I never would have cheated on him. I loved him and love was supposed to bring you home. At least it always brought me back.

I picked up the hospital phone and dialed Kenyon's number. After the third ring, he picked up. I said, "I really hope you're happy with yourself, I'm going to die because of you. I never did anything but love you, stand by you, cheer you on and you give me a disease that's going to kill me in return. I hate you and I hope you rot in hell, you miserable bastard."

Before he could respond, I disconnected the call. I placed the phone back in its cradle just as the first sob escaped my lips. My pain was palpable. My body began to shake with sobs. This was what dying felt like.

JUSTICE

An hour had passed since the nurse did the test. She just left the room and I was in shock. No, shock isn't the right word for what I was feeling. I couldn't believe what she just told me. There had to be some mistake. There was no possible way that I was HIV-positive. I wanted to cry but the tears wouldn't come. I wondered if Kenyon was still locked up. I needed some answers. I deserved some answers. I pulled my cell out again and dialed his number. The first time I called, I got his voicemail. It took calling fifteen times back to back for him to pick up. I wasn't leaving a message.

When he answered, he sounded harsh. "What do you want?"

I was quiet for a moment.

He said, "You've called my phone fifteen times Justice. Don't sit there and get quiet now. What do you want?"

He didn't have a right to be angry. I was the one laid up in the hospital. "Do you have HIV?"

I saw no sense in beating around the bush. He was quiet. That scared me. "Do you have HIV ?" I asked again. Still no response.

"Kenyon, I'm laid up in this hospital and they require all patients to have an AIDS test done. Mine came back positive. I've got HIV. You were the only person I've been with. Do you have HIV and if you do, how could you do this to me?"

Again, I was met with silence. I wanted to slap him. "Answer me," I said through gritted teeth.

"I don't know."

That was it. Was he serious? "What do you mean you don't know? How do you not know?" He sighed. He sounded tired. I almost felt sorry for him until I remembered the reason for the call. "Did you infect me on purpose?"

I wondered if that's what it was all about. If he was the type of man that had been scorned by some woman in the past and wanted to hurt as many women as possible. I thought about Genesis. I was definitely calling her now; she needed to know that she should be tested. That was the least that I could do for her after sleeping with her husband. I guess this was my karma.

"I said I don't know."

The sound of his voice was grating on my ears. I hung up. I didn't need his lies or his excuses. The phone started to vibrate in my hand. I looked at the display. It was Kenyon calling back. I didn't answer. Just let it go to voicemail. He had nothing else to say to me. I picked up the hospital phone and called Genesis' room.

"Hello." She sounded weary. Like everything in her world was wrong.

"Hello," she said again.

I cleared my throat. "Is this Genesis Swan?"

"Yes. This is she."

It was now or never. "You don't know me, but I've got something very important to tell you and you'll probably think I'm crazy but I need to let you know something important about your husband. I really hope that you won't hang up on me and just hear me out."

I could hear her shifting around. "Who is this? And how do you know my husband?"

She had every right to sound angry. It sounded like the anger was taking more of her strength. "My name is Justice. Justice Denson. I won't bother lying to you. I've done enough damage and I want you to know that I'm truly sorry for all the pain that I've caused you. I'm not sure if you know anything about me or not. I've been having an affair with your husband for quite some time now. I'm four months pregnant with his twins. I'm in the same hospital as you. I saw you earlier today when I was being admitted. That's how I knew you were here. I'm here because Kenyon beat me up when I told him that I was pregnant."

I stopped talking to see if she had something to say. I could tell she was crying. I felt bad. I never meant to be the source of this woman's pain. Truth is I was. She was hurting now because of me.

"You're her? The other woman? I didn't know anything about you until last Thursday. That was our anniversary. He came home and told me that he was having an affair with not one but two people. You're one of them."

She said all this through her tears. Had I heard her right? Two people? I wasn't the only other woman in his life? He was cheating on us.

"Did you say that he said he was having an affair with two people?" I knew I had no right to question her but I needed to make sure that I'd heard her right.

"Yes. You and some man. Addison I believe was his name."

I dropped the phone when she said that. I could hear her saying hello over and over so I picked the phone back up and placed it back against my ear. "I'm here."

I'd called her to tell her something about him and here she was with surprises of her own. I felt like the biggest fool. How could I not know that he was cheating on me too? . Ironic. "So, no, you're not the only one. Did you know that he was married from the beginning?" she asked.

It was a fair question. I thought she'd be irate but she was actually being civil. "I didn't. Not in the beginning. We'd been together for nine months when I found out about you. And I only found out about you because I saw him on the cover of Essence with you. I asked him about you and he told me that he wasn't happy. He told me that he planned to leave you soon. Only soon never came and I had already fallen in love. .I never meant for things to go this way."

She said, "Have you been tested?" It caught me off guard. It meant she knew. I was silent. "My results were positive. If you haven't been tested yet. I suggest you get tested."

I wasn't sure what to say, so I said, "Why are you here? If you don't mind me asking."

"Not that it's any of your business, but I had a miscarriage. I lost our baby."

That hit me hard. I had no idea that she was pregnant. "I'm sorry." "Save your pity. I don't need it. You're the one I feel sorry for. Yes, I lost my baby. Yes, I've been diagnosed as HIV-positive. But, you must be one lonely, pitiful woman to have to sleep with and get pregnant by a married man. I will not wish any harm on those babies you are carrying; they are innocent in all of this, but you aren't. You deserve everything you get." She said that and then she hung up.

I sat there with the phone in my hand for quite some time before I heard the noise indicating the phone had been left out of the cradle for too long. I placed the phone back in the cradle as tears began to fall. She was right. I was pitiful, lonely and pathetic. How had I ended up here? And now, I was going to die. I wondered if my babies would have the disease. I pushed the button for the nurse to come back in and when she did, I asked her to send one of those counselors in. I had some questions.

When she walked out of the room, I said a simple prayer, "Lord, please, let my babies be alright. Please don't punish them for the sins of their mother. I know I was wrong and I'm sorry. I never meant for any of this to happen, but I know that children are gifts, especially from you, so if it be in your will for me to have these babies, God, please let them be negative. Don't make my babies pay for what their father and I have done."

KENYON

I'd received two calls in less than an hour from the two women in my life, both telling me that they were diagnosed as HIV-positive. I was still at the hospital with Addison I still hadn't told him that I'd already been tested. There was no point.

I stepped out of the room when I felt my phone vibrating in my pocket. So, Addison had no idea that I'd talked to either woman. Well, he didn't know about Justice. I wasn't going to tell him. The truth had caused enough problems as it was. It was much easier living a lie. There was a song out called "Live a Lie" by Jasmine Sullivan, and to be completely honest, I could sure relate to the words at this point in my life. *If a lie gone get me through, I'd rather not know the truth.* Truth was I'd infected two people with a disease that I had no intentions on contracting. I thought Addison and I always practiced safe sex. Well, almost always. I guess that wasn't enough and now he's progressed to having full-blown AIDS. I wondered what that meant for him, for me, for all of us. Eventually we'd all reach that stage. I sat down on the couch in the visitor's waiting room with my head between my hands. I hadn't cried in all this time but now the tears flowed freely. We were all going to die. I had no idea where things went wrong in my marriage. How had I ended up here? An HIV-positive, 29-year-old man with a set of twins about to come into the world by a woman that wasn't my wife and in love with a man. Genesis deserved better than this. I realized it now. I hated all that I'd put her through but there was nothing that I could do about it. I couldn't rewind the hands of time.

When I met Justice, it was all friendly. I never intended to fall for her. She was beautiful; there was no denying that. 5'3, dark chocolate, and the brightest smile you ever did see. When she walked in the room, everyone stopped. Even me. I was captivated I admit. She was the total opposite of Genesis. Where Justice was short and thin, Genesis was tall and thick. Where she was dark chocolate, Genesis was Café au lait, a cup of coffee, three creams. Where Genesis wore her hair long and in soft curls that framed her face, Justice's hair was short and curly, feisty. Where Genesis was laid back and conservative, Justice was spunky in a way that I really couldn't explain. She was on her way to becoming a missionary when we met. She'd told me she was very involved in the church, but I'd met her in a club. She was fine and I had to have her. My wife was gorgeous, but she was boring. Something was missing. I never could pinpoint it but when I met Justice and Addison I felt like I'd found what was missing.. They brought an excitement to my life that hadn't existed in a long time. It was almost like once we got married, all the fun Genesis and I used to have with each other stopped. She got more serious about pursuing her dream of being a writer. She didn't have time for me. Once she finally finished her novel, it was like her career took off over night. When her dream became reality that was all she cared about. I mean I traveled a lot for work but then she was gone all the time. She was doing book signings and speaking engagements. It wasn't like she didn't ask me to go along with her when she was on the road but I never did. I had found someone to keep me occupied and I didn't want to let them go.

Truth told I still didn't want to let go. I was sorry that I was the reason Genesis and Justice had been sentenced to death. I wondered if my babies would be alright. I was angry when I first found out about the babies but they were mine. I couldn't just forget about them as if they didn't exist. Truth was they were here now. It was too late to do anything about that.

I dried my tears and walked back to Addison's room. When I opened the door, he was wiping his eyes. Guess he'd been crying too.

"Hey what's wrong?" I asked walking over to the bed. I was going to hold him until he fell asleep. Then I'd leave. I had a lot of things I needed to figure out.

ADDISON

Kenyon finally showed up at the hospital. I had no idea that the reason I hadn't heard from him was because of all that had happened that day. I didn't know that it was their anniversary. I never would have told him to leave her on their anniversary. Yes, I wanted him but I wasn't completely heartless. I told him that I had AIDS. I wondered what was going through his mind because he didn't say much after that. He got up and walked out of the room. I realized it was a lot to digest, especially since losing a child. I felt bad for him. That's why when he left I'd called Jeremiah and told him that maybe we would be able to work things out after all and that I'd give him a call back soon and let him know. It all depended on what Kenyon wanted. I wouldn't press him to be with me now. He still had his whole life ahead of him. I wasn't sure how much time I had left but I knew that it wasn't going to be very long.

When I asked had he been tested, he didn't answer me, which led me to believe he hadn't. I knew he had to be afraid but I was honest with him from the very first time we'd made love. I gave him the option of getting out before we crossed that line, and we'd always tried to practice being safe. There were a few times when the passion was just too much to let go. I remembered the first night we were together like it happened yesterday. It was perfect. I wasn't sure that he was going to go for it, but we'd been out several times over a couple of months, so I invited him to my house. No longer using business as a pretense, I told him that I was feeling him. I was an openly gay man.

He had to know that by now. He told me that he'd never been with a man but he'd thought about it several times. That he felt like it was a part of him that he'd been fighting for a long time. I had my opening so I took it.

"So, now's your chance. I'm not going to lie to you. I've been attracted to you since day one, but I wasn't sure if you felt the same way."

I touched his locs. I could tell he was nervous.

"I don't know Addison. I mean I'm married and..." His voice trailed off.

"Before anything happens between us, there is something that I need to tell you. " He looked at me but he didn't speak. "Kenyon, I want you. There is no denying that, but I want to give you the chance to walk away from this before you get in too deep. I have HIV."

He looked shocked but he didn't say anything. I wasn't sure if that was a good sign or not. "I promise you that we'll always be safe, if you agree to this, to us."

He didn't leave. I took that as a good sign. When he continued sitting there, I took my chance. Got up from where I was sitting and stood in front of him. "Look at me," I commanded. I was about to school him on what it was like to be loved for real. What a woman could give him was nothing compared to what he'd get from me. He looked up. I looked in his eyes. He wanted this just as much as I did but he would never make the first move. I kissed him. And just like I'd expected, he'd kissed me back. More forcefully than I expected but I liked that in him. I ran my hands through his locs. He was the one to break the kiss.

Out of breath, he said, "Are you sure about this?"

I answered him by taking his hand and leading him into my bedroom. The rest of the night would be a pleasurable one for him. If those walls could talk, they would have told tales of love that was unreal, passion that was unbridled, and sex that was out of this world. Oh, yes. That night I'd made him mine. He couldn't get enough and from then on, we'd been together every opportunity we'd had. Like I said I loved him. I knew that he loved me. I'd never felt this way about anyone before and for that reason I was willing to let him go. His happiness meant that much to me. Just thinking about ending things with Kenyon after all this time made me cry. When I saw the door to the room opening, I wiped my eyes and hoped that he hadn't seen my tears. I wasn't ready to tell him that if he wanted, I'd set him free.

GENESIS

I couldn't believe his mistress had the nerve and the audacity to call me in the hospital and tell me that she was sorry. What kind of woman does something like that? I wondered if she expected to hear any of what I told her. If I was the innocent one in all of this, why should I be the only one to suffer? Lose my baby and end up with a death sentence? I pushed the little red nurse's head on the remote that was attached to the wall. I wanted to know if it was alright if I got out of this bed and walked around. I needed to pay Ms. Justice a visit. I wanted to see what she looked like and since she told me that she was also a patient in the hospital what better time to do it than now? I was feeling vindictive. I wasn't sure what I'd say once I laid eyes on her but something in me had to see this woman. I had to know what the woman who'd been sleeping with my husband for the past year looked like.

The nurse finally buzzed back. "I was wondering if I could get up and walk around. I'm tired of sitting in this bed. I need to move."

She said, "Hold on let me check," and within a few minutes, I had permission to walk around. That was all I needed. I'd have to drag this God forsaken IV with me but I could deal with that as opposed to sitting in the little bed and staring at the beige walls. It was driving me crazy. I was ready to be released. I should be able to leave in a few days at the most, but tomorrow would be nice. I'd have to let that worry about itself though. Now I was on a mission.

I picked up the phone and dialed zero. All I got was a busy signal. I forgot this was a hospital not a hotel. I picked up my cell and dialed the number for the hospital. I asked for patient information and was quickly given the room number. I put on my pink robe that my mother had bought along with the plush pink slippers and padded slowly out of the room. I was still in a bit of pain but if I hoped to get out of here and back to some semblance of a normal life, then I'd better get used to moving again. I walked down to the third floor and located the room I was looking for. I didn't bother knocking before I walked inside. I didn't think she deserved that much courtesy. I held my breath when I walked in to the room. She was sleeping. She looked so at peace. She was beautiful. I was angry. I wasn't sure what I expected but she definitely wasn't it. She looked so young, childlike almost. I found myself feeling sorry for her and taking back all the ill thoughts I'd had against her. I wondered how old she was. I walked over to her bed and stood there. I was glad that I'd opted for the slippers; they didn't make much noise. I sat down in the chair that was near the bed and watched her. I knew that this seemed kind of odd but I wanted to be there when she woke up

JEREMIAH

So he'd finally come to his senses. I wasn't expecting to get the phone call that I'd gotten a little less than an hour ago from Addison but I was glad that he called. He was thinking about giving us another chance. I knew that things between him and Kenyon could never work but he'd set himself up for that when he fell in love with a married man. I tried to reason with him before. I knew that we'd been together for a long time and maybe he was seeking something different. Maybe he wanted some variety but I was willing to let him have his cake and eat it too as long as he promised never to leave me. He didn't think that was such a good idea because he'd already developed feelings for this man. I'd thought about taking the life of Kenyon Swan since day one. He took the only thing that had ever meant anything to me and yes, he would pay. I'd take something that was dear to him. Even if I managed to salvage things with Addison, Kenyon was still going to pay. He owed me for my pain and suffering but I didn't have time to take him to small claims court. Besides the price he paid would be far greater than what he'd cost me. He had no idea. Neither did Addison. Oh, yes. They were both going to pay for making me look like a fool. That was a given. I loved Addison but what he had done to me had been unforgivable. I loved him so I'd overlook it until I could find the perfect opportunity to execute my plan. Revenge was on my mind.

Addison had no idea that if given the chance, he would soon be sleeping with the enemy. I laughed. Though there was nothing really funny about what I was planning to do to either man. Death and destruction would soon strike the doors of Kenyon Swan and Addison Limón. I was going to make sure of that. I'd gotten played, but I would have the last laugh. I took the top off of the pill bottle I'd been holding in my hand. It was time for my meds. See, I was an AIDS patient. Yes, full blown. I wasn't sure how much time I had left but for now, I was well. As long as I took my meds and stayed away from most sick people, I never really got sick anymore. In the beginning, I stayed sick. I was glad that part was over. I popped thirteen pills and chased them with water. Then I had two glasses of wine. I was celebrating. I blew out the candles and got in bed. Tomorrow was another day.

KENYON

I left Addison as soon as I knew he was sleeping soundly. I kissed his forehead and left as quietly as I possibly could. It was hard for me watching him lie in that bed and know that there was nothing I could do. Love had a way of making you want to protect people, even when you knew in your heart there was nothing you could do. I wanted to take all of his pain and make it my own. That's how much I loved him. I was fooling myself or at least trying to talk myself out of it. Telling myself that what we had was just a deep infatuation with each other but I had to stop lying to myself at some point. I was in love with him.

I tossed and turned all night in the hotel room that I'd gotten. I wished that I could have gone home and slept in my own bed but I knew that my in-laws were there and as long as they were, there was no way that I could be. So, I rented a room at the Hyatt. I wasn't sure how long I'd be there but for now this was home. My mind was so full. It kept replaying the conversations with both Genesis and Justice. I gave them both HIV. I picked up the phone to call the doctor's office. When the attendant answered, I said, "I need to make an appointment for today." She scheduled my appointment, gave me all the information I needed and told me that I should arrive at least thirty minutes early for the appointment since all patients were required to talk to a counselor at each appointment. I thanked her and hung up. I needed to try to eat something; I hadn't eaten since I'd gotten to Justice's house. I was hungry. I got up, dressed, and went down to the complimentary breakfast bar they offered at the hotel. Once I made my plate, I picked up the paper and on the front page was an article about Genesis. Someone from the hospital must be leaking information; there was no way that her publicist would have agreed to this. I wondered if she knew that everyone in the area was aware that she was HIV-positive. I hung my head. My appetite was gone. I'd ruined her life. I never even stopped to think of what this would do to her. All I'd thought about all this time was myself. What I wanted. What I needed. What I felt I was lacking at home. Now because of me, she was sick, she'd lost our baby, and her business was plastered all over the front of the newspaper. I felt tears well up in my eyes but I wasn't going to cry. I put the paper down and glanced at my watch. I needed to leave if I wanted to make it to the doctor's office thirty minutes early. I had a thirty-minute drive ahead of me. I hoped that traffic wasn't out of control.

Luckily, traffic wasn't heavy and I pulled into the lot of the doctor's office just in time. I walked into the office, gave the lady my name, filled out the necessary paperwork and waited for the counselor to call me back. I sat in the office that was brightly decorated and looked at all the sad faces. I wondered how many other people were here for the same reason I was. There wasn't a happy face in the room, with the exception of the nurse who seemed to be too chipper for this setting. I wanted to slap her for smiling at me. Didn't she know that I had nothing to smile about?

Once my name was called for the counselor, I told her that I already knew that I was HIV positive but my lover had just been diagnosed as having full-blown AIDS. I wanted to know the timeline, how long the progression from one to the other usually took. I wanted to know if there was anything I could do to keep from developing AIDS.

"Well, I won't lie to you. That can happen really at any time. It's a case-by-case things so I can't tell you that it will take ten or fifteen years for you to develop the AIDS virus. You are already disposed being that you have HIV. I know that you'd like for me to give you good news but the truth is, I have none to give. The only thing I can suggest at this point would be for you to see your doctor."

She couldn't give me good news? Was she serious? I felt the room start to spin when she told me that it was a case-by-case basis. I'd always assumed that it took years for the virus to progress. Now she was telling me that wasn't true. I wasn't prepared for everything that she told me. The good thing about it is that I knew the person that had infected me as well as the others that had been infected by me. They had already been tested. They were already positive. I told her that this was only an informational visit. I needed to know what I had to look forward to from now on. What we all had to look forward to. She looked at me like she pitied me. I knew she was really thinking was that I deserved whatever I got. Truth was she was right. I did deserve it. After the meeting with the counselor was over, I saw the doctor. I decided to take that time to walk and clear my head. My thoughts were all over the place. There was always something about hearing a person tell you bad news when you already knew that the bad news was there. Acknowledgement made everything real. As long as I didn't acknowledge it, it didn't exist. That was wishful thinking.

It was a nice day out. Too bad everything in my life seemed wrong. I used to love days like this; now I had a feeling they would only remind me of the day my life changed.. I could tell from the somber look on his face that the news he had for me wasn't good.

"I'm sorry to be the one to inform you, Mr. Swan, but your viral loads are coming back abnormal. It appears that one of the medications that we have you on currently is no longer working. What I'll need to do is add two new medications to your treatment regimen in hopes that one of them regulates those levels." I felt like I'd been punched in the chest.. I couldn't even explain it. It was like for the first time since I'd been diagnosed months ago, the reality that I was sick was just setting in. I felt the tears falling before I could stop them. "Are you going to be okay?"

Am I going to be okay? Was he serious? I was HIV-positive. Was there any such thing as okay anymore? I wasn't sure. All I knew was that this wasn't something that I'd ever thought would happen to me.

"What happens now?" I asked before I thought about it. I think I was talking more to myself than to him but he answered any way.

"Now, we find out the best course of treatment to slow the progression of the disease. We run tests. You keep living. That's what happens now." He sounded so certain. I wasn't certain of anything except that I'd just had my life cut short. "Schedule another appointment for a week out and I'll see you then. We're going to fight this tooth and nail. I can't tell you that you'll beat it, because there is no cure, but you will have a longer life than you would have had you been diagnosed twenty years ago. I'm sorry you have to go through this, but I'll be here with you every step of the way. Make sure to inform your lovers of your status. It's illegal not to."

I thanked him, made my next appointment and left. Once I got in the car, I broke down. I hated myself. I was headed back to the hospital to be with Addison. Now there was no reason to end any of the relationships with the exception of my marriage. I knew that there was no way Genesis would ever even consider being with me now. I considered saying another prayer but I knew that it would be a waste of time. God wasn't trying to hear me. I'd caused too many problems, ruined too many lives.

JUSTICE

I woke up to a woman sitting in the chair near my bed, I wasn't expecting visitors. It wasn't my sister. I rubbed my eyes and tried to focus. I'd fallen asleep with my contacts in and they'd moved when I rubbed my eyes, so I couldn't make out her face. She didn't speak. She just continued to sit there as if this was the most natural thing. Once I got my contacts right, I looked at her again. I was shocked to see her sitting here. I didn't think that she'd be bold enough to come to my room. Genesis Swan didn't strike me as the confrontational type. So, I didn't know what to expect.

"What are you doing in my room?" I asked trying to put some attitude in my voice, although what I really felt was fear. "You can calm down, sweetheart. I only came to see what you looked like. I had to know what the woman who was bold enough to continue sleeping with my husband even after she found out about me looked like. I must admit you aren't at all what I'd expected."

She wasn't rude. She wasn't condescending. She was honest. "I feel like you owe me an explanation so I came to get it. I've been here for a while. You looked so peaceful while you were sleeping, I didn't want to wake you so I waited."

Wow. She sounded motherly, even, like she held some concern for me. I ran my hands through my short hair. I wasn't sure what she wanted me to say, so I said nothing.

"Why did you do it? What made you sleep with my husband?"

"I didn't know that he was married when the affair first started.

I told you that when we spoke on the phone. I was infatuated with Kenyon. He made me feel beautiful when I needed it. He gave me compliments. I gave him my body, my heart. I love him."

She didn't speak, just looked at me as if to say is that all?

"Once I'd found out about you, I was in too deep. I figured what you didn't know couldn't hurt you. Felt like maybe you were treating him wrong. What other reason would he have to be unfaithful? He said he wasn't happy. I believed him."

She shifted in the chair. "So you were desperate? Is that it? I mean I realize that once you fall in love with a person it's hard to leave them, but he is a married man. You should have stopped."

"I know. You're right. I can't tell you how sorry I am but I realize that sorry doesn't change anything. It doesn't make it better."

She was staring at my stomach; I saw the tears in her eyes. I felt horrible. "So you're going to have the babies I take it?" She didn't sound mad, just envious.

"Yes, I'm going to have them. He wants me to get rid of them but I don't believe in abortion. Truthfully, I was trying to get pregnant. I figured if I did, he'd leave you and be with me."

She chuckled softly. "You aren't the only one. I told you that. Even if he left me, which he has, it wouldn't be for you. He left me to be with that man. I guess you were just going to be his side-piece. Let me ask you this, did you ever think that he would do that to you?"

That was something I'd never even considered. "To be honest with you, no. I didn't. I guess hindsight is 20/20.."

"You said you never meant to hurt me? You didn't hurt me. You couldn't. You have no obligation to me. The only person that you hurt is yourself and those babies. I feel sorry for you." She'd just been told that her husband was leaving her for a man, that he was sleeping with me too, that I was pregnant and she'd just lost her baby, but she felt sorry for me. I didn't understand how that worked exactly.

"You feel sorry for me?"

She looked at me like I was stupid."Yes, I feel sorry for you. See, my life has been ripped completely apart. Turned upside down. Everything I knew to be true wasn't. I thought he loved me. I was wrong. I've lost my marriage, my child, I've been told that I'm HIV-positive but at the end of the day, even with all that is wrong in my life, I can sleep at night knowing that none of this was my doing. I didn't cause this. I didn't deserve this. I'm the innocent one in all of this. Me and your babies. We are the victims of unfortunate circumstance. Could I have been more attentive to Kenyon? Sure. But I have a career and he was supposed to be supportive of that. He was supposed to love me enough to tell me that he felt neglected. Yet, instead, he made the choice to turn to someone else. Even when I was traveling, I never thought about sleeping with someone else. Do you know why? My heart belonged only to him. So yes, I feel sorry for you because you deserve whatever happens to you. You brought this on yourself. You have no one else to blame for being here. You were a willing participant in your own downfall.."

I hadn't thought about it that way. When she put it like that, I felt sorry for me. This was my fault. I'd been so busy blaming Kenyon that I'd never stopped to take responsibility for my own actions. I was the reason I was in this position.

"Oh," was all I'd said in response to that. I really wanted to cry.

"How old are you?"

I didn't know why she was asking me this but I answered anyway "I'm twenty-three. Why?"

"I'm asking because you look young. I just wondered how much younger you were than me. Well I've gotten the information I came to get. I'll leave you to yourself now. I'm sure you have a lot to think about. I'll be praying that your babies aren't infected. Have a wonderful evening."

She got up, tightened the rope on her bathrobe and walked out of the room without so much as a backwards glance. I was in awe. Even though she'd just come and made me feel like crap, she was so classy. Was it stupid that I still wanted her autograph? She'd given me a lot to think about but I'm sure she knew that's what she was doing. I envied her. Even in the midst of all that was happening in her life, she had somehow found the strength to take comfort in something. I was mad at Kenyon for cheating on her, for cheating on me. I'd been played but that's what I got for falling for a married man. I'd played myself. So, I guess she was right; I deserved what I'd gotten. God how had I let my life spin out of control like this? I needed to find my way back to what I knew was right, what I knew was true.

GENESIS

She wasn't anything that I'd expected. Young and seemingly not as dumb as I thought she'd be. She appeared to have her head on her shoulders. I said what I had to say and walked out of the room. I truly felt sorry for her. Desperation and low self-esteem caused her to end up in a place that no woman should be at twenty-three years old, a place that no woman should be ever. I really did feel sorry for her. I was beginning to come to grips with things. I had no other option; feeling sorry for myself would get me nowhere. I realized that. I also realized that it was time for me to get back to God. I had left him and look where I'd ended up. My father told me that things were going to have to get bad before I came back to God and I'd always told him that he was wrong, that I'd make time to get back to God when life was less hectic. Only life hadn't gotten less hectic. It had only slowly gotten busier.

I married Kenyon against my parent's wishes. My father was the one to try to tell me that Kenyon wasn't the man I thought he was. I'm not sure why I didn't listen. I was young and dumb and wanted to assert my independence. I was seventeen when I met Kenyon. I'd never forget the first time I met him. We were on a college tour together. Several schools had gathered at Howard University so that the graduating class had the chance to tour the campus. We bumped into each other in the student union and as I bent down to pick up the things I'd dropped, he had done the same. When we both stood up I was staring into the most beautiful pair of eyes I'd ever seen on a man. For me it was love at first sight. We spent the next couple of hours talking while we were given the chance to break from our groups. He told me that he was from my hometown and attended the high school across town. No wonder I'd never seen him. I didn't go to many games or school activities. I spent most of my time in church being the daughter of a preacher and all. Once we made it back home we started doing a lot of talking on the phone. I'd begged my father to let me go on a date with him and to my surprise he agreed that Kenyon could escort me to my senior prom. I felt like Cinderella that night. From that moment on we were inseparable. Kenyon said he didn't believe in God. I should have run then but he excited me. Slowly I'd stopped attending Bible study and all of the other services that I attended on a regular basis. I started arguing with my parents. Something I'd never done before. I told my father that as far as I was concerned if God didn't want us together he never would have allowed us to meet. My mother disliked him more than my father, but Daddy told me that if I wasn't careful Kenyon was going to hurt me in ways I'd never imagine. He'd said that anyone that took you in the opposite direction of where God was trying to take you was nothing but the enemy wrapped in flesh. I just blew him off. Kenyon treated me wonderfully at first. We both graduated and ended up attending the same college. Girls were always throwing themselves at him and I wanted to believe that he was faithful. I knew he wasn't though, but I told myself it didn't matter because I loved him. He told me one night during our junior year that he thought we should take a break and see other people. I went for it and I started dating another guy from campus, but my heart always belonged to Kenyon. He got mad when rumors started going around campus that I'd slept with the other guy. That was part of the reason he wanted to take a break because I refused to give him my virginity. I wanted to wait until we were married. I'd ended up going to a party one night and though I'd never gotten drunk before that night. I'd had one too many drinks and ended up in the dorm room of the guy I was seeing. When I came to I wasn't sure exactly what had happened but I was sure that we hadn't slept together. Kenyon confronted me about it. That was the first time he'd ever raised his voice to me. He said that I'd hurt him but he's the one who wanted the break. I apologized over and over again. Finally in our senior year, right before graduation he told me that he missed me, that he'd forgiven me and he asked me to be his wife. I said yes. I wanted to prove to my parents that they couldn't run my life. I wanted to show them how wrong they had been about Kenyon. How silly I had been.

I should have listened to them, should have listened to my heart when it told me that he wasn't the one for me. But I wanted to believe in us. So we got married and then my career took off; I was an instant success. It was as if I'd written the first book and, overnight, it was on the best sellers list. My father said that was the favor of God in my life. I told him that was my talent landing me where I deserved to be. Amongst the stars. I was a household name. I was happy, or so I thought. Then I found out I was pregnant. That dream was taken away from me and my life was turned upside down. I hadn't told anyone about the first miscarriage. I figured Kenyon would be devastated if he knew. That was six months ago. Since then I'd been trying to get pregnant. I wanted nothing more than to be a mother. But it was as if a cyclone had hit my life and left nothing but destruction its wake. I was a fighter. This wouldn't destroy me. I couldn't say that it wouldn't kill me because, unfortunately, eventually it would. My responsibility now was to make the most of the time that I had left. I refused to sit around and get sick. No, I was about to live my life like each day was my last. This whole thing put things in perspective for me. I'd taken so much for granted, especially my relationship with God. I was faithful to my husband. But I'd cheated on my father, God, with the devil and look where it landed me. I was truly sorry. I wondered, though, if I was sorry because of all that had happened because I wasn't faithful in my relationship to God or if I was sorry because I failed God. This time I decided to pray like my parents taught me to pray when you had a sincere request. I sincerely wanted God to forgive, redeem and restore me. I needed strength. I needed restoration. I needed God to make it through the rest of this trial.

7 months later...

JUSTICE

I couldn't believe that so much time had passed. I gave birth to the babies. Two little girls. They were beautiful. I fell in love the first time I laid eyes on them. Kenyrah and Keniyah. I know I probably shouldn't have but since they both looked exactly like Kenyon, I thought it was fitting. They were beautiful babies. Both paper bag brown, light green eyes and one dimple, each on different sides. I didn't think it was possible to love anyone or anything as much as I loved these girls. They had my heart wrapped around their little fingers. This was what love really felt like. I would do anything to protect my babies. Thank God that they both tested negative consistently since being born. God had answered my prayers and kept them safe. The sins of the mother wouldn't affect them, at least not health wise. They were perfect.

Kenyon made an effort to be a part of their lives. I was thankful for that. I told him after talking to Genesis that day in the hospital that there was no way we could be together ever again. I deserved better and so did his wife. I wasn't going to lie and say that it wasn't hard every time I saw him because God knows that it was but I was making an effort to get my life back on track. I started attending church again. The guilt that I carried with me in the beginning was no longer there. I was forgiven; not only had I been forgiven by God but I'd forgiven myself and Genesis had forgiven me. I wrote her a letter after I rededicated my life to God and told her again how sorry I was and that I needed to know that she could forgive me and I asked her to do something else for me. Something that no one else but she and I were aware of.

Should anything happen to me, I wanted her to have my babies. Most people would probably think I was crazy for this but I believed that she would give them all the love she had. She wrote back and told me that she would forgive me, not because I really deserved her forgiveness but because she, too, was trying to get her life with Christ right and she realized that in order to be forgiven she must first learn to forgive. She also told me that should anything happen to me she would take the girls. That she was honored I even thought of her to be their guardian. I didn't care what her reason was as long as she was able to forgive me and I was able to move forward with a clear conscience and leave this world knowing that my children would be well taken care of.

The girls would be two months old in a few days. Time had passed in a blur. One minute I was being told that I was sick and the next it seemed like my water was breaking. I was in church the day I went into labor. I was on the altar getting prayer when I felt this terrible pain rip through me. I had to sit down; not five minutes later my water broke. I was rushed from the church straight to the hospital via ambulance and delivered two healthy babies. Thank God. I was sure that he was going to punish my babies for what I did. I had to be reminded that God doesn't operate like that. Once I realized that, I had peace about things. It felt good to have some sort of normal life back.

Don't get me wrong; things were nowhere near easy. So far, I was healthy and my doctor assured me that as long as I was careful and took my meds like I should, I'd be okay. I didn't know what it was but for some reason lately I felt like I didn't have much time left, so I tried to make sure that all of my affairs were in order and that all of my legal documents could be located in one place. There were insurance policies and the guardianship papers, which I'd had drawn up right after Genesis agreed to take my children. Kenyon had no idea that he would not be taking care of our children once I was gone. I think he assumed so but he never asked and I never brought it up. Truth was I didn't trust him to do what was best for them. I mean sure he came around and he sent his support payments on time but other than that, he was uninvolved. He couldn't even tell the twins apart.

The phone rang and it was Kenyon. I didn't feel like talking at the moment, so I didn't answer. I just let it go to the voicemail. He apparently didn't want anything because he didn't leave a message. I didn't bother to call him back. I was slowly but surely pulling away from him. There was a man at my church who had recently started expressing interest in me. I thought about seeing where that could go. It had been enough time since Kenyon and I were actually together. The day he hit me was the last day that I actually even thought about him in that way. God knew that it was hard because he was all up in my soul but I knew that he was bad for me and he'd caused enough destruction in my life. That ship had sailed and I was thankful. The only concern I had about getting to know Jared was that I'd have to be honest with him about my status. I wasn't comfortable telling anyone that I was HIV-positive as of yet. I was sure that there were rumors; you know how people talk but I didn't know what he'd heard and what he hadn't. I guess the only way to find out would be to ask him. Besides, going to dinner and a movie couldn't hurt anything and it would give me a chance to see if I even liked him. The next time he asked me out, I'd tell him yes. I was tired of being alone and it wasn't even the sex I missed; it was just the companionship.

KENYON

My daughters were born healthy. Thank God. When they tested negative every time they went to the doctor, I had a little more hope that they wouldn't ever test positive. I missed Genesis. I missed Justice. Neither really wanted anything to do with me now. I couldn't say that I blamed them. I just wondered why neither of them felt like I deserved a second chance. I was taking care of Addison. He'd been sick a lot lately but I guess that came with the territory. He was the only one who even acted like I was still worth the time, worth the love.

I really wanted to try to make things work with Genesis. I prayed that God would bring us back together but I'd broken her heart and she wasn't trying to hear anything that I had to say. As much as I hated to admit it, I was miserable without her. I'd just called Justice to check on Kenyrah and Keniyah but she didn't answer. I hadn't spent as much time with them as I should have but I had a lot going on. I wasn't even really sure that I wanted to be a father most days. Knowing that I was responsible for someone else's well-being wasn't something I was sure that I could handle. I was trying though. I still couldn't tell them apart, which pissed Justice off. She thought that I should be able to tell them apart but I wasn't her and I didn't spend as much time with them as she did.

"Did you reach the mother of your children?" Addison was still pissed. I didn't tell him about Justice until the last minute. To be more specific, I didn't tell him until I got the phone call saying that she was in labor. Then I was forced to be honest. I never meant to hurt him. I never meant to hurt anyone; that's just the way things happened.

"No. I didn't." I wasn't in the mood for this argument again.

"Kenyon, why can't you just fight her for custody and we raise the babies?"

There he went again. Did he forget that he had AIDS and I was HIV-positive? Did he forget that I was married when I involved myself with him and with her? Did he really think that a judge was going to actually give me custody of two infant girls? I was sure that he didn't think about all of that. I didn't feel this today. Not today.

"Can we not do this? Please. It's getting old. I'm not interested in taking the twins from Justice, Addison. Besides, no judge in his right mind would take them away from her and give them to us. It's just not realistic. You may as well get over it already."

"Get over it? Kenyon, get over it? Seriously. You were cheating on me with her and I'm just supposed to get over it? You've got a lot of nerve."

I knew where this was headed. "I wasn't cheating on you with her. Let's be real about it. I was cheating on my wife with both of you."

For some reason this was an issue lately. I wasn't really sure what his problem was but I was definitely getting tired of him and his dramatic, self-entitled attitude. Did he realize that I didn't really owe him anything? It was like all of a sudden he was turning into some nagging woman, except he was a man. Even Genesis never nagged me. I was really missing her these past few months. So many times, I'd picked up the phone to call her but I could never bring myself to dial her number. Truth was I loved her. I'd always loved her. I think it took me all this time to find out exactly how much. Sometimes you have to walk away from a person to realize that they really were the person you wanted to be with. I just prayed that it wasn't too late. Although I was certain that it was past too late. I knew that saying sorry wasn't going to fix what I'd broken. Her life would never be the same because of me. I hated myself for it. My guilt was tearing me up. I spent so many days crying and asking God to fix the mess I'd made. If not in my life, then at least in Genesis' life.. Justice and Addison weren't innocent. They were both willing participants. Addison was well aware that I was married before anything ever happened between us. Justice claimed that she didn't know but I think she did. I never removed my ring. She wasn't that naïve.

"Are you really going to sit here and ignore me?"

I guess I'd tuned him out and gotten lost on my stroll down memory lane. "I told you I wasn't in the mood, Addison. I meant that."

"You know what? I'm getting really tired of you blowing me off. You keep treating me like my feelings don't matter."

"I never said that they don't matter. It's just that you keep complaining about something that isn't going to change. No matter how much we want the reality of the situation to be different, it isn't. You need to understand that. Now if you want to push me away, keep talking. Otherwise let it go."

I meant that. He was close to losing me. I guess that's what he wanted. I'd find out soon enough. I knew one thing, if this conversation kept coming up then I was leaving. I couldn't take it anymore.

GENESIS

Seven months had passed and so much had happened. I wrote two more books. I was still a household name; only this time it was more so because of all that had happened in my life than because of my writing. Someone in the hospital leaked information to the press about my HIV status so all of my fans were aware that I was HIV-positive. I held a press conference and came out with the truth. All of it. My Bible says that we are overcome by the words of our testimonies. So I told mine and I felt better. There was a plan at work here. Something bigger than my understanding. I didn't question God about it. I simply used my test as a catapult into another arena of fame. Now I was a motivational speaker as well. I traveled all over speaking to young women and young men about how their decisions affected more than just themselves. I didn't end up in the place I was in because I had been sleeping around or anything like that. I ended up here because I trusted someone to love me enough to care about me. I trusted someone to love me enough to take care of me and not do anything to put my life in danger and I was betrayed. I was learning now, though, that sometimes betrayal is necessary. Sometimes it's needed to usher you into the place that God wants to take you. This was what it took for God to get my attention and now He truly had it.

Not only was I doing speaking engagements, Justice and I kept in touch. I was to be guardian of her daughters if anything ever happened to her, something Kenyon knew nothing about. I was fond of those little girls and I loved them as if they were mine. Some days I couldn't help but wonder how our baby would look, would it have been a girl or a boy. Some days my heart ached so badly from the emptiness, but it was in those times that I prayed like there was no tomorrow. So far I was lucky or blessed enough not to have been really sick. I was really careful of germs and being around sick people. Sometimes I was too careful. I can't lie and say that I wasn't still afraid because I was, but I knew that fear was natural. I wasn't operating in fear; it was just a feeling that I had sometimes. I didn't know what was going to happen but I trusted that God would work it all out for my good.

Today, though, I'd filed for divorce. After much prayer and much thought, I was sure that I could never trust Kenyon again. Not after the way he changed my life. He took so much away from me that I didn't know if I'd ever be able to forgive him, but then, one day, while I was praying, I heard God clearly tell me that in order to move forward I'd have to forgive him. It took a while, but finally, I was able to.. I knew that I'd forgiven him with my heart and with my soul because I was no longer angry. Now I only felt pity for him. I felt sorrow when I thought of him. No longer love, no longer hate, just sorrow. I prayed for God to turn his heart and to bless him. I prayed that God keep his health. I knew that if I was sick he had to be too. He'd ruined so many lives with his selfishness, but I knew that the same God that had forgiven me would forgive him too.

I hadn't talked to him since the day he told me what he did after I woke up in the hospital. My father made it clear that he was to stay away from me if he knew what was good for him. That made it that much easier to file for divorce. I was ready to be completely free of that part of my life. I'd started a new chapter. I wasn't ready to be with anyone else just yet. My focus was just on getting better emotionally, getting back to God spiritually and staying healthy physically. Yes, I was going to be alright. I had an assurance that things were going to work out for my good so I wasn't worried. I wondered, though, if Kenyon was going to contest the divorce. I prayed that he wouldn't put up a fight. Only God knew just how much I'd have to pray on that.

ADDISON

I don't know who Kenyon thought he was, but I did know that he would be sorry for treating me like what I felt or thought concerning his whore and his brats didn't matter. He thought that he needed to keep reminding me that he was cheating with me as well. I already knew that but I didn't feel like I counted because I wasn't a female. I was all man. I should have been enough for him. I guess I wasn't. I was seeing Jeremiah behind Kenyon's back. He took a lot of out of town business trips for his job, so whenever he was out of town, Jeremiah kept me company. I missed him. I didn't realize just how much until the first time we were together again. It was like picking up where we left off. There was no fumbling. He hadn't forgotten and neither had I. The passion still existed between us. I thought I was falling in love with him again.

Would I tell Kenyon? Absolutely not, but if he thought that his threatening me was fazing me, he didn't know how wrong he was. He was the one who'd better tread lightly before he found himself out in the streets. He couldn't go back to his precious wife. He'd ruined her life. She was now infected like everyone else. It really was unfortunate that things had turned out this way. I never meant for anyone to be hurt in the ways that those women were hurt. All I wanted was him to be mine and he was. But it cost two other people in the process. I had no idea that he was still sleeping with his wife and I definitely didn't know anything about the mother of his children. I felt betrayed because I thought that I was the only other person in his life.

That was the reason I didn't feel bad for sleeping with Jeremiah. Kenyon betrayed me first and we all know that what goes around comes around. Oh yes, he was going to get what was coming to him. I couldn't wait. Although his wife had held that press conference telling her story, she never named names, well no names except for her and her now "estranged" husband. She never said that his affair was with a man. Only that he had extra marital affairs and, because of this, she was HIV-positive and they were no longer together. It was my job to finish that destruction. I was going to ruin him, so that he had nowhere else to turn but to me when his world came collapsing down around him. I sat back with my drink in hand and smiled at the thought. There was more than one way to get what I wanted. I always got what I wanted when I wanted and he was about to find that out the hard way.

JEREMIAH

Obviously Addison thought I was a fool. Yes, I gave him what he wanted but he wasn't the only one planning to destroy someone. Looks like we both had secrets. I knew that he was only back with me because he was mad at that boy he'd been with lately. I wasn't as stupid as he thought I was but I was sexing him something serious because I wanted to. I missed him, but there was definitely a method to my madness. In due time, he'd see just what playing with my heart was going to cost him. I wondered if when it was all said and done he'd think it was worth it. Foolish, foolish man. He'd soon see just how big a mistake he was making. I allowed myself to be played like a fiddle but only for so long. He had no idea that I was on to him, nor did he have any idea that he stood to lose a whole lot more than his little lover.

Oh, yes, I would have the last laugh. He knew that I wanted us to be together. I wanted us to die together. I knew in the beginning when he got sick that we would be together forever. After all, how many other men would willingly be with a man who was HIV-positive? Then that boy came along and changed everything. He ruined my life, but not only my life; in midst of ruining my life, he inadvertently ruined his own life. He lost his wife because he infected her with the disease and had two children with another woman that he infected. He was lucky that those women hadn't pressed charges on him. He could have been charged with conspiracy to commit murder or actual murder, if, and when they die from the disease he gave them. Ultimately, he'd handed them a death sentence. Sure modern medicine would prolong the effects of the disease. It would save their lives for a while but no one knew when it would take a turn for the worse. No one knew when they'd go into that one illness their immune system could not recover from. Nope. No one knew. That was the one thing about this disease. You never knew when that day would come. I didn't think I had that much time left.

I beat the clock. I was sick for years. I was sick before I met Addison but I didn't tell him in the beginning. Hell, I didn't even tell him until he told me that he'd tested positive. I remember that day like it was yesterday. He was sick with a cold he couldn't seem to get rid of, so he went to the doctor. He got some cold meds and came home. A few days later, he was supposed to have his annual checkup, so he went in and he began telling his regular doctor about all the symptoms he was experiencing and the doctor asked him if he'd ever been tested. He told the doctor no, that there was no reason for him to be tested, but he took the test because that's what was suggested. About ten days later, he got the call. I walked in the house and he was sitting in the chair staring out the window with this blank look and tears streaming down his face. I sat down next to him and took his hand in mine and asked what was wrong. I was thinking maybe someone had died. What he said was music to my ears.

"I'm dying Jeremiah. I have HIV." Inside I was smiling. It had taken longer than I wanted to infect him but it had been done. I played it cool though.

"You've got what?" He turned to look at me as if he'd just noticed I was in the room, like he was seeing me for the first time.

"I just got off the phone with the doctor. I haven't been sick because of a cold. I've been sick because I've got HIV. I just… I don't…"

Then he broke down. I held him and let him cry. He then told me that he'd had so many lovers during the past ten years that he wasn't sure where he contracted the disease. He didn't want to lose me and thought I should get tested as well. He wouldn't make love to me until

I did. That's when he found out that I was sick too. It was hard to pull off but I managed to keep all my medications hidden from him the whole time we'd been dating. After we were both diagnosed, things between us were good. Until he met Kenyon. That's when the down-hill slide began. He never knew about my lie, and since no one else did either, there was no one who could tell him that I was the one to give him the disease. Then again since he'd had so many lovers there was no telling if I was actually the one to give it to him. There were a few more of the men he slept with that tested positive for the disease.

I was hurt. This man was my life. My whole world and he turned on me. He didn't love me enough to be faithful after all that we'd been through. I was the one who took care of him when he was sick. I was the one who wiped sweat from his face. I was the one who held his hand. Me. This was the repayment I got. I went from his main thing to his side thing. That's some mess that only happened to women. I don't know who he thought he was. I had a love for him that was bordering on hate. After all, there is a thin line. Soon enough he'd see that he'd gambled and he'd lost. I was just biding my time. I couldn't wait. Soon as the opportunity presented itself, I'd be sure to take it. He wouldn't know what hit him. Oh yes, this was going to be good. The wheels had already been set in motion.

AURELIA

Months had passed since Genesis was released from the hospital. So far, she seemed fine. I was thankful to God for that. The illness that she was diagnosed with somehow hadn't affected her at all. She showed no symptoms of being ill. Something else that I was thanking God for. I didn't believe that my daughter was sick. It was something I was still in denial about. God was merciful. I couldn't allow myself to believe that He would punish her this way for something that she didn't do. That wasn't the kind of God that I served. I knew that this thing would work out for her good.

I was, however, glad that she was in the process of getting a divorce. I never did like Kenyon. I tried to tell Genesis before she married him but she didn't want to hear it and all I wanted was for my daughter to be happy. So, I kept her in my prayers and things seemed to be okay until he told her that he was cheating on her. Her world began to spiral out of control. She managed to regain some semblance of order in her life. I was happy for her. We were trying to get her to move closer to us but she said that would only be running and that she wasn't running from what had happened. She wanted to face this head on. I asked her the last time we spoken if she had spoken to Kenyon and she told me that she hadn't heard from him since the day he walked out of the hospital room and Judah told him not to come back. He moved all his things out while we were still there and I wondered where he was now. How could he just ruin her life and leave like it was nothing? He couldn't have ever loved her, not to do these things to her. I guess it wasn't my call. I prayed for him. He needed God to touch his heart more than anyone else involved in this sad situation. God was going to get the glory. Of that, I was certain.

JARED

I'd been trying to get Justice to go out with me for quite some time now. I knew that her situation was different. I just wanted a chance to prove to her that all men weren't like that last man. I watched her closely. I knew that deep down she was a good woman. She was just struggling and searching for something that she still hadn't found. I could tell that she had gotten sidetracked although I wasn't sure in what way. She had two adorable green-eyed little girls that I absolutely loved to be around. They were just infants but they smiled each time I held them. She seemed to trust me with them and for that, I was at least glad. If she trusted me with her children, maybe she'd trust me with her heart one day. That's all I could ask for. I wasn't really sure what it was about her that drew me to her. I just knew that I wanted a chance at getting to know her.

I got her number from one of the ladies at our church but hadn't mustered up the courage to call her. I figured I'd ask her out again if she made it to Bible study. Hopefully, she would say yes. All I wanted was a chance but I wouldn't push.

JUSTICE

It was time for me to do something different. I couldn't live the rest of my life in fear of being hurt. I knew that God was love, and if he loved me, then someone else would too in spite of my situation. God was too good a God to let me live the rest of my life alone. I didn't know what this feeling was but I felt like I didn't have much time left. For some reason, I felt like death was swarming around me. I didn't know what, when, or how but I did know that I wasn't going to be here that much longer. It was an odd feeling but strangely, it was one that I was at peace with. It wasn't something that I made a habit of telling people. It was just one of those thing you have to make peace with within yourself. I thought it was necessary to make sure to live my life to the best of my ability each day and make sure that I ended the day with no regrets and much repentance. Daily, I made it a habit to end the day asking God to forgive me for the areas in which I fell short. I knew that He was faithful to do that as long as I was sincere with what I was saying to Him. All I wanted was to make the most of the days that I had left. I wasn't sure how much time that was but what I was sure of was that whether it be a day, a month, a year, or ten years, I was going to make the most of my time and live each day like it was my last. That was the reason why I said, "Yes" the next time Jared asked me out. I was determined to see where this could go and I felt like I gave myself enough time to get over Kenyon. He was no longer in my heart., at least not like that. I had purged myself of him. I just wanted to make sure that I wasn't going to punish another man for his mistakes.

When Jared asked me out, I sat him down and made sure that he knew what he was getting into. I didn't know that he had already heard about my situation, about the babies and the disease. He said that he didn't believe that either of those things defined me. They didn't make me the woman that I was and the fact that I smiled through and praised through it was what attracted him to me. I was shocked but I was thankful to God for the opportunity to find out what it was like to be with a man who had no hidden agenda. If I was lucky, before I left the world. I'd be fortunate enough to find out what it meant to be loved. I believed that God would give me that one desire of my heart. It was rare that I asked Him for anything else but this had always been my prayer. It had always been my desire.

GENESIS

My reprieve was over. It had been a nice seven months but I knew that once I signed those papers and had them sent to him, he was going to flip out. I knew that he didn't believe I'd ever file for divorce because I didn't believe in it. But, there was a time that I didn't believe he'd be unfaithful again and we all know how that turned out. My beliefs had changed. Nothing was as it once was and I wasn't sure that things would ever be again. Now, everything was a case-by-case basis. Personal. There was no one belief for a group. I'd take situations and deal with them as they came. I knew that once he got the paperwork in his hands he was going to call. I was right. He tried calling the house. He called my office and cell. He got an answer at the office, but I wouldn't take his call. For what? There was nothing left for us to say to each other. He left a message on my cell saying how sorry he was. Begging for forgiveness. Now? I forgave him before but did that mean that I had to be the same fool twice? I didn't believe that it did. Biblically, adultery was the only reason to get a divorce. I knew this, but I believed that if his infidelity had been simply with another woman, I could learn to trust him again. It wasn't. He betrayed me, not only with a woman, but also with a man, a sick man at that. He had taken away my child, he had compromised my life and my health and I was supposed to believe that he loved me. After all of that? I didn't think so. Love doesn't keep a record of wrongs, and yes, I still loved him. He was the only man I'd ever loved, but I was no longer in love with him. Now, I only loved him because I was a woman who believed that salvation saved my life. And because God is love, I must love, even my enemies.

Forgiving him had been a process but once I understood that it was necessary for my freedom, I did it. It hurt. I won't lie and say that I didn't fight God on it because I did. It felt like a slap in the face. After all he put me through, I had to forgive him. But a really good friend of mine explained to me that my forgiving him was not for him; it was for me. I would be stuck as long as I held on to the malice and hatred in my heart toward him. I just wanted to know why. And I was going to find out. I needed an explanation. I deserved an explanation and an apology. I'd settle for the reason though. He could keep his sorry's; life had already given me enough.

My phone sat on my desk and once again, it rang. It was Kenyon. Something told me this time to answer it. I looked up at the ceiling. *God, are you serious?* I heard the gentle urging to answer. So, I did.

"Hello." I turned on my business voice. As far as I was concerned, that's exactly what this was--business.

"Genesis?" There was a question in his voice, like he couldn't believe I actually answered. Shoot, I couldn't believe I actually answered.

"Yes, this is Genesis Maicott." I'd gone back to my maiden name. There was no reason for me to continue using his name.

"Maicott? Are you serious?"

"As serious as the disease you gave me." I took a deep breath. I could feel the argument brewing. I silently prayed for God to keep my temper in check because I knew that he had the ability to take me to a place I didn't want to go.

"You're still married. How can you be using your maiden name?"

I didn't want to get into a long and drawn out debate with him. "Is there a specific reason you called?" I was careful to keep my tone professional and not allow my irritation to come through.

"I got the divorce papers today."

Something in his tone had changed. He sounded sad. I'm not sure what it was but I felt a pang of compassion. I said a pang. I wasn't ready to go running back to him. That love was nonexistent. All I wanted now was to get out of this unholy union. I knew in my heart now that our marriage was never in God's plan for my life. It was too late to redo it. I just had to be free of it.

"Good. That was the intent. I'm glad you received them."

I was going to listen to him and not be rude but I wasn't going to be pulled in by his charm. Not this time. That power had been broken with the words HIV-positive.

"Why are you doing this? You don't believe in divorce."

Inside I laughed. I knew that was going to be his first thought. "Correction. I didn't believe in divorce just like I didn't believe that you would stick your penis in a man. Now I know anything can happen." There was a moment when he didn't speak. "Kenyon, I'm busy. What do you need?" I was getting irritated.

"Genesis, I love you. I want another chance to make things right. I know I messed up but baby, please?"

Did he just? I know he… "Messed up? Is that what you think you did? Messed up? Kenyon, you gave me a death sentence. You did more than mess up. Your selfishness and self-centeredness ruined lives. Not just my life. But you ruined Justice's life and the life of those babies. We were all pawns in your sick game. If you had only played with your life, maybe that would be different, but you gambled with the lives of everyone involved and we all lost. There is no chance that we will ever be back together. Do I love you still? No. Not like that. I don't. I love you because God has commanded me to love you. But I'm not in love with you. I don't trust you. You hurt me in a way that you can never make up for. So, yes, I filed for divorce. If you love me like you say you love me, you won't fight me on this. You will set me free once and for all."

I could tell that he was crying but I didn't care. "Wow. I didn't realize that you felt that way. I'm sorry."

I closed my eyes and rubbed my temples. My head was beginning to hurt. "Yes. You are sorry. You can save it though. I've had one too many; there's nothing I can do with them. I'd rather not have yours too. You made a choice. Now you have to live with the consequences of your actions. I will continue to pray for you but I'd prefer if you didn't contact me anymore. There is nothing more for us to say. Good bye."

I hung up. I couldn't contain the emotion that had begun to well up in me. Hot tears fell from my eyes like rain drops. One after another, they fell and for the first time, I didn't stop them. For the first time since all of this had happened, I allowed myself to grieve. I cried for myself. I cried for Justice and her children. I cried for the child I'd lost. I cried for the years I wouldn't see. I cried for the pain that I'd endured in the name of love. I cried because I realized that I'd placed my faith in the wrong man. For all those reasons and for no reason at all, I cried and when the tears stopped falling, I felt a freeness that I hadn't felt before. I thanked God for this time, for this lesson. Now I could move on. I said a quick prayer that Kenyon would heed what I said to him and not fight me on the divorce. He wouldn't win. I didn't want anything from him except my freedom.

KENYON

I received the papers that Genesis sent to me. Divorce papers. It was so unexpected. I knew there was a chance we would never get back together but I didn't think she would actually file for divorce because she didn't believe in it. I figured that this had to be some kind of joke. Genesis was not filing for divorce. She loved me. She always had. In my heart, I knew that she always would. So, when I was served with the papers it was like time stood still. My whole world froze as I read over the petition for divorce. Seven months ago, it had been me preparing to file for divorce and end our marriage because I felt like I was missing something. Hindsight, is definitely 20/20. I wanted to go back to the day I told her about the affairs and just celebrate that day with her. It could have been the happiest day of my life; instead, I turned it into a nightmare.

I sat down on the couch and stared out the window. I had to fight for her. Fight for us. I hadn't talked to her since the day Judah told me to leave his baby girl alone. I picked up the phone and dialed every number that I had for her. I needed to hear her voice today. I called the house and she hadn't had the number changed, which was a surprise. She didn't answer but I wouldn't stop calling until I reached her.

I tried the number at the office and she finally answered .I had to make sure that it was her, even though I would never forget her voice. It was a part of me. She was a part of me. We were meant to be together. I honestly didn't expect her to answer but I was glad that she did. I took the opportunity to tell her that I still loved her and that I was sure she still loved me. Her response was so unexpected. She told me that she was over it, that there was no chance we'd ever be together again, and that she wanted me to leave her alone. Then she hung up. I was left with my mouth hanging open and wondering if she really meant everything that she said. How had my mistakes cost me everything? I thought that I was lacking something, missing something when I first started the affairs. I saw now that everything I'd ever needed and wanted was right in front of me the whole time. There were nights that I didn't sleep because I couldn't get Genesis out of my dreams. There were nights when I relived the day that all of my secrets came out, the day that I told her I wanted a divorce. It didn't turn out the way I planned. Everything had gone so wrong since then. Addison was beginning to get on my nerves. Justice had taken my children from me. She didn't want me around them and on top of all that I had been getting sick lately. I had this cold that I couldn't get rid of. I could only think to myself *and so it begins*. The error of my ways was catching up with me. I wasn't sure if I could deal with the loss of it all.

I dialed Genesis' number again. This time she didn't answer. I left a message, "I know that you asked me not to contact you anymore, but there's so much that I need to say to you. We don't have closure. There's still something left between the two of us, whether you admit that or not. We have a history. We are connected and we belong together. Whether you admit it or not, our hearts beat as one. You're the only woman I've ever truly loved, even though I failed to show you that I loved you. I do, love you, Genesis. It hurts me that I caused you so much pain. I know I can't go back and fix what's already been broken. All I can do is try to make things right from here on out. Let me love you, Genesis. Let me love you right."

I hung up. Hopefully, she would at least return my call. Maybe I could convince her to meet me face to face and listen to what I had to say. I didn't know if that would ever happen but one could only hope. One could only hope.

JEREMIAH

"Addison."

I called his name and tapped him on the shoulder. He was sleeping so peacefully that I hated to wake him but we needed to talk. He needed to explain to me where this was going. He'd been here for a few days, told Kenyon he was going out of town on business. I believed they were growing tired of each other. The novelty was wearing off. That made me glad.

"Addison," I called him again. This time I kissed his lips after I called him. Finally, he stirred. It took a minute but I sat back and waited until he was fully awake.

"Good morning. We need to talk," I said when he sat up.

"Talk? About?"

He was in a mood. I woke him up before he'd planned to get up but so what. I was tired of this being about him. Today, it was about me. He would just have to deal with it.

"Talk about what? Talk about us, Addison. What do you think we need to talk about?"

He sighed. It was his here-we-go-again sigh. I didn't care.

"Yes. About us. What are we doing?"

He looked up at the ceiling, then toward the door almost like he was debating getting up and walking out. "Don't think about walking out on me. We're going to discuss this. You owe me at least that much."

Rubbing his head, he said, "I don't know what we're doing. At first, I wanted to make Kenyon jealous, but that doesn't seem to be working.

He doesn't even seem to notice that I'm gone."

I couldn't believe that he was honest but I appreciated the fact that he was; lying would have only made things worse. There was no more room for dishonesty. There had been enough lies, so many that I was blanketed by the lies he told. I clung to them and they kept me warm when he was gone. It didn't make much sense, but I'd forced myself to not think about whether or not he was being honest most of the time. It was easier living with the blinders on. Stupid? Naive? Yes, It was probably a bit of both, but it was my reality..

"Do you love me? At all?" I needed to hear him say yes or no. If he gave me a yes, I'd put my plan off for just a while longer. If he gave me a no, then I'd move into phase two of my plan. He would regret the day he chose to play games with my heart. That was a promise I could keep.

"Do I love you?" He looked at me, put his head down, and looked at me again. My heart skipped a beat. I wasn't sure what his answer would be. I didn't speak. I just waited. It seemed like an eternity before he spoke again. "What is love? I wonder if it's a simple feeling. Is it a word? Does it truly have meaning?"

He was about to make me mad. "Don't try to be Plato. Just answer the question. *Do you love me?*"

He shook his head. I thought he was saying no. My anger began to rise. My flesh became hot.

"Yes." There it was. One simple word and all the anger blew away like leaves in the wind. "I love you, Jeremiah. I suppose I always have. I suppose I always will. I just wish that things were different, that this was another time and place. I love you. But I love him more."

My emotions were on a pendulum. ~~Swinging back and forth~~. I wanted to slap him for being so bold. In reality, all I could do was appreciate his honesty. It was time to set my plan in motion. If there were no Kenyon, nothing would keep Addison and me apart. This, I knew for sure. Addison was the type of man that despised being alone.

He went from relationship to relationship. There was no space in between. It was him or me. He and I. There would always be an us no matter where he was because I was part of him. He knew this and so did I. I didn't give up that easily. I may have pretended like I'd moved on but, he should have known that this was till death do us part. I'd kill us both before I allowed him to leave me for good. I could watch him love another as long as he loved me too. When that was threatened, he had to go. It was nearing that point.

ADDISON

Jeremiah was really trying me. He woke me up talking about we needed to talk. We'd been down this road before. This was just a fling but he was crazy and I'd never tell him that. I knew that Kenyon was still in love with his wife. I hadn't been home since he and I had gotten into it the last time. I didn't care to be around him with all his dramatic ways right now. Everything was a fight because he couldn't stop thinking about his precious Genesis or those babies. I didn't do second place too well, so I returned to familiar. I knew that, to Jeremiah, I was number one. There was no one above me in his eyes. I relished that. I cherished it. I needed it and he gave it to me. Not only sexually, but in every other way, he lavished me. If I told him I wanted it, he got it. If I looked like I was thinking about it, he got it. Who wouldn't love a man like that?

I couldn't. I mean I did, just not the way he wanted me to love him. I loved him because he was familiar, because we had history, but not because I was still in love with him. Our hearts were connected, I admit. But those feelings were gone. Don't get me wrong. The sex, my God, the sex, but there was no real love there. He was serving a purpose for a time. That's all this was about. I knew that he wanted it to be something more but I couldn't bring my heart into it. It would only serve to complicate matters more. So when he asked me if I loved him, I simply said yes. No explanation. No "I love you likes" just yes. It was a safe answer because truth was I did love him. I would always. I just wasn't in love with him. Had I said that, it would have caused major problems. I looked at him. He looked so sad. So frail. Like he was missing something. I just wasn't sure what.

I didn't want to ask. We didn't talk about our health. We didn't talk about our dreams. Our hopes were off limits. Our goals were forbidden topics of conversation. This was just about satisfying the flesh. No more, no less. He was giving me what I needed right now and I was giving him what he wanted. At least until Kenyon came to his senses and realized that what he had at home was more than what he spent his time wallowing in regret over. Even as a man I was more woman than Genesis Swan would ever be. I knew that he was cold in her shadow. He'd had a chance to feel the sun shining on his face and now he wanted to go back to being her husband. She was never his wife. It was always the other way around. He was associated with her.. No one ever said to her, "Oh you're married to Kenyon Swan." Even when he and I were out together, people would come up to him and say, "It's you. The husband of Genesis Swan, how could you have done that to her?" No one knew who I was, so I didn't bear the brunt of it or any of it for that matter. Still it was upsetting to me. He would always say that he had made a mistake and that if given the chance, in a heartbeat he'd make it right. I guess the saying is true. "You don't miss your water until your well runs dry." Maybe I needed to leave well enough alone and walk away before my heart was broken into even smaller pieces, but there was something holding me hostage in his life. He had this pull on me that wouldn't let me go. I both loved him and despised him. I loved him for all the reasons he'd given me to love him. I despised him for hurting me. For breaking my heart and not even knowing or caring that, that's what he was doing. I wasn't a praying man, but I'd said a couple in the time that he and I had been together. I needed him like I needed air to breathe. His love was necessary. He was my everything. I'd put him in that position and I felt like that's what I was about to lose. Everything.

JARED

I'd been blessed to spend some time with Justice. She was a breath of fresh air. Refreshing. Nothing like the women I dated in the past. I knew that this was my wife. I just hadn't told her that yet. I knew that from the first time I laid eyes on her that she was going to be the woman I married. Her name was already woven into the threads of my heart from the beginning of creation. She was my missing rib. I was complete before her because of my relationship with God, but when she was there, I felt that all was right with my world. There was no void. No missing pieces. No blank spaces. Every line was filled. Every T was crossed and every I was dotted.

She was the woman God created just for me. I don't even know how to describe our first date. It felt like finally I was where I belonged. Nothing had ever made me feel better than finally being with this woman and being able to bare my soul to her. She thought she was telling me something I didn't know when she said that she was HIV-positive. I already knew. I'd heard the talk and I had made up my mind that I didn't care. I knew how to be safe. Any time that we were apart, she was in my thoughts. I dreamt of her. Yes, she was under my skin. And I loved every bit of it. I knew that we had only been out a few times but I was ready to ask her to marry me. I didn't see the point in waiting. Time was only bound by the limits that we imposed. Love happened when we let our hearts be free to feel instead of trying to keep them locked and imposed a time limit on the flow of God. I loved her. She was my wife. I wanted to marry her immediately, but because I wasn't sure what she felt, I would wait for just a little while longer.

GENESIS

Kenyon just wouldn't stop. He kept on calling. This time I didn't answer. I had said all there was to say. He left a message on the voicemail. He wanted me to meet him for dinner or something so that he could say what he wanted to say to me face to face. There was so much he claimed he needed to say, but I didn't even see the point in it anymore. He said all that he needed to say to me. He was sorry and he was right. Sorry wasn't even an accurate description but it was the only description he had for himself and I wouldn't even bother with trying to find another word for that. He had gotten enough of my time. There was no more time for me to devote to him. He lost. In the end, I would win. I knew that God would see to it that I would come out of this victorious. That was the promise that He made to me and I thanked Him for the promise each day. Learning to trust God proved to be the best decision I'd made since all of this had happened. He was showing me daily that there was nothing or no one that could be better to me or for me than He was. I appreciated God for all of the things He did for me. I could have been sick. I could have been near death. I could have been any number of things, but fact was that even though my marriage had failed, I was given a disease that would ultimately kill me, and my husband had children, the one thing I'd always wanted, with someone else, I was well. Spiritually, mentally and emotionally. Genesis Maicott was well. This was honestly the first time I could say that and mean it since I'd met Kenyon and allowed my life to change. God shouldn't have forgiven me but I'd learned through Bible study that *Forgiveness always followed failure.* If I was sincere in asking to be forgiven, God would forgive me. I knew that no matter what happened from here on out my relationship with God would remain intact. I wouldn't run from him when I messed up. Instead I'd run to Him and allow Him to chasten and love me.

Even though I wanted to blame Kenyon for where I had ended up and for hurting me, I had to accept and realize the part that I had played in allowing myself to be hurt. He didn't break me alone. I had relinquished my power to him because I had put not only my trust, but my faith in him. I allowed that man to take the place of God in my life. You never trust another person so fully that they have the power to break you. That was my first mistake. My second mistake was not realizing until it was too late that God created me to be deposited into, not to put out. I gave so much of myself to Kenyon while he never gave anything back to me. I confused lust and sex with love and I'd made my bed. Now I was lying in it. But, I was able to lie in it with no regrets because God had shown me the error of my ways and He was changing me from the inside out. Daily I could feel myself becoming better as I let go of the hurt, the anger, and the animosity. I was growing. It was all a process. Sometimes painful, sometimes joyous, but a process, nonetheless.

I was preparing for a speaking engagement. I had to speak to a group of a thousand young women. What message did I want to leave them with in all that I had learned? That was easy. Love God first. Love yourself second and never make the mistake of allowing a man to take the place of God in your life. Yes, it was okay to love. I would never tell them that it wasn't, but I would tell them to make sure they know to the best of their ability the person whose hands they were placing their heart into. A man can't hold your heart if he has both hands hidden behind his back. I had to learn this the hard way but I was grateful for the lesson.

I was going to wrap up for the day. I had a busy evening ahead of me. Since I'd been sick, I made it a habit of not writing a speech. I would only speak what God had laid on my heart. The rest would be vain words to glorify Genesis. It was no longer about the fortune or the fame. It was funny how God got your attention, the things He used to place you into the destiny He had created for you. I finally felt like I was fulfilling my purpose. There were days when I was just sad that I had to go through so much loss to reach this place. My father told me, "Never despise the journey. It prepares you for the destination." Those were the words I'd opted to live by. Whenever I felt tempted to complain about things I remembered that it was necessary for God to get me where He wanted me to be and I became thankful that even though I'd lost so much, I still had my life.

JUSTICE

Some days it was hard to smile, but I managed. God had indeed given me reason to smile. That man. Whoo, Jesus, where do I even begin? I was glad that I had followed my heart and said yes to him. He had made this the best time in my life. There was something about that man that connected with my soul and made me feel as if I was home. This had to be what heaven felt like. I prayed and asked God that if He saw fit to give me more time, I'd appreciate it because I wanted to see where we would end up. Yes, we were a we and I loved every bit of it. He loved the girls and they immediately took to him. That was a plus. It was more important to me than anything that when someone else was in my life, my children took to them. I was very protective of my babies. They were all that I had and I would make sure that no one would ever have the chance to hurt them the way that I'd been hurt. I didn't believe that God entrusted me with two beautiful little girls because He had nothing better to do. Truthfully, I never really wanted to be a parent but now that I was, I couldn't imagine my life without them. Kenyrah and Keniyah were my life. My world. All I did from the time they were born revolved around them. . It was no longer about me. It was about my children. Every day, I thanked God for them and for Jared.

Back to Jared. Like I said, that man was refreshing. There was nothing I felt I couldn't share with him. Strangely enough after Kenyon, I never thought I'd find love, especially true love but I was beginning to think that that was God's way of giving me a ray of sunshine in the midst of a great storm. He was my double rainbow. I was in love. I wouldn't tell him that until he said it first. I had a tendency to fall in love too soon, too hard, and too deep. But I had to admit to myself that I was in love. The man had captured my heart and was holding it hostage and I didn't have a problem with it. I was ready for the journey. I'd let go of all the animosity and expectations. I was learning to love without them. They did no one any good. I was leaving us both free to love each other without restrictions and constraints. I wanted this time to be different from anything I'd ever felt before. I wanted this to last as long as it could. This could possibly be my chance at love. All I wanted to do now was be happy with what I had. Satisfied. I was at a place of contentment and I was learning with the help of God to be content whatever the situation.

Being diagnosed with HIV had given me a whole new outlook on life. The big things no longer seemed so big. Every day given to me was a blessing and I would do my best to let God know that I was thankful. So many changes had occurred in my life in so little time. No one knew how far I'd come spiritually. Leaps and Bounds. I was back to where I was before Kenyon. It took God allowing this to happen to me for me to get it. Sometimes, we have to suffer on purpose for purpose. Some things we go through, we go through because God wants to get our attention. I strayed far from Him because of a man, someone who should have never caused my focus to shift, but the Bible tells us not to be unequally yoked with unbelievers. I used to believe that referred only to marriage, but now I realized that it meant in any area of your life. Don't get caught up with people who didn't believe as you believed because they could cause you to stray away from where God had you slowly but surely. If you walked away from Him, He would give you gentle nudging to remind you of where you were supposed to be but He would not force you to stay in His will. This was a place that I had to be in, but I also knew that I wasn't going through this for me. This was for someone else. It would help me be more effective in ministry. This last year had been a journey for me, but I was a better woman for it and strangely, I wouldn't change any part of this journey.

AXTON

I'd noticed her first in church as she gave her testimony. She came with one of my members and had been visiting off and on ever since. I could sense the anointing on her. She was beautiful. Tall and full of class. I loved her smile. She got up to give her testimony one Sunday and I think that's when I knew that I had to have her. It was like Boaz meets Ruth. I saw her and all I wanted to do was care for her, take care of her. I wanted to be to her what he wasn't able to be. But for some reason I hadn't been able to get close enough to her to even make my presence known. I wasn't going to give up though. I was told that when you met the person that God had created for you, you would just know. Well, I just knew. I was ready to introduce myself to her and made up in my mind that the next time I saw her that I was going to do just that. I didn't believe in love at first sight but I did believe that two hearts could connect and, out of the connection, God could bless and ordain a union. I knew that there was something in her that connected with something in me. For that reason all I desired to do was cover her.

When I heard the testimony that she had to give, I cried because I wanted to take away her pain. I wanted to take away all the wrongs that had been done to her. I wanted to make sure that each day from here out she wore a smile. I wanted to be the man in her life that made her believe that God was love and that love was real. I wanted to love her like God loved the church.

I wasn't your average man. I'd been through hell and back and, because of where I'd been, I'd learned many valuable lessons. I had learned to go after what I wanted and to live life without regrets. I also learned to not let my good works be evil spoken of. I was a man of God, a man of prestige and position and for this reason, I had to guard my witness. I had to be very careful in my approach of Genesis. I'd do all of those things but I would end up with this woman. Not only would I end up with her, I would become her husband. She was going to be my First Lady in every since of the word. I knew that her father was a prominent pastor in another city. I'd preached for him before. I was going to call him and let him know where my head, heart and intentions were. I would do nothing without her father's approval. I didn't think that he would have issue with it.

Now, it was time to go into prayer; we know that these kinds of requests come only by fasting and prayer. I put my head between my hands, wiped the tears from my eyes as I thanked God for his revelation, stood and joined in with the praise. I was preparing to bring the word of God on this morning and as I looked out over the crowd, I noticed Genesis in her usual spot, second pew, end right seat. One row up and she would have been in the First Lady's seat. For now, there was no first lady, but that was going to change. If I had anything to do with it, she would stop visiting every so often and become a permanent fixture here.

I smiled. My heart was happy just knowing that she was there. I was preaching from St. Luke 7:36-50 with a sermon topic of "There's a story behind my praise." I walked to the podium and looked over the crowd, "Good morning people of God. Please stand with me for a word of prayer. God, our most gracious father , we come to You this morning asking that You shower down Your spirit upon the people in this room today. Oh God, we come asking that You open deaf ears and give sight to blinded eyes. Lord, we come to You today on bended knees with broken hearts asking that You open the windows of heaven and pour out blessings of healing and hope, God. Lord, someone may feel as if they cannot make it another day. Touch in the way that only You can. We decree and declare that bondage will be broken and breakthroughs will be given in this place and in Your name on today, Father. We thank You in advance for all that You're going to do, God. We love You, not because of what You have done but because of who You are. And we call it done in the name of Jesus."

I opened my eyes and saw people all over the building thanking and praising God and it made my heart rejoice. This was what I loved to do. "Open your bibles to St. Luke chapter seven; we are going to begin reading at the thirty-sixth verse:

"And one of the Pharisees desired him that he would eat with him. And he went into the Pharisee's house, and sat down to meat. And, behold, a woman in the city, which was a sinner, when she knew that Jesus sat at meat in the Pharisee's house, brought an alabaster box of ointment, And stood at his feet behind him weeping, and began to wash his feet with tears, and did wipe them with the hairs of her head, and kissed his feet, and anointed them with the ointment. Now when the Pharisee which had bidden him saw it, he spake within himself, saying, This man, if he were a prophet, would have known who and what manner of woman this is that toucheth him: for she is a sinner. And Jesus answering said unto him, Simon, I have somewhat to say unto thee. And he saith, Master, say on. There was a certain creditor which had two debtors: the one owed five hundred pence, and the other fifty. And when they had nothing to pay, he frankly forgave them both. Tell me therefore, which of them will love him most? Simon answered and said, I suppose that he, to whom he forgave most. And he said unto him, Thou hast rightly judged. And he turned to the woman, and said unto Simon, Seest thou this woman? I entered into thine house, thou gavest me no water for my feet: but she hath washed my feet with tears, and wiped them with the hairs of her head. Thou gavest me no kiss: but this woman since the time I came in hath not ceased to kiss my feet. My head with oil thou didst not anoint: but this woman hath anointed my feet with ointment. Wherefore I say unto thee, her sins, which are many, are forgiven; for she loved much: but to whom little is forgiven, the same loveth little. And he said unto her, Thy sins are forgiven. And they that sat at meat with him began to say within themselves, who is this that forgiveth sins also? And he said to the woman, Thy faith hath saved thee; go in peace. Turn to your neighbor and say, 'There's a story behind my praise.'"

KENYON

She hadn't called back and things had only gone downhill from the time that I'd left her the last message. Addison finally decided to come home. Not that I wanted him there, but he was. He must have thought I was stupid. Hello, I was the one who was having two affairs. I knew when someone was cheating, but I lacked the energy to care. I had more pressing things that I had to deal with.

He stood in the doorway to the office. I pretended not to notice he was there. He cleared his throat. I kept typing. If he couldn't open his mouth to speak after being gone a whole week, then I would not acknowledge him. It was simple as that. I was ready to move out. I was ready to get my own place and I planned on telling him that soon. I had no more tolerance for the games. It was old now and I wasn't in love with him. I still loved my wife. It had taken me a very long time to realize it but that was the truth. With Genesis was where I wanted to be. It was where I belonged. Getting my wife back was my focus although she had planned to divorce me. I wasn't accepting that things would end this way. If there was a God, there was no way He would take away what He had blessed me with. He was the God of a second chance, right? Well, I needed a second chance. I may not have deserved it, but how many people really do?

"Are you just going to act like you don't know I'm here?"

I drew in a breath as quietly as I could. I turned around in the chair and faced him. "I was waiting to see how long it was going to take you to speak. Didn't your parents teach you to speak when you enter a room?" I turned back around and continued reading over the proposal that I was writing for work. I didn't have time for it.

"What is the problem, Kenyon?"

Did he really have to ask? "What is my problem Addison? Are you serious? Did you enjoy your trip? Or do you think I'm stupid? I know that you weren't out of town. Did we forget I was the king of cheating? I know that you are having an affair and I don't even care. He can have you. I'm done. I'm moving out."

This was just the time I needed. I hadn't planned to tell him like this, but the opportunity presented itself and I took it. Finding a place wouldn't be an issue, especially since I'd been looking for a while.

"Moving out? What do you mean moving out?"

Was he stupid? "If moving out has an alternate meaning, I'm unaware of what it is. I'm getting my own place. I can't stay here anymore."

He walked around to the front of the desk so that he could look at me. He was wearing a slate gray button down with some black dress pants and Ferragamo dress shoes. He'd let his goatee grow out and gotten his hair cut low. He was looking good but I had to maintain my focus. Now was not a time to let his good looks trip me up as they had so many times before. I refused to look him in the eye. Instead, I looked past him. As he talked I stared out the window at the stormy sky. I watched as the lightening danced across the sky. I listened intently as it was followed by the boom of the thunder. I allowed myself to be taken in by the storm.

"Are you listening to me?" He snapped his fingers twice to get my attention.

"Addison, I'm leaving."

"Did you hear anything that I just said to you?" he asked. I looked up at him and remembered what it was about him that had drawn me in the first place. The man was gorgeous. Shorter than me at 5'6, dark brown, like he'd been dipped in Hershey's chocolate, muscles for days, hazel brown eyes, a goatee and one dimple, right side. He had a smile to die for. Whenever he smiled at me, I felt warm all over. Today when he smiled at me, I felt sick. The love was fading but the lust was ever present. I wanted to do things to him right now that were illegal. Hmph, the man was fine.

"Kenyon you can't leave me. I love you. I was away on business. I told you that."

I had to cut him off before the lies got to flowing. I didn't care to be lied to today. "You weren't away on business, Addison. I called the office. Unless it was a personal business trip, would they not have record of your travel arrangements? You never left the area. Save your lies and tell me the truth."

He looked like the cat that swallowed the canary. Caught in a lie and he didn't know how to rebound. Foolish man. "Well, where were you? You can always just not say or you can stick with your lie about being out of town. It's up to you. It doesn't matter to me either way. I'm leaving. I'll be out by the end of the week."

He looked like he wanted to cry. I could see the anguish in his eyes. He felt guilty about something. "Why can't we just sit down and have a conversation about things. Why can't we try to make this work? I really do love you. I just feel like lately you've been so caught up in those women that it's causing a rift between the two of us."

I inhaled deeply. Here we go again. "Those women? My wife and the mother of my daughters? Are you referring to *those* women?" He knew that pissed me off but he was insistent on saying it. "

Yes, those women, Kenyon. Do you want them or do you want me? You need to make a choice. I won't be some little side thing that you're keeping dangling on a leash so that you have somewhere to come back to when it's not working out with them."

He was really about to get on my last nerve. Whining like some little… "That's why I'm leaving. I'm tired of the whining. You expect me not to have anything to do with my daughters and I'm not willing to choose you over them. Justice already doesn't want me to see them as long as we are together and yes, I miss my wife. I want to make things right with her. If that hurts you, then I apologize, but she still has my heart. I made a mistake. Now I want to fix it. I know you can't or won't understand that, but it is what it is."

I got up and left him standing there with his mouth open. As far as I was concerned, there was nothing else to talk about.

ADDISON

I sat down in the chair in the office after he walked out. I wasn't done talking but he apparently was. For months, things between us had been getting worse and worse and no matter what, I still loved him. It seemed like the more we fought, the deeper in love I fell with him and now he was telling me that he was leaving. I wouldn't let him see me cry but it hurt me in a place that no one else had ever been able to touch. I wanted to hate him but all I felt was love. It wasn't fair. I wanted to hurt the women who were taking the love of my life away from me. This was the reason why I'd never dated a bisexual man before. They went any way the wind blew and you never knew which way they would land..

I should have just told him the truth. I should have told him that I'd been with Jeremiah the last few days, hurt him like he had hurt me, but I couldn't. I wondered who he had spoken with at the office. I had to learn to cover my tracks better.

My cell phone vibrated in my pocket; I took it out and looked at the screen. It was Jeremiah. I should have known. I pushed the button to answer the call. "Yes."

"Don't sound so happy to hear from me. I miss you." I hadn't been gone two hours and he missed me?

"I haven't even been gone long enough for you to miss me."

"Addison, I'm not you. I'm not chasing behind some wet behind the ears dreadlocked youngster."

He was going to piss me off. "Watch it or this conversation will be over before it even begins."

I knew that would stop the madness. "I just called to tell you that I was thinking about you and that I love you. I wish you would have stayed the rest of the week but I understand you had to get back to work."

"I'll be back sooner than you think. Don't worry. There will be more time spent between you and me. I can't really talk right now, I'm preparing for a meeting. I'll call you later."

I hung up. I had issues with the word goodbye so I very rarely said it. It made people mad but they would get over it. They didn't really have much of a choice. It wasn't personal, just my own hang up. Literally.

After I hung up from Jeremiah, I thought about trying to force Kenyon to talk to me but I decided against that. He wanted to leave? Let him, but this was far from over. I always got what I wanted and I wanted him. I had Genesis' number. I thought maybe I would call her. We needed to have a conversation. I wondered if she would talk to me. More than likely, the answer was no but if all else failed, I'd go to her office. I needed to let her know that I would fight her every step of the way for the man I loved.

I went and closed the door and locked it so that Kenyon couldn't walk in unexpected. I sat down at the desk and pulled out my rolodex, located the number and dialed it. I didn't expect an answer, but I got one on the second ring.

"This is Genesis Maicott. How can I help you?"

"This is Addison Limon. You and I need to talk. There are a few things that I need to make perfectly clear to you." I wasn't sure if she knew who I was or not but I didn't care, by the time this conversation was over she would know exactly who I was.

"Do I know you sir?" She still had her business voice on. How professional.

"Oh, I'm sure you've heard of me. I'm the man that your husband left you for. Remember me *now?*"

"Why are you calling me? We have nothing for us to discuss." She said all that, but she didn't hang up.

"Oh yes, we have plenty to discuss."

"You have Kenyon. What else is there? Looks like you've won the game, doesn't it?"

Ha! "One would think. That's how it seems, but that isn't how it is. I love Kenyon but he's pining away for you, like he's made some great mistake by leaving you. Personally, I don't see the great sense of loss; after all, you're *only* a woman. I just called to tell you that I will fight you to the death for this man."

"Are you threatening me?"

"Threat? Oh no honey, I'm not threatening you. I don't make threats. That, my dear, was a promise. You may still carry his last name but I have the man. I want his heart. He has mine. And anyone and any thing standing in my way has to go. If that means you, then so be it. I have no problem taking you out to keep him."

I wondered if she was mad yet or would she continue to play nice. "Listen, you can have Kenyon. I don't want him. He's done all he can do for me. I've filed for divorce. He has the papers. He knows that there is nothing left between us . This is a waste of conversation and a waste of my time. I hope the two of you live happily ever after. Goodbye."

With that, she disconnected the call. I stared at the phone. She had the nerve and audacity to hang up in my face. At least I knew that she wasn't the one with the issue. How could I get him to realize that it was over between the two of them and he just needed to be happy with me?

GENESIS

I was so tired of Kenyon and all his games and foolishness. I just wanted to be done with it. All connections severed. I needed this part of my life to be over. I was trying to be free of it, free of the drama, but it just kept popping up at my door. Still I could not hate him. I felt sorry for him and the life he'd chosen for himself. I couldn't believe that his little boyfriend had the audacity to call and threaten me over Kenyon. Was he crazy? Well, obviously, because he'd threatened me but I didn't think that I'd be getting any more calls from him after telling him that he could have Kenyon. I didn't want him. They could live in HIV bliss for all I cared. There was nothing that I wanted from Kenyon. Not even his apologies at this point. I just wanted him to leave me alone and let me be free. I guess, in a way, I did want one thing from him: my freedom, but that was it.

I went to visit Justice and the twins earlier. I didn't think that she and I would ever be friends but we'd gotten to be really close since she asked me to be the girls' guardian if anything ever happened to her. I thought it best that we build a relationship so that they weren't coming to live with someone they didn't know, if, God forbid, something happened to her. Those girls looked so much like Kenyon it was scary. They had his color, his eyes, and his dimples but they had grown on me. I loved them like they were my own. Looking at them made me wonder if our child would have looked like this, but that's something I would never know and for that reason alone, I didn't let myself think about it. I'd have children of my own one day. If not, I had those two beautiful girls who would always love auntie Genesis.

My life was getting back to the place it was in before all hell broke loose and I was thankful for it. That phone call threw me though. I couldn't concentrate now. I wanted to call Kenyon and tell him to keep his little boyfriend in check.. I put my work on hold; there was no use in trying to write now. I picked up my phone and dialed Kenyon's number.

When he answered, I didn't give him time for the casual talk. I got straight to the point, "Don't ever have your boyfriend call me again! Not only did he call me, but he threatened me. I don't appreciate it. I let him know that there is no need to be upset because I do not want you. Matter of fact, all I want from you is my freedom. Check him or I will have someone else do it. I'm a saved woman but I will not tolerate that kind of foolishness. I've put up with enough from the likes of you and him, don't you think?"

"Genesis, what are you talking about?"

Oh, he wanted to play dumb? "Kenyon, what I said was what I meant and unless you've suddenly gone hard of hearing then you heard *everything* I said."

"When did he call you and what did he say to you? Addison hasn't been here in a few days."

"I don't care.. He called me less than fifteen minutes ago and told me that he had no problem taking me out over you. Hear this and hear it well, if anything happens to me, the police have been notified and you and your little friend will be spending the rest of your pathetic lives in jail. Try me.. I suggest you put a stop to the madness quickly."

"I didn't know he called you, but I will definitely find out what that was about. I'm sorry."

I was so sick of hearing him say that he was sorry. "You're right. We've already established that. Either you talk to him or I will have someone else talk to him and I'm sure that's not something you want. Remember this, I'm covered by the blood of God, and nothing else that you try will be able to hurt me."

"Genesis, I love you, I wouldn't ever do anything to hurt you."

I cut him off. "You've already done a lot to hurt me but you won't ever be able to hurt me again, I promise. I didn't call to hold a conversation about us. I have to go. Put a stop to it, *now*."

I hung up. I'm sure that he wanted to keep the conversation going but I was done. I didn't even feel like working anymore, so I called my mother. It had been a while since we'd talked and I was overdue for a visit. She didn't answer so I decided that I'd leave the office, stop home, and then drive to my parents' house. I needed the break.

KENYON

"Who the... Who do you think you are Addison?"
I was trying to stay calm. He had no idea that Genesis had called me and told me that he'd threatened her. He was standing there with this stupid look on his face like he didn't know what I was talking about. "I don't care how much you claim you love me; if you ever so much as dial Genesis' number I will hurt you."

"Oh, that. What are you going to do, Kenyon? I meant what I said. If she stands in my way, I will take her out. You think I'm just going to let you go without a fight? After all I've invested. You're crazy if you think so. You can move out if you want but this is far from over. Believe me."

He was crazier than I thought he was if he really believed that I would allow him to threaten her and me. "Have you lost the better part of your mind? You don't make threats like that and just expect people to sit idly by and wait for you to fulfill them. If I have to kill you myself, I will. You don't believe me, do something to Genesis."

He must have thought this was a game but it just got serious. You don't threaten the woman I love and think that I'm going to just let that slide without doing or saying anything. I don't care how fine I thought he was or how much I loved him, Fact was I didn't love him more than I loved her.

"So you're threatening me, Kenyon? Really? Over your *beloved* *Genesis*? Boy please. I'm not afraid you're going to do anything."

He'd pushed a button that had never been pushed and before I knew it, I was on top of him. My fist connected with his jaw and it was on from there. We fought like two men who didn't know each other. If you'd walked in on this fight, you would never have guessed that we were lovers. I didn't stop punching him until he begged for me to stop. I stood up out of breath and asked him, "Do you believe me *now?*" He must have never thought he would see that side of me. I looked at him again; the hatred I felt was thick enough to cut with a knife. I walked out of the room and left him lying on the floor in a bloodied heap. I went back into the bedroom and began throwing my things in a suitcase. I had to leave and I had to leave now or this day was only going to get worse. He hadn't been home an hour and already things had taken a turn for the worse. There was truly a thin line between love and hate because if you asked me right now if I loved this man, I'd tell you no and mean it with all that I am. Yeah, this relationship was drawing to a close. The time had come for us to part ways.

Addison

I couldn't believe that he'd actually put his hands on me. Things had quickly gotten out of hand. I wasn't sure what would happen next or how he even knew that I'd called Genesis. He was nowhere near when I had spoken to her. The only thing that I could think was that she called him. I hated her. She was costing me everything I'd worked so hard for and I'd be damned if I was going to allow her to take from me everything that was mine. If he thought this was the end, he was sadly mistaken. I'd let him leave, only to keep the peace for the time being but he was mine. If that meant that we had to die to be together, so be it. I'd lived my life and death was already a sure thing for me. The only thing I wasn't aware of was when I'd take my last breath.

I sat down on the bed and looked around the room. Everything here reminded me of Kenyon. The colors were ones he'd picked out: silver and black, his favorites. The comforter held his scent. I lay in his spot and inhaled. I didn't want to fight. What I really wanted right now was to be in his arms. I couldn't imagine not being with him but I would kill him if the situation called for it. They say if you love something, set it free. Death would be freedom for him. He would be free of all his obligations to these women and free of his thoughts of leaving me. The more I thought about it, maybe killing him would be the best thing to do. Screw her; she wasn't worth the time. I could certainly see the two of us leaving this world together. *Together*. That's all that mattered to me. .

My phone vibrated again and I knew it was Jeremiah. I didn't want to speak with him at the moment, so I just allowed it to vibrate as I lay in the spot Kenyon had been in not hours ago. I dozed off with sinister thoughts in my head.

AXTON

When church was over, I made sure that I greeted the members but I was really longing to make today the day that I
was able to talk to Genesis. I had my armor bearer send word to
her that I'd like to speak with her. Once I was done greeting the
people I made my way to the office, careful not to appear too excited. She was seated when I came in.. Up close, her beauty was
breathtaking. I felt a magnetic pull. I had to play this carefully.

"Sister Maicott, I'm glad that you were able to make it."

She turned to face me in her seat. "Pastor, how are you this afternoon? I really enjoyed your message today. I was a little shocked that
you wanted to meet with me, though. Is there something wrong?"

I smiled. "Quite the contrary. I just wanted to get a chance to
sit down and talk with you. It seems like every Sunday, you're gone
before I have a chance to greet you. I was determined to change
that today. I've wanted to sit down and personally talk to you since
you gave your testimony."

She was blushing. It was cute. "Oh really? I had no idea. Was
there something particular that you wanted to know?"

That was a loaded question. I decided to be honest. I wasn't the
kind of man to beat around the bush. "Yes, in fact. You." It was out
there. Now the ball was in her court.

"Me? I don't understand."

"Yes, you. I want to get to know you. I know it may seem a
bit forward but I don't believe in playing games. You may find it

strange, especially for a pastor to make his intentions known up front, but like I said I don't do games. So, I asked you to meet me here so that I could tell you that I'd love the chance to get to know you. Not only that, but I believe that you are the woman God has sent for me."

I sat back and laced my fingers together atop the desk. The look on her face was priceless and she was speechless. "I know it all seems odd to you but ever since the first time I've laid eyes on you my heart has longed for you. I know that you're just getting out of a bad marriage and may not be prepared to start dating and I understand that. I'm willing to wait however long it takes for you to be ready, but please know Ms. Maicott, that you are the woman God has ordained to be my wife."

I was done talking. I'd let her have it. "I really don't know what to say. I'm kind of shocked, but I appreciate the fact that you were up front. Right now, if I need anything in my life, it's honesty. However, you guessed right, I'm not ready to date.. It's mainly because I'm still a married woman and as you can probably under-stand, I intend to honor those vows until the final divorce decree has been issued. I intend to remain blameless in the sight of God."

I could only commend her for wanting to be faithful to a man that had obviously not been faithful to her and it only made me fall for her more. That's what a true woman of God would do. "I respect that and I'll wait however long it takes. Just allow me the pleasure of getting to know you first as my friend. I promise that you will see in due time that I am the man God has always intended to be yours."

I ended the conversation there. We made plans to meet later on in the week to discuss some plans for a program that she wanted to implement for the young women in the church. I thought it was a good idea to make sure that they were informed about the

AIDS virus and how to protect themselves from it. I was sure that many people would disagree with my approach to ministry but I believed that people should be informed about all aspects of life, both physical and spiritual.

GENESIS

That was unexpected. I had no idea that Pastor Axton was interested in me. To tell the truth I was kind of glad to hear that he was. I would never tell him this but I was interested in him as well. I'd wondered if he was dating anyone, but I knew that with the way things were in my life now I needn't be entertaining thoughts of another man until my divorce was final. Axton seemed to be everything that Kenyon was not. I knew that somewhere out there, there had to be an opposite of what Kenyon had been. Perhaps Axton was that opposite. I knew that only time would tell, but I was willing to find out. Love hadn't been kind to me but I knew that God answered prayer and I was praying that the prayer I prayed in regards to love was being answered now.

It's miraculous the ways that God works. Just when I was beginning to feel that everything was falling down around me, there was a bright spot and the sun seemed to shine again. I was looking forward to meeting with Axton in regards to the program I wanted to implement for the young women in the church. I had thought about including the young men and perhaps that could be done as well but they could get their training from one of the males in the church. I just believed that they needed to be informed and not be caught off guard like I had been. Being blindsided by something that you didn't expect was hard but every day was getting better. The closer I got to God, the easier things were for me. I still hadn't been sick and for that, I was thankful. If it weren't for the fact that I had paperwork saying that I was HIV positive, I wouldn't even know that there was anything wrong with me.

Speaking of which, I was due to be at the doctor in a while. I packed up my belongings and headed to my appointment. I wondered what he would have to say this time. There was always something different but so far things were good. I had to mentally prepare myself for whatever they had to say every time I had an appointment. I prayed the whole way there. I pulled up to the doctor's office and noticed that there was a car parked in the lot that looked a lot like Kenyon's but I didn't think that we had the same doctor. I just shook it off. I parked and walked into the office and who did I see other than the devil himself sitting in the lobby. It was too late for me to turn around and walk out because he was looking toward the door when I walked in. He stood up and immediately began walking towards me. I wasn't in the mood. This was the first time I'd laid eyes on him since the day he admitted his affairs and doggish ways. I'd wondered what it would be like when I saw him again. I wondered what I'd feel, what I'd think. The only thing I felt was regret at wasting so much of my time loving him. I wanted to slap the taste out his mouth, but it wouldn't do any good.

"Leave me alone, Kenyon. We have nothing to say to each other," I said when he finally got to where I stood. I wanted to walk away, but for some reason I was rooted to the ground like I was growing from this very spot. Shoot, I thought to myself.

"We have a lot to say to each other Genesis. I miss you."

I just looked at him. Really, was he serious? "This is not the time or place for this, Kenyon." He had to know that the doctor's office was an inappropriate place for the conversation he was trying to have, one I wasn't interested in having with him ever.

"I love you, Genesis. I know that I haven't shown you that lately and I know that I was wrong but I've had time to think about all the wrong that I've done and I want you to forgive me and give me another chance." He couldn't be serious. I wasn't going there with him.

Not today, not if hell froze over. I was done. I was finally getting back to loving myself. There was no way that I would sacrifice that for him. Negative like my test should have been.

I turned and walked toward the check-in counter before he could say another word. When I got to the counter and gave the nurse my information, she told me to have a seat and that the doctor would see me shortly. I'd gotten into the habit of reading my Bible in my spare time, and although I really didn't want to sit down because I knew that as soon as I did Kenyon was going to have something else to say to me, I found a seat in an empty corner and took out my pocket sized bible that I always carried with me. I was reading the book of Ruth. There was something about this story that gave me hope. Not because I had a mother-in-law that I would follow to the ends of the earth. Kenyon's mother had passed before he and I had met. It gave me hope because in Ruth's faithfulness, God blessed her with a man who wanted to protect her and love her the way she deserved to be protected and loved.

I couldn't stop thinking about Axton lately. Ever since the meeting with him, I couldn't stop replaying what he said. He knew I was his wife. For some reason I wasn't as skeptical as I should have been. I think part of me just wouldn't allow myself to be hopeful because I thought Kenyon was the man I'd spend my whole life with. I couldn't survive anymore heartbreak, so I was hesitant to let Axton in but the more I tried to stop thinking about him, the more he stayed on my mind. It was odd but in a good way. Maybe love would finally be kind to me.. Ruth and Boaz remained my inspiration. All I knew was the next man that I gave my heart to would have to go through God to get to me. That was a promise I was keeping to myself.

I looked up when I saw that the sun had gotten dim, only to see that Kenyon was standing in front of me. Inwardly, I sighed. I was not in the mood for him. "Genesis, I really wish that you would allow me to tell you how I really feel about you. I realize that I've made some mistakes but all I need is for you to give me another chance."

He was wearing on my last nerve. "Kenyon, I don't do second chances. You've caused me enough pain and I won't allow you to hurt me anymore. Your power over me is gone. I've come to my senses and I know that you were merely a distraction that Satan used. The thing about destiny and God's promises is that I can't die before they come to pass in my life, so see, it doesn't matter what you've done to me, I win because I am a child of God."

The nurse called my name. I gathered my belongings and walked away from Kenyon with his mouth hanging open and my spirit was soaring. I was feeling good. I'd wondered how I would handle that and I handled it well. I was proud of myself.

KENYON

I couldn't believe that Genesis was coming in the door to the doctor's office. I thought my eyes were playing tricks on me but when she walked in the door, I knew it was her. My first thought was to take her into my arms and kiss her, but I thought better of that. I knew that wouldn't go over well with her so I just walked up to her and asked her if we could talk. I'd been trying to get her to talk to me for the longest and she just refused continually, each time saying we had nothing else to say to one another. Of course, I felt differently now. I missed her. It was true what they said. You never missed your water until your well ran dry. My whole life had changed for the worse since we'd been apart. I couldn't even put into words the emptiness I felt since she had been gone. I dogged her out but I was the one who had ended up with a broken heart. I hadn't believed in Karma before this but let me be the one to tell you, I'd been introduced to her and Karma was indeed real. It was like everything I'd done to her was being done to me in one way or another.

She looked good, very good. It was like being without me had proved to be the best thing for her. She hadn't been this happy since I'd first met her. I guess I hadn't realized until now that maybe I was the reason that she wasn't happy. It was a huge wake up call. I knew just from her reaction to what I said to her that she was truly moving on. It hurt. I couldn't even lie and say that it didn't. I felt like my heart was being ripped right out of my chest and I had no idea how to stop the pain. There was emptiness inside of me that I hadn't realized was there until the very moment that she walked back with the nurse. I wanted to call after her but it would have done no good so I just let her go accepting once and for all that it was over between me and the woman I loved. Had someone told me that my ways would have cost me her love, maybe I would have listened but I thought that she loved me enough to forgive me no matter what I did. Strange thing was she had forgiven me. She just hadn't chosen to stay. I couldn't go back and do things differently now.

I felt the tears begin to fall so I went and sat over in a corner where no one else was sitting and I allowed myself to cry. For the first time since all of this had started, I felt. I'd shut my feelings off. I guess because I didn't want to admit that I knew I was wrong for hurting her. I knew from the beginning that she didn't deserve to be treated the way I was treating her. I knew that I had a good woman at home and yet, it wasn't enough because she was boring. She wasn't exciting enough. All she seemed to care about what was working and starting a family. She never wanted to go out. She didn't drink. She was a good girl. That was what had attracted me but sometimes the very things that make you love a person are the things that push you away. After a while, it started to bother me and I strayed. The vows we took in front of God, family, and friends meant nothing to me. I guess that's because they didn't mean anything to me when I said them. I was an adult when we got married but I wasn't grown. Going through this had grown me up and I wished with all that I was that I could go back and do things over. It was too late. I lost everything and for what? A death sentence. I wished to God that I had never met Addison or Justice. Maybe then things wouldn't have turned out the way they had but who was I kidding. I was the only one at fault here. I should have had enough respect for my wife and enough self-control to remain faithful.

Whatever happened to me now, I realized that I deserved it. It was sobering. I was dying. I felt it inside and out. The man I once was, he was gone. In his place, there was I. Sad, confused, regretful, dying me.

I felt my phone vibrate in my pocket. I knew it was Addison so I didn't even bother to look at it. He was mad because I had moved out. I couldn't stand to look at him anymore, especially after he'd called and threatened Genesis. That was the straw that broke the camel's back. I'm not sure what he thought this was, but as long as I lived I wouldn't ever allow another person to cause her pain. I'd done enough of that. The least I could do at this point was protect her and I would if it was the last thing I did. She didn't know that I felt this way and after what she had said to me today, she never would. I would give her space. She deserved it. I had her. I lost her. Now I just prayed that the next man lucky enough to get her treated her right.

I was waiting for the doctor to call my name. I'd been feeling badly for the past few weeks so I decided to make an appointment and see what was going on. Here I was. I knew the news was going to be bad. I could feel it. Just then, the nurse stepped out from the back and called my name. I felt weighted down. I moved slowly and as I made my way to the back I began to pray to a God I wasn't sure even existed. *Please don't let them tell me that I'm going to die. Amen.*

ADDISON

I had been calling Kenyon for days and he wouldn't accept my calls. He moved out like he said he was going to do after I threatened Genesis, but what he didn't realize or obviously understand was that it wasn't that easy to walk away from me. I knew that he was at the doctor's office today. I'd made copies of his day planner before he moved out so I knew just about his every move but he didn't know that I knew that. It was just a matter of time before I started to show up where he was. I was trying to give him time to get his act together and answer my calls. We needed to talk. I didn't take kindly to being ignored and he was about to find that out the hard way.

I tried to call again and once again, I was sent to the voice mail. This was beginning to thoroughly piss me off. I wasn't going to be played or ignored. I'd take him out before I allowed that to happen. If I couldn't have him, no one could. I thought I'd made that clear to him. He apparently thought that this was a joke. My feelings were nothing to play with. I loved this man. I don't think that he truly understood the depth of the love that I had for him. Perhaps he thought that it was just a fling, something that meant nothing to either of us, but he couldn't have been more wrong. I was sleeping with Jeremiah, but he no longer meant anything to me. That was simply sex, skin-to-skin contact. My heart was not involved. My heart longed for Kenyon but he had shut down on me once he realized that his precious Genesis was never coming back to him.

That was too bad for him and all, but I was better for him anyway. I took care of him, at least I had before he decided to leave me, but this wasn't over. I had been reading my favorite Shakespeare play *Romeo & Juliet* and if we had to end tragically then we would. I'd gone through too much to give up without a fight. I still had my plan in place. Hopefully, he would realize the error of his ways and come home without force. I'd hate to have to hurt him to get him to come back to me.

My cell rang. I looked down at it hoping that it was Kenyon calling back. It was Jeremiah. We were supposed to be meeting for lunch but I'd changed my mind. I didn't feel like being around him. I only wanted to get this mess straightened out with Kenyon. This was my focus. I let the call go to voicemail. I knew that he wouldn't understand if I tried to explain so I didn't even bother. I knew how to shut Jeremiah up and trust me I was very good at making him change the subject. I sat outside the doctor's office in a rental car so that Kenyon wouldn't notice that I'd been following him. Where he went, I went. I needed to know his every move. I'd taken a few weeks off from work. You can do that when you're the boss. This was important. For me, this was life or death, life *and* death. At least that's the way it felt. Have you ever felt like you loved someone so much that if they were gone you had no air? I couldn't breathe without him. He was oxygen; he was healing to my soul. I didn't want to live without him and I wouldn't. I'd already made up my mind that if we both had to die to be together, then so be it. I'd already given him my disease. I thought that was insurance that we'd be together forever but he'd been fool enough to sleep with her without protection and had therefore, infected her and Justice. Now there was no insurance, not if either of them would have him back.

I sat there for what seemed like an eternity when I saw Genesis go into the building. At first I thought I was seeing things but her face was all over the newspapers lately, so I knew that it was her. Was he meeting her here? Couldn't be. I started to get out of the car but I knew better than to blow my cover, so I called him again. Once again, he sent me to the voicemail. I was getting pissed. He thought I was just going to sit back and take this. No. I wasn't. I told her that I'd kill her and honey, I meant that. She better watch herself.

GENESIS

The doctor ran several tests and now I was waiting. The nurse kept coming back to draw blood. I finally asked her if there was an issue. She looked at me kind of strangely and shook her head no, everything was fine. The doctor just wanted to test my blood again to make sure that his results were correct. Something was wrong. I had no idea what but I felt it in my spirit. The spirit of fear tried to grip me but when I felt myself getting scared, I began to pray.

God, You know the state of my health. So far, You have blessed me to not be affected by the diagnosis that the doctor gave me. Now I'm sitting here in the doctor's office again and I am uncertain. I have no idea what's going on, Lord, and I am afraid. I'm asking You first to comfort my heart where the fear is trying to rise up. God, I know that even if the doctor comes back with bad news, You are the ultimate healer and You have the final say. I'm putting my trust solely in You, Father. Guide the doctor's hands; regulate what needs to be regulated. I speak healing over my life in the name of Jesus. I know that by Your stripes, Father, I am healed. Satan, you have got to go. There is no room for you here. Light and darkness cannot dwell in the same place. I speak to the spirit of fear and rebuke you in the name of my savior Jesus Christ. By the blood of Jesus, I am healed. I will have peace. I am set free. In Jesus' name, I pray. Amen"

When I finished praying, I felt much better. I was at peace and I knew that no matter what the doctor had to say things would be just fine because I was in the hands of the Master Potter. I was glad that I brought my Bible with me, so that I could keep my mind focused on the word, especially when my mind started to roam. I looked through my bag for the Bible when there was a knock on the door and the doc-tor peeked in. "Do you mind if I come in?"

I looked up. "No. Come on in. I was just looking for my Bible."

I couldn't read the look on her face at first and then she broke out in a broad grin. I was confused. I had no idea what she could be smiling about so I just sat there and looked at her..

"Genesis, I've got some really great news to give you today. I'm sure you were wondering why I kept having Angel come to draw blood after the first two times, right?"

"Well, yes I did wonder, but is everything alright?"

She smiled again. "Things are better than alright. The test results that you were given in the hospital were wrong. They were someone else's results. The doctor faxed over your blood work and there were two files in your folder. One was for you. The other was for another patient that had been tested the same day as you with the same initials."

I wasn't sure what she was saying but I didn't want to get my hopes up so I sat down in the chair.

"Your test was negative, Genesis."

I just stared at her. I couldn't have heard her correctly. "That's the reason why we did so many tests. I wanted to be sure that the results I was getting now still matched your actual records from the original testing. They did and you're perfectly fine. Your iron is a little low but other than that, sweet heart you are in perfect health."

I sat there and tears began falling from my eyes. I was fine? I wasn't HIV-positive? I lifted my hands and praised God right there. A miracle? Yes, I was; this was. I looked up and she was crying and praising with me.

"I prayed for you. I heard all about what happened and I didn't think that God would allow something like that to affect someone like you. God bless you, Genesis. If you don't mind, I'll be sharing your testimony with members of my church without giving your name of course!" I didn't care who she told. I was going to tell the world what

God had done for me. I was so undeserving but He had blessed me yet again. "Thank you, Jesus!" was all I could say. I hugged the doctor and sat back down. I was in awe. The tears wouldn't stop. I tried to compose myself but it wasn't working. I wanted to call Axton and tell him. You'd think that my mother and father would have been the first people that I wanted to call but they weren't.

I wanted... no, I needed to see Axton. This miracle had sealed the deal for him. I was going to live my life to the fullest. I had just been given another chance at life. Satan had tried but my God had blocked it. He had placed this opportunity in my hands and I wasn't going to let it pass me by. I was a lot of things, but a fool wasn't one. I thanked the doctor and hugged her again, gathered my things, and headed to the door. I was glad to see that Kenyon was no longer in the waiting room. I wondered if his results were wrong too. I doubted it. I couldn't honestly say that I cared. I would say a prayer for him but I had someone that I had to see.

When I got to the car, I placed my belongings on the front passenger's seat and dialed Axton's number, set the phone to hands free, and waited for him to answer. When he finally picked up, I said, "You won't ever believe the news I just got!"

He chuckled. "I'm glad to hear from you too. How are you?"

I felt silly. "I'm sorry. I'm just so excited. God is too good to me. Can you meet me for lunch? Are you busy?"

I really hoped that he was able to get away. "Are you actually asking me to lunch? Or are you accepting my invitation finally?"

He was going to enjoy this, I could tell. "Both. Now, are you free?"

"Absolutely, I've been waiting for this call for a very long time. I have one question though, is this a business lunch or a date?"

There it was. This was definitely a date. "This, Pastor Axton Kyle, is a date. Can you meet me at Completion in thirty minutes?"

"Completion, huh? This is going to be good. I'll see you there. Oh, and Genesis, I love you."

Did he just? I didn't know how to respond to that. "I'll see you when you get there." I hung up before he could say anything else. I was sweating because I was nervous, but you know, I think I loved him too. Oh yes, God was on a roll. I laughed to myself through my tears. Stopped at a red light, I lifted my hands one more time, said, "THANK YOU JESUS!" and sped off toward my lunch date.

AXTON

I couldn't believe that Genesis called me and asked me to lunch. I hadn't been able to get her off of my mind since I told her that I had feelings for her. I was a bit skeptical about it, thought maybe I had stepped outside my boundaries and acted outside of God's will but so far, things seemed to be going well. I was thankful. She had been heavy on my mind earlier in the day, so much so that I stopped what I was doing and prayed for her. I didn't know what was wrong but I knew that God was impressing upon my spirit to send up a prayer on her behalf. Maybe at lunch I would find out exactly what was going on.

I told my secretary to cancel all my appointments after I checked my calendar and made sure that I had nothing pressing to do that day. Thank God, it was pretty much a clear day and the things that were on the calendar my associate pastor could handle for me. I closed out the message that I had been working on when she called and headed out of the office. It was a beautiful day, the sun was shining and the birds were chirping. Maybe she would agree to go for a walk after lunch. One could only hope. Baby steps, I kept telling myself. It was hard because I knew that if she agreed, I'd marry her today.

I got in the car, let the window down and backed out of my parking space. I made it to the restaurant in record time and when I pulled in, I saw Genesis getting out of her car. She was dressed in a lilac pantsuit that fit her perfectly, her hair was pulled back into a bun, and her opened toe pumps were sexy. Yes, I noticed. I had a thing for feet and this woman was always put together. At 5'7, she was incredibly attractive, the color of caramel, with the prettiest head of jet black naturally curly hair that, when loose flowed down her back, and her smile lit up any room she entered just like it lit up my heart. This woman was gorgeous. I couldn't deny that even if I wanted to. I sat there for a few more minutes admiring God's gift to me. I watched her sashay to the door and enter the restaurant. She removed her sunglasses before going in. I waited five minutes before I got out of the car. I needed cool down time. I was a man of God but I was still a man and that woman always turned me on. Lawd! I chuckled to myself as I walked across the parking lot. I took out my breath spray and squirted it twice before I reached the door, placed it back in my pocket and walked into the restaurant. There she was waiting for me.

"Hello, Ms. Maicott." I decided to be formal. I knew that would throw her off. She turned around, obviously not expecting me. I saw her look me over from head to toe in what she thought was a discreet fashion and then she flashed that smile. My heart rate sped up. The thoughts I was having right now were downright sinful.

"Hello, Reverend" Ah. So, she was going to play along. I loved that in her. "I'm glad that you could meet me for lunch at such short notice."

I gave her the once over. "I told you, I've been waiting for this moment for a while now, so when you called it was my obligation to answer. I'm just glad that you called." I wanted to hug her, kiss her, touch her but I kept a safe distance.

"Well, this is cause for celebration and I wanted to celebrate with you."

I was shocked to hear it but glad. I knew that God was working in my favor. I wanted to do a fist pump but I acted civilized. "Oh really, what are we celebrating?"

She smiled again. "Wait until we've been seated and I'll tell you." She walked over to me, held my hand, and kissed my cheek. I guessed that was better than nothing. The hostess finally seated us at a table in the back corner, perfect spot for the two of us to be alone. There weren't many people in the restaurant now and I was thankful. Not because I didn't want to be seen with her, but because I wanted her to keep my undivided attention. People were a distraction since I was a people watcher. I seemed to be always looking for opportunities to share the word of God with someone. It didn't matter where we were if the opportunity presented itself, I would take it. Today, I just wanted to enjoy her company.

Once we got to the table, I pulled her seat out for her and waited until she was seated and comfortable before taking my seat. My mother had raised me to be a gentleman. I was thankful. When I sat down, I was ready to hear what the cause was for this celebration.

"So?" I asked anxiously. "What are we celebrating?"

Her eyes filled with tears and I was worried for a minute until she said, "We, my dear pastor, are celebrating the goodness of God and my miracle."

I was confused so I just sat there expectantly. When I didn't respond, she continued. "I went to the doctor today. My appointment was at 10:30. When I got there, Kenyon was there. I thought at first that maybe he was following me, but that wasn't the case. He was there to see his doctor.. Anyway, I went back into the exam room and I just sat there. The nurse took some blood and then the doctor came in and we talked for a while. She did her regular short exam, said that things looked well, but she wanted to run a few tests to make sure. I started to get worried once 11:30 rolled around and I was still in the exam room and the nurse had come in two more times since the first time to draw more blood. I was getting scared, so I began to pray."

She stopped for a moment and looked at me I guessed to gage my reaction. Now I knew why I felt like I needed to stop what I was doing and pray for her. 11:30 was the exact time that I had begun praying. "I prayed for you today at exactly 11:30. God had me stop what I was doing and pray now I know why," I said and I told her to go ahead with her story. Now I was very interested in hearing what happened.

"When I finished praying, I felt so much better. Like God had dispatched angels of peace to be with me. So, I was looking through my bag for my Bible when the doctor finally came back in, about noon. She had this odd look on her face and then she started smiling. I didn't know what was wrong with her, you know? I was wondering if she had lost her mind. But I didn't mention that. I just waited until she started talking and guess what she told me."

"I don't know. What did she tell you? Is everything okay?"

She laughed. "Everything is better than okay. My original results were mixed up with someone else's with the same initials as mine. I am negative. I've never had HIV. It was all a mistake."

By this time, tears were streaming down her eyes and I was crying along with her. I knew that this was nothing but God. I grabbed her hand across the table and said, "I told you there was nothing that God couldn't do." I reached across the table and wiped her eyes. "So, do you still want to do the classes that you were planning to do?" I still wanted her to facilitate the classes.

"Oh yes, definitely, this is something that, even though God blocked, is near to my heart. It's become my cause if you will and I still think that people need to be educated about it. Just because God saw fit to reverse it in my situation doesn't mean everyone will be so lucky. If I can help in any way, I plan to do just that." I smiled. Another thing I loved about her. "I haven't even told my parents. You were the first person I wanted to tell. I kind of have a confession to make. Axton, as you know my divorce isn't final yet, but for some reason since you told me that I was your wife, I can't seem to stop thinking about you. No matter what I do or how much I pray that God take the thoughts of you off my mind, you're there. You are the first person I think about in the morning, the last person I think about at night, and I pray for you every time I talk to God. I didn't even feel this way about my husband. This is all new to me but I know you are right. We are meant to be together. I have some unfinished business to take care of first but when my divorce is final, I promise you that I will be yours. There's no use fighting what God has ordained. And to say that I don't love you would be a lie, so I won't say it. I appreciate the time you're giving me and I truly appreciate the fact that you can be patient in waiting for my divorce to finalize."

I sat there with my mouth open. I wasn't expecting any of that. "Genesis, I will wait for you. I told you that and I meant it. I've dated a lot of women but none of them ever captivated me like you do. None of them ever made me feel like a day without them would end my world. You brought the Son's shine into my life. Even though I have Christ, I don't think that I realized his love for me until I saw you the very first time and I knew then that you were bone of my bone and flesh of my flesh. You were my missing piece. The sum of you and me is equivalent to God's love. Infinite. The possibilities are endless when we are together. I am your covering. But I see God's hand on you and I am blessed to have met you. However long it takes, I'm here. There isn't another woman that will ever take your place. You will be my first lady, my last lady. You are my Eve. I am your Adam. God created us for each other. I truly believe that you are the reason God gave me life. I was starting to doubt God, then I met you and honey, you're all the reason I'll ever need to learn, to live, to love, to simply just believe."

She was crying again but she needed to know just how serious I was about us being together. There was nothing in this world that would keep me from getting the gift that God had created just for me. Not even her soon to be ex-husband.

JEREMIAH

Who did Addison think I was? I had already told him I wasn't going to sit around waiting while he pined after that lil' punk Kenyon. No, I'd take them both out if need be. I loved Addison but I knew that he didn't love me and trying to get him back was taking up more time than I cared to keep investing. I wanted them both dead. Like always, I was biding my time. Waiting for the perfect time to catch them both together and catch them both off guard. I was a man with nothing to lose. Lately I'd been sicker than I'd been in years and I knew that it was only a matter of time before I would be dead.. I was at peace with that. I was also at peace with the fact that I was headed to hell for the sins I'd committed. Yes, people had tried to preach me straight, they had tried to preach me right but it didn't help. I was who I was and I was going to be me until the day I took my last breath and gave up the ghost. Yes honey, I knew what the Bible said. I read it faithfully. I had just never gotten all into religion like everyone else. My favorite people in the bible were the men in Sodom and Gomorrah. I could relate to them. No matter what people did, they were true to their inner desires, just as I was and I desired Addison Limón. He was everything that you could want in a man but I think I'd said all that before. Now he was the thorn in my flesh and rather than pick out that one thorn, I wanted to kill the whole damn bush.

You see, I'd gone into a confessional a few days earlier and told the Father to forgive me because I was planning to sin. I bet that was the first time someone had confessed a sin that hadn't been committed yet. That poor Father was like, "My son whatever do you mean?" Just by the sound of his voice, I could tell that he was one of us. Yes, Father McSweeny liked to get the weenie honey. Ha. I laughed every time I thought about it. He was just as gay as me, sitting up in this lil' booth, probably fantasizing about what he was going to do to his lover. Who ever thought that priest weren't getting them some sex was a damn fool. Those men were rocking it out. Trust me. I could always tell a well-sexed man when I heard him and Father here was very well taken care of. So anyway, back to my confession. I told the good Father, "I'm going to kill my lover and his boyfriend as soon as I can catch them together. He's played with my heart for way too long and I am tired of being a toy. I don't have Mattel stamped on the bottom of my foot. This is not a game. I love this man, but he doesn't love me back the way I deserve and so he has got to go."

I chose a Catholic confessional because they were bound by law to keep the secrets of their parishioners and those they never even met, so I was safe. "My son, life and death isn't ours to decide. Only God has the power to give and take life."

Okay, I admit he had to give it his best shot but it wasn't working. I wasn't moved. I'd made up my mind. I had already planned to burn down Addison's business. I just had to make sure that all of his employees were gone. He wouldn't miss it. I knew that he was insured and would gain a lot of money from the little campfire I planned to start tonight. I was getting ready to make his life miserable.

"Well Father, that's good to know, but I'm about to play God, so I'll talk to you later."

I slid the curtain back on the confessional booth and slid out while he was talking. I was sure that by the time he realized I was gone he was wishing that he had asked my name or something. It was getting dark. I left St. Andrews and drove to Addison's building. I had stolen all of his keys and had each and every one of them copied. I was wearing gloves and bags over my shoes so that I didn't leave any finger prints or shoe treads that the police would be able to identify. I had also tied my hair up, although I wasn't too worried about a hair being left behind. I had on a facemask, just in case I had to cough or something. I didn't want my saliva to be the reason I got caught.

It was 9:30, the office closed at 8:00. I made sure that all the lights were off and made sure to disable the alarms and turn off all the surveillance equipment. Oh, honey it was about to go down. I couldn't contain my excitement. My adrenaline was pumping and I was psyched. I walked around the whole building pouring out gasoline as I went. When I made sure that each office in that building had been saturated with gasoline, I walked outside, lined the perimeter of the building with gas as well, lit a cigarette, threw the match down on a very wet spot, walked back to my car and watched the flames engulf the building. It didn't take long for the flames to dance all around the building. It was like a pretty orange-red-yellow light show of my very own creation performing for me. I started to leave him a message but I was sure that he would know this had my name on it once he got a look at things. Before I got sick, I was an arsonist for a living. I was paid to burn down businesses so that the owners could collect the insurance money. It was a job that had paid very well. That's how I was still able to live the lavish lifestyle I lived. You would think that knowing this about me, he wouldn't want to try me but they say love made you do some stupid things. Stupid was putting it lightly.

I sat there for a few more minutes until the entire building was engulfed in flames. I put my cigarette out in my ashtray, gave a salute to the building and told the wind that Addison Limón could kiss my... well you know. This was only the beginning of my plan to destroy him. I wondered if he would think that playing with my heart was worth all it was going to cost him. I started to call him and let him know about the fire but then I thought better of it. I went to a local bar to make sure that I had an alibi. I'd stay there for a few hours so that there would be people who could attest for my whereabouts. I'd done this a million times and I knew that this time would be no different. I would get away with it. I laughed as I changed clothes in my car and headed to the jazz club Imagine on the other side of town.

KENYON

The doctor said that my illness was progressing very quickly and that we needed to try some new medication because the ones that I was on before didn't seem to be working. Long story short, if my body didn't begin to respond to the meds I was going to die and soon. Things were looking bad for me on every avenue it seemed. All I could think was, "What goes around comes around." This was the universe's way of making me pay for all the hurt and pain I'd caused others. I knew that I'd have to pay sooner or later but I never imagined that I'd have to suffer like this. . All I could think about as I sat in the doctor's office was what Genesis had said to me. I'd decided that when I got back to my apartment, I was going to sign the papers and give her the freedom she deserved. I knew that it would take a while for her to even think about being with someone else; she was always faithful to me, and of this, I had no doubt. She was raised that way.

I wanted to cry but I knew that mourning the loss of my wife was pointless. It was my own fault that she was leaving me and if I was honest about it, I deserved for her to go. I didn't deserve a second chance. I had been banking on the fact that she loved me and was forgiving but I guess some things you can forgive and others you can't. She said that she had forgiven me, not for me but for her, because holding on to what I had done to her would only cause her to die a faster death and she wasn't willing to give me the satisfaction. I wanted to be mad. I wanted to blame someone else for the place I found myself in, but I couldn't. So, I told the doctor that I was willing to try a new medication and asked him about making a will, if he knew a good estate planning lawyer. Even though I was going to give Genesis the divorce she wanted, everything I had would be left to her and my daughters. It was only fair, something I hadn't been to her the whole time I'd known her. I knew that I was no good for her, yet, I married her any way, and ended up ruining her life. I was sorry but my sorrow couldn't make her well or erase the pain and hell I'd put her through.

I was planning to go to the lawyer Monday and have my will drawn up, just in case my time was cut short. I wanted to be prepared, at least as prepared as one can be when their death seemed to be staring them in the face. When I left the doctor's office, I looked for her but it appeared that she was already gone. I wanted to see her one more time. I looked across the street and there was a blue sedan parked on the corner. The guy in the driver's seat looked like Addison but it couldn't have been him; he didn't know where my doctor's office was. I shook off that thought, got in the car and drove off toward home. I had to locate all my bank records, insurance policies and financial records so that I could have my will drawn up first thing Monday morning. Since I hadn't done right by her in life, I was going to do right by her in death. That was a promise I intended to keep.

JUSTICE

Things were going so well between Jared and me. I was so happy. I don't think I'd been this happy in all my years of living. He loved the girls and they adored him. We had quickly become a little family. He asked me to move in with him but I turned him down. I didn't think that was wise. I was trying to make better decisions about my life. We were going out tonight. He said that he wanted to take me someplace special, somewhere I had never been. I got dressed and waited. I opted for a formal look since I was sure we were going someplace nice. I was wearing a black dress that came to the floor, silver sexy heels, and my back was out. I knew that he liked it when I was dressed up, so I decided to do it up for him this evening. My hair was swept up in the back and curls framed my face. My make-up was just right and if I could say so myself I smelled delectable.

The doorbell rang. I waited a minute before answering. I didn't want to seem too anxious. When I opened the door, I felt my breath catch in my throat. I'd never seen him look like this before. He looked amazing. He'd gotten a fresh haircut, was wearing a black tuxedo and his scent had me wanting to skip dinner and go straight for dessert. Lord knows that I wanted to sleep with this man, but I promised myself that the next man I gave myself to would be my husband.

"Keep it under wraps, Justice," I said to myself.

"Well, are you just going to stand there staring or are you going to invite a brother in?"

We both laughed. "I'm so sorry. I'm just not used to seeing you look like this. You look amazing."

He stepped into the foyer and we kissed. We'd been doing a lot of that lately but I was very careful not to let it get out of control. He was good at keeping things legit too. When he felt himself starting to want to go further, he'd pull back and get his things and leave. This was another reason I wouldn't move in with him. "Are you ready?"

"I am. Just let me get my purse and we can go." I went and kissed the girls. I told the sitter I'd call if I was going to be late. I grabbed my cover and we headed out.

In the car, he told me that he needed to blindfold me because he didn't want me to have any idea where he was taking me. The element of surprise! I was never much for surprises but I went along with him. I was interested to see how this night was going to turn out. When the blindfold was on tightly and I was in the car with my seat belt on, he got in and we were off.

We drove in silence for what seemed like ever until I asked, "So, where are you taking me?"

He laughed. "If I wanted you to know, I wouldn't have blind folded you, now would I?"

I guessed he had a point. Still, I was nosy and I wanted to know where we were going. Just when I got ready to start a game of twenty questions, the car stopped. I could tell we weren't at a light because I felt the car being backed up. I heard his door open and close. Then I felt my door open. He took my hand, undid my seat belt and helped me out of the car. He was such a gentleman. I loved that about him.

He kissed my hand and said, "Trust me. Let me lead you."

I held his hand and wanted to feel with my other hand but he advised me to keep it down. I did as I was told. We walked up a ramp and I had no idea where we were. Once we had stopped walking, he undid the blindfold and I was pleasantly surprised. We were on the new dinner ship The Fusion. I looked out at the water and all the lights surrounding the city. It was beautiful. This was going to be a good night. I could feel it. After we'd been seated and ordered our food, he said that he had something he needed to ask me. I had no idea what that could be. The violinist came over to the table and began to play softly. I thought this was just a part of the dinner set up until Jared got down on one knee and took a little black velvet box out of his left pocket. Tears welled up in my eyes immediately. This wasn't happening. I pinched myself because I knew that I had to be dreaming. This was real.

"Justice, I know that we've only been dating for a short time but I've known since I first asked you out that I wanted to marry you. You're my inspiration. Your strength and resilience and beauty are like none I've ever seen in a woman. You've survived hell and you still manage to smile and I love you for that. You make me want to be a better man. I want to protect you. I want to love you. I want to grow with you. Will you marry me?"

I didn't have to hesitate. I grabbed his hand and said, "Yes, yes, yes."

There was never any doubt in my mind that when he asked I'd say yes. This man was what God intended love to be and I knew it from the first time that we'd talked. I didn't think that he would ask me to be his wife so soon but I was overjoyed that he had. In my mind, at that moment, we became one.

"I love you Jared. I didn't think that you would want to marry me but I am so thankful to God for sending a man like you into my life." This was truly the happiest day of my life and I just realized I had no one to share this news with. I wouldn't let that bother me though. This was a cause for celebration and celebrate is exactly what I intended to do.

JARED

I was on my way to pick up Justice. It had been a few months since we'd started seeing each other but I was certain that I didn't want to go another day without this woman as my wife so tonight, I planned to ask her to marry me. I should have been nervous but I wasn't. Instead, I felt at peace, like God was giving me the go ahead. I'd prayed about this on numerous occasions and I knew that she was the woman that God had sent for me. There was a magnetism that drew us together. It was like we were the missing pieces of each other. Our minds worked as one; our hearts beat as one. I knew that I was a lucky man to have found the woman that God had made from my rib. I had gone through one of the darkest periods in my life right before I met her.

I'd been working for the fire department for about four years, was happily married and very much in love when I got a phone call while I was out on a call, that I needed to come to the hospital right away. Once I made it to the hospital, I was too late; she was gone. My wife had been hit by a teenaged girl texting and driving. She ran headfirst into my wife and she died on impact. I didn't think that I'd ever get over the pain of losing her. Most days I wanted to die myself. I'd started drinking and took a leave from the department. I was mad at God. I stopped going to church. I stopped doing everything. Until one day my Pastor came to see me. He said some things that changed my life. He told me that sometimes, God allowed bad things to happen as part of his plan for our lives because we were to use them to help someone else get through, that the bad times in our lives were rarely about us and usually about someone else. I didn't want to hear it at the time. He helped remind me that God performs miracles in the dark. Out of the dark, He created the world. In the dark, He created Eve from Adam. Technically, it wasn't dark, at least I don't think it was, but God put Adam to sleep and that's darkness and out of that darkness God created a miracle for Adam. He created woman. Bone of my bone, flesh of my flesh. Not every man was lucky enough or blessed enough to find that part of him. I thanked God daily for allowing this woman to come into my life. She made me better. She brought out the best parts of me, parts I was unaware even existed..

I'd asked her to move in with me and she graciously declined. I think she knew that we wouldn't be able to remain celibate if we were spending all day and all night together. She would only allow me to spend the night at her house if it had gotten too late for me to drive home and then I was only allowed to sleep in the guest room while she slept in her bedroom with the door locked. I appreciated the fact that she was serious about her vow of celibacy. It only made me want her even more. She was the forbidden fruit. I hadn't considered what would happen to me if she had somehow told me that she couldn't or wouldn't marry me. I never allowed myself to think along those lines.

I had an amazing evening planned for us and it was a total surprise. As I was getting dressed, I found myself wanting to call her but I would see her soon enough. It seemed like time was flying today and it was time to pick her up before I knew it. When I rang the doorbell and she opened the door in this black long formal gown with one arm out and the other covered and her back out, my mouth hit the ground. I couldn't stop staring. To say she was gorgeous would be an understatement. The man in me wanted to skip dinner and take her straight to bed. The God in me wanted to make her my wife right then, so that I could skip dinner and take her straight to bed. Hey, I was all man. What could I say? I laughed to myself.

She got her things together and we were off. I blindfolded her. I wanted this to be a surprise. Once we got to Fusion, the look on her face was priceless. I wished that I had brought my camera. Tonight was truly a night I wanted to capture but I would always have the memory of how the next moments would go. We were seated and before long, the violinist came to the table. That was my cue. I stood and got down on one knee. When I pulled the ring box out of my pocket, tears began to fill her eyes. I wasn't prepared to see her cry but I figured they were tears of joy, so I didn't bother to wipe them away. I had planned a whole speech to give her and I delivered it flawlessly and the next thing I know she was in my arms and I was engaged. I was the happiest man alive. I couldn't wait to share this news with the world. As far as I was concerned, we could go to Vegas right now and do this. I didn't need to wait but this would be her first marriage. I knew that she would want a big wedding because we had discussed it. Perhaps we could compromise. Big weddings took a long time to plan and I didn't want to wait any longer to make this woman my wife.

We finished the night off with dancing and then took a long walk along the river. It was peaceful. This had to be what heaven felt like. I silently thanked God once again for blessing me.. I felt like I'd won the lottery. Love was definitely in the air.

ADDISON

My phone rang about 11:00 and I wondered who could be calling me. I usually didn't answer restricted calls but something told me that I had better answer.. I picked up the phone. "This is Addison." There was silence on the other end. "Hello?" I guess the person hadn't heard me answer at first.

I didn't recognize the voice on the other end that said, "Is this Addison Limón, owner of Disclosure?"

It is. How can I help you?"

"Sir, your building is on fire."

Fire? Did I hear him correctly? Was he telling me that my office was on fire? "I'm sorry, did you say that my building was on fire?"

I waited for him to respond. "Yes, sir. That's exactly what I said. I was given your number by some man and he told me to call you and tell you that your building would be burnt to the ground in less than twenty minutes."

I had no idea what was going on. "Thank you. Have you contacted the police or fire department or anything?" By this time, the caller had disconnected the call. I sat there for a moment. I was in shock but I quickly got up and threw on some clothes. By the time I arrived there were sirens blaring and flashing lights coming from everywhere or so it seemed. I threw my car in park and jumped out. My whole office had burned down. Tears began to fall everything I had worked for was literally up in smoke. I had no idea who would do a thing like this to me.

I wanted to call Kenyon. I needed him right now. I picked up the phone to dial him and then I thought better of it. I didn't call. After I talked to the officers and the firefighters, I drove over to his apartment. He couldn't ignore me if I was in his face. It seemed like everything I had worked so hard for was falling apart right before my eyes.

GENESIS

Lunch with Axton turned out to be just what I needed. I had to be honest. When I was with him, it felt like I had finally found my way home, like this was exactly where I belonged. I had been nervous about it at first but that soon faded like the day into night. We laughed, we talked, we cried. Then when lunch was over, we decided to take a walk. I'd never done anything so simple and had so much fun doing it. I noticed small details that I'd never noticed about him before. He had the biggest smile, deep dimples on both sides, and his hands were firm, strong. I liked that about him. Kenyon's hands felt softer than mine. I should have known then. He was very attentive, seemed to hang on my every word and I knew that he was sincerely interested in what I had to say. He asked me questions. I asked him questions. I felt like I'd known him all my life by the time we parted ways. We'd made plans for dinner the next night. I was excited. I could tell that this was going to be very whirlwind, fairytale like, the kind of relationship every girl wanted. God truly had favored me.

I got back to my car and as I was driving home, my phone rang. My first thought was that Kenyon was calling, but it was my mother. I had forgotten to call her when I left the doctor's office and I knew that was the reason for her.

"Hello, Mama. How are you?"

"Don't hello mama how are you me, young lady. You were supposed to call me as soon as you left that doctor's office. That was almost six hours ago."

I took the phone away from my ear. It was very rare that my mama yelled but she was yelling today. I knew that no amount of apologizing would calm her down so I didn't bother. I told her the truth. "I know, Mama but I had a date and I kind of forgot. I was going to call you as soon as I got home. . I promise."

"A date? What do you mean you had a date? You're still a married woman. You can't be out gallivanting with these men."

I laughed. "Mama, I wasn't gallivanting. I had a lunch date that kind of prolonged. I had a very nice time. I deserve it. It was just lunch."

I heard her suck her teeth. My mama was one of the most sophisticated women you'd ever see in public, but at home, her country ways sure shined through. You had to love her.

"Well who is this young man you had *just lunch* with?"

She truly had a way with words. I pulled into my garage. "Mama, why the interrogation? You don't trust me?"

She clicked her tongue. "Trust you? Honey, this has nothing to do with trusting you. I just want to make sure that you're a better judge of character this time around. I don't want to see you getting hurt anymore. You've been through enough. Your father and I just want the best for you."

I knew she was telling the truth. I couldn't blame her, not after the way things had gone the last year of my life. I was finally getting back to myself, truly. "Since you must know, Mama, I had lunch with the pastor of my church. He's been trying to get me to go out with him for quite some time now and I finally accepted his offer and I'm very glad that I did."

"Oh, you were out with Axton, were you? Well Judah will be so glad to hear that."

What was she talking about? I knew that Axton knew my parent's but why would my father be glad to hear that I had gone out with him? It was time for a little interrogation of my own. "Mama, why will daddy be glad to hear that I was out with Axton?"

"Oh child, now you know that man does things the old fashioned way. He called your daddy about four months ago to let him know that he was interested and to ask your father's permission to ask you out. He knew all that you had been through. He sat your father down and explained to him that you were the woman he believed God had sent to be his wife. Your father told him that, ultimately, it was your decision but if it was indeed God then in due time things would work out as they should. It looks like that young man was right. I'm happy for you, baby."

I was in awe. I had no idea that he had gone to my father to ask his permission to take me out. For some reason that just made me fall in love with him more. Any man that wanted my father's approval, well that was unheard of in today's time.

"I can't believe you didn't tell me. Mama, you know you can't hold water." I laughed and so did she.

"Girl your father made me swear on that big white Bible in the living room that I wouldn't say a word. He didn't want me trying to talk you into going out with that young man but I'm glad to know that I didn't have to because you made the right decision."

Well at least now, I knew that I didn't have to worry about introducing him to my family and worrying about whether or not they would think that I was doing the right thing by moving on. That made things a lot easier for me.

"So, I have something that I need to tell you," I said to my mother changing the subject. I knew that she called to find out how my doctor's appointment had gone.

"Oh?" It was the old fashioned nosy oh, like I was going to tell her something juicy. I had twisted the cord to my hands free headset around my fingers and was untwisting it as I sat down.

"Yep, I know that your reason for calling was because I went to the doctor today." I didn't want to worry her but I tried to hide the excitement in my voice.

"Well yes, since you said that you were going to call me as soon as you left the appointment. Is everything okay, Genesis?" Her motherly concern was back. That didn't take very long.

"Yes ma'am, everything is okay. As a matter of fact, things are better than okay. Things are wonderful. Mama, God is such a great God. I'm not sick at all. I don't have HIV. According to the doctor, I never did. She said that she wanted to double check some things because my test were all coming back normal when I was there today. Well come to find out, there was someone else in the hospital with the same initials as me and their test was positive. I'm so thankful, Mama."

By this time, I was crying again. The goodness of God just kept overtaking me. I loved Him so much. She was crying too. "Baby, that's wonderful. I've been praying that God would heal you."

As far as I was concerned, no one deserved it but I was the only one who didn't have a willing part in the downfall of my marriage.. I would continue to pray for all involved but I was so thankful that God saw fit to give me vindication and vengeance. Grateful didn't describe the way I was feeling.

I finished the call with my mother and reflected on the day I'd had with Axton. I still couldn't believe that he had talked to my father about his feelings for me. I said a prayer and thanked God for sending him into my life. It looked like things were beginning to look up for me again. I forgot that I hadn't checked the mail so I walked out to the box. It was such a beautiful night. The sky was clear, stars all over the sky. It was nights like this that I truly felt the presence of God. I took the mail out of the box and there was a large manila envelope that had no stamp on it. It had a post-it note on the front: *You were right. I'm setting you free. You deserve better than what I've given you. I hope you find it somewhere in the world. Here's the divorce papers, signed and uncontested. I won't bother you again. Despite what my actions said, I do love you.*

-Kenyon

I really was not expecting that but for some reason I wasn't surprised. I guess today really was a day for miracles. I thought that he would drag this divorce on forever. I said one more time, as I'd been saying all day, "Thank you, Jesus!" Now I could really begin my journey. I did a little dance and went back inside. Grateful. Yep that's what this feeling was, gratefulness.

AURELIA

I had just gotten off the phone with Genesis when Judah came into the kitchen, smiling and smelling good. Even after fifty years of marriage, I still loved this man like we were newlyweds.

"How was your day?" He asked with a smirk on his face and a twinkle in his eye. I knew what he was thinking but that would have to wait.

I chuckled. "It was alright. Very uneventful, but I do have wonderfully amazing news about our daughter. Unless you'd rather she tell you herself." He cocked his head to the side. "I just got off the phone with her. She asked for you but I didn't know you were home. You're welcome to call her back if you'd like to hear it straight from her."

"Oh woman, just tell me what's going on with my baby girl. There's no need for me to call her back if you've already talked to her. Once I know what's going on maybe that will change."

"Well, do you want the short version or the long version?"

I was going to mess with him now since he wanted to get smart. He rolled his eyes and said, "Short version because if I get the long version from you, we'll be here all night and I'm hungry."

I swatted his hand and we both laughed. "Okay, short version it is. She went to the doctor today and her test results were wrong. She doesn't have HIV, bless God."

I stopped and let him digest what I just said. The shock and thankfulness all registered on his face within seconds. Tears welled in his eyes. My husband was never a man that was afraid to cry and I appreciated that because men who won't show emotion take it out on the women in their lives. Not this man. He cried and I cried with him. That's what love was about: sharing everything.

Once he was calm, I went on. "And she's finally giving Axton the time of day. They had lunch together today; she's getting her happy back."

With that, he smiled, waved a hand of praise and said, "I had no doubt it would work out for her good. All praises be to God. Now let's eat."

KENYON

It was after midnight and someone was banging on my door. I felt like I'd been asleep forever, but then there was a boom, boom, boom on my door. I glanced at the clock on my nightstand and wondered who could be knocking at this time of night. I threw the covers back and banged my toe on the edge of the door leaving the bedroom. I was already upset; that just made things worse. I snatched the door open without looking through the peephole. Whoever this was was about to catch it.

"What the...?"

Addison was standing at my door looking like he'd been drug through the mud. Since I'd known him, I'd never seen him look like this. I took a deep breath. "What are you doing here?"

He stood there looking defeated but didn't say a word as tears fell from his eyes. I could tell that whatever was going on had to be very serious. I'd never seen him cry before. I pulled him into the apartment and we sat down on the couch. I wrapped my arms around him. "What's going on Addison?"

He pulled away from me and said, "It's all gone. Everything I've worked so hard for is gone. I don't understand. I've lost you, now my business. What else can go wrong?"

I didn't have any idea what he was talking about. "What do you mean you've lost your business?"

Tears started falling again. He wouldn't look at me; instead, he got up from the couch and walked over to the window, pulled back the curtain and looked out. It was kind of like he was looking at something that used to be, a memory maybe. I just sat quietly and waited for him to go on. "Someone set my building on fire tonight and by the time I got there, the whole building was burned to the ground. You don't love me anymore. I'm dying. My life is over. I was looking forward to growing old with you, but who am I kidding? Neither of us is going to grow old. I've made so many mistakes and I won't have time to correct any of them. I never meant for things to turn out this way." He turned to face me, "I love you Kenyon. I need you and I don't think you understand that."

I didn't really know what to say. I got up and walked over to him, took him by the hand and made him come back over to the couch. "I'm so sorry to hear about your business. I know that you worked so hard to get where you were, but you can always reopen in another location. Maybe this was a blessing in disguise. Are you sure you have no idea who would want to do something like this to you or even if it was something someone did?"

A look passed over his face but I couldn't really be sure what it was. "I have to wait for the firemen's report to come back but he said that shouldn't take very long. One of the firemen at the scene told me that a fire usually doesn't burn that quickly without the use of an accelerant. They think it was arson."

I wasn't sure but I had a feeling that Addison's ex had something to do with this fire so I said, "Didn't you tell me that Jeremiah threatened to make you sorry that you'd left him? Would he do something like this?"

There was that look again. He rubbed his face with both hands and said, "I don't want to believe that he would be that conniving, but he used to be a fire starter.."

"I mean, I understand that you don't want to believe that he'd do something like this but fact is, he's had a history of doing it and he did threaten you. I just don't want to see you be foolish."

Fact was, even though my heart wanted Genesis, I knew that she was better off without me. She didn't want me back anyway; she'd made that very clear. I had been thinking about Addison and going back to be with him since I dropped the divorce papers off at Genesis' house. There was no need for either of us to end up alone. I loved him. I just wasn't in love with him but having someone was better than not having anyone, wasn't it? We were both sick and I didn't think I'd be here much longer anyway. Something inside told me that for all the dirt I'd done my days were numbered. I'd made peace with the situation that was most pressing to me. I'd given Genesis her freedom. She deserved a lot more than what I'd ever been able to give her and I realized that now. Next on my list was to make sure that Justice and my children were taken care of. I made preparations for trusts to be set up in each of the twins' names so that when they reached eighteen they wouldn't have to worry about a thing. I'd also left Justice a nice sum of money if I was to die before the girls grew up. I paid child support already and I'm sure that many people thought it more than enough, but I knew that it wasn't. This was my way of making amends. I knew that I'd never been able to take back the fact that they were both sick because of my carelessness and selfishness. I could never take back the death sentence that I'd handed them, but I could try my best to make things right. It wasn't much.

I turned to Addison and said, "I've been thinking and I'm sorry. I'm sorry that I acted the way I did but I was so mad when you threatened Genesis. Anyway, I signed the divorce papers. She and I are through. If you still want to try to make this work, I'm all for that."

He didn't respond at first. Then he took me by the hand and led the way into the bedroom. I guess this was his way of saying all was forgiven.

JEREMIAH

I paid a man at the bar to call Addison and tell him that his precious little building would be burnt to the ground in a matter of minutes. By the time he arrived at his building, it was no more. Phase one was complete. I watched the anguished look on his face from a distance. He had no idea I was there. I started to call him and then I thought better of it. I wondered if he had even begun to connect the dots yet. Knowing him, I never even crossed his mind.

I got back in the car I rented for the night and followed him when he pulled off. He pulled up outside some apartment building but I had no idea where he was going. I'd never been to this place before. It was nice. I wondered why he hadn't gone home to his boy toy, then it dawned on me. The last time we were together he said that Kenyon was moving out because they weren't getting along. That's when I thought that maybe he was going to come back to me once and for all, but I was wrong. Sitting outside that building, I realized that he went just where I expected him to go: to Kenyon. I thought maybe this time he'd come running to my arms. It was time to step this game up a notch. I wasn't going to be ignored. His beloved building was phase one. Maybe his car and house should be next. Let's see if he thought this was a game now. I got out of the car, walked over to where he was parked, took out my keys, and wrote on the hood of his car, "YOU'LL BE SORRY." Maybe then, this silly man would get the picture. This was not a game. I'd been played one time too many. I was done being nice.

After I left there, I drove to his house, found his spare key, broke out every window in the place, tore up his television, cut holes in all his clothes, broke his computer monitor and took his laptop. I was worse than a woman scorned and he was just about to feel the fury. Whoever had come up with the saying "Hell hath no fury like a woman scorned" had apparently never been involved in a lovers' quarrel involving gay men. 'Cause honey, I was pissed and it was about to be on.

Axton

I don't think I'd ever had such a simple date. We had lunch and we walked and talked. I felt like I was in heaven the whole time. I felt like I'd known this woman all my life. Things that she had been through I had been through. We almost had identical childhoods, both being preachers kids. However, I'd done a lot more dirt and damage than she had. From what I could tell, the worse thing she'd done was marry Kenyon against her father's will. Other than that, she was an all-around "good girl," definitely not the type of girl I was used to dating. Maybe that's why I was so attracted to her. She wasn't the type I was used to. I hadn't told her that I'd already spoken with her father about my feelings for her. I was old fashioned that way. I needed to get her father's permission before I pursued his daughter. Besides the fact that her father was a well-respected minister, he was one of my favorite preachers. I'd never do anything against his will, but I wanted to be sure that it wasn't just lust that was making me feel like this was the woman God had created just for me. I asked him to pray with me as I sought God's direction for this relationship and when he came back and told me that God had told him I was the one, I knew that it was time for me to make my move.

I was sitting on the edge of my bed watching the Knicks game when the phone rang. No one ever called me at this time of night so I knew that something had to be wrong. I picked up my phone and looked at the display before answering. It was Genesis. A smile appeared on my face before I could even realize it.

"Hello." I tried to sound casual, knowing I probably sounded all goofy and what not.

"Uh, hey. You're not busy, are you?"

She was being formal still. I thought we'd gotten past that today. "Even if I were, I'll always make time for you. What's up?"

"Oh, nothing. I just called to tell you that I really had a nice time with you today. I've never had that much fun just walking and talking with someone. I felt at peace and it was just… nice."

We must have been thinking the same thing. On one accord, that's what kept going through my mind. I felt connected to her. I wondered if she felt the same. "I'm glad that you had a good time. That was my intention. To make you fall for me even harder. I had to put on my secret charm." I laughed and so did she. I wondered how long this courtship would last before the wedding actually took place. I was aware that it wouldn't be long. Like I said, if she said yes I'd marry her today.

"So I have some news." She sounded serious now. The playfulness was gone in her voice. I wondered if she was getting ready to drop a bomb on me. I moved around on the bed to get comfortable and braced myself for what she was about to say to me.

"News?" I couldn't really say more than that at this point. I was a bit worried now.

"Yes. When I came home today and checked my mail, there was something in the box that I wasn't expecting."

"Like a check or something? You got another blessing? Praise God" I knew that she hadn't said that but I was hoping that's what it was.

"It wasn't a check. It was my divorce papers signed, sealed and delivered. He's no longer fighting it. There was also a note that said he was going to release me to find what it is I should have had all along. He knows that he can never give me what I deserve."

I said a silent *thank you, Lord*. "Really?" I tried to keep the excitement out of my voice. Things were moving faster than I'd thought they would. "How do you feel about that?" I knew how I felt about it but what I felt about it really didn't matter. This wasn't about me; it was about her. Whatever she said I had to be sure to just let her guide this conversation. I'd follow her.

"I'm ecstatic. I thought that it would bother me when I finally got the papers but I feel nothing less than free. I'm thankful. God is working things out for me and I don't know anything else to be."

She was ecstatic? I hadn't expected her to say that but since she had, I allowed myself to feel the same way. "So, does this mean that now you can be with me?" I saw no reason to beat around the bush. She knew that I wanted to be with her and I told her that I would respect her wishes no matter what, but she had told me that when her divorce was final she would be with me. I didn't want to wait much longer.

"Well, the divorce isn't final yet but I do have the papers in hand and it will be finalized soon, since he's not contesting it anymore." I didn't respond. She still hadn't said yes so I just waited for her to speak again.

"Yes, Axton, we can be together. I see no reason to keep waiting. I know that I'm not going back to him. I love you. You love me. Let's make this happen."

"That's what I'm talking about!" I was excited. I knew that things would definitely work out for the best now. "Genesis, listen, I told you that I'd marry you today if you'd say yes. I don't know how slow you want to take things but I don't really see a reason for waiting. However, I'll do whatever makes you most comfortable."

"Let's take the time to get to know each other. We've already decided that we are going to be together. I believe that you are the man God ordained to be my husband. You've confirmed I am your wife. It will happen when it's meant to happen. We've taken the first steps.

Now let's enjoy this journey. We have a lifetime to make memories."

I couldn't argue with that so I didn't. I just told her that it was fine with me. We ended our conversation and I smiled until I fell asleep that night. Things were definitely coming together. What an awesome God I served!

JUSTICE

I could not believe that I was engaged. I never imagined that I'd be the woman that a man wanted to marry, although I had always wanted to be a wife. This night had turned out to be magical. I felt like a princess. Nothing could bring me down.. I didn't allow myself to think about the fact that I had no friends or family to share this news with. I looked at Jared as an idea popped into my head. Since I had no friends or family, I didn't need the big wedding. I didn't want to wait anyway.

I grabbed his hand across the table and said, "Let's do it tonight! Let's get married."

I knew that he was going to be caught off guard by that and the look on his face let me know that I was right. I laughed. "Are you serious?"

"Of course I'm serious. I don't have any reason to wait. I don't need the big wedding. Would I like one? Of course I would. What girl doesn't want the fairytale wedding? But let's be honest, I'm not your average girl and I don't have the friends or family that people invite to weddings. More than the wedding, I want you. I want to be your wife. I want to be able to make love to you. You have no idea how badly I want to do that. So let's do it. Let's fly to Vegas and let's get married."

I think he was still in shock because he just sat back in his chair like he had a lot on his mind. Looking at him leaned back in that chair with the night sky and the stars surrounding him out there on the water just made me want him even more. I took out my cell phone and called the sitter. I wanted to let her know what my plans were and see if she could stay with the girls until later tomorrow. Tonight, I was getting married. I was already in a formal gown, although not white and not a wedding dress it would do. White was for those who had led chaste lives. I stopped being chaste long ago. And he was already in a tux. Tonight was the night. There are some opportunities that when they present themselves you seize them. For me this was one of them.

I grabbed him by the hand and said, "Let's go to the airport". He got up and followed.

We arrived at the airport and booked the first thing going to Vegas. I was excited. All of my wildest dreams were about to come true. I felt a little pang at having no one to share the news with but it passed quickly. I was used to being alone and not having friends. I never really had a lot of friends. I mean, I'd made some along the way but when you grow in foster care you don't really bond with anyone. The closest person to me was my mama and she'd passed away years ago. My older sister stopped talking to me when she found out that I'd gotten pregnant by a married man. She told me "Mama raised us better than that." The day she picked me up from the hospital was the last time that we'd talked. I guess I was a bigger disappointment than I originally thought. She wasn't my real sister anyway so it didn't much matter. It just meant that once again I really had no one to turn to. That was part of the price you paid when you became the scandalous one, but I knew that if God could do this for me, he could restore my relationships as well. Maybe it was time to start making amends. But that would have to wait.

We boarded the plan and all I could think about was how my life was getting ready to change. I said a silent prayer thanking God for loving me even in the midst of my mess and for sending Jared into my life. I was happy, truly happy for the first time in a long time and I could only hope that I remained this way.

JARED

She looked at me and said, "Let's do it." For a minute, I was a little confused. I thought she meant let's *do it*. You know, let's make love. What she meant was let's get married. Tonight. She wanted to fly to Las Vegas and say I do. And I was all for it. Just in case she was pulling my chain, I didn't allow myself to get too excited. I didn't want to make a fool out of myself just yet. Y'all know how women can be. Say one thing and mean another and then when you respond like a man is supposed to respond, they flip out on you. We were having a good night. I was enjoying her company and the fact that she had agreed to be my wife. For now, I was content. She didn't have to rush this for me, but if she was serious, we would get married tonight.

She said the word and now we were on our way to the airport. Inside I was soaring. I was the most ecstatic I had ever been. I was getting married. We arrived at the airport, purchased the tickets and boarded the flight. She laid her head on my shoulder and all I could think of was growing old with her. I had never loved a woman so much that I waited for her, but Justice wasn't just any woman. There was something special about her. I loved her resilience. She could be depressed and angry, yet she chose to smile and enjoy life and now we would enjoy life together.

We made it to Vegas in what felt like little to no time. I asked the lady at the ticket desk where the nearest 24-hour wedding chapel was and she gave me a laundry list of them. I had to admit it was kind of funny but I guess this was Sin City and nothing was forbidden here. We looked at the list and decided on Allure. She liked the way the name sounded. I wanted to go to A Little White Chapel for obvious reason but she declined. Ater all this was more about her than it was about me, so *Allure* it was. I was pleasantly surprised. I was also glad that I'd opted to wear a tux tonight instead of a regular suit. We looked good even if this wasn't going to be your traditional ceremony.

The guy that came out when we first got there made me laugh. He kind of looked like he should have had a starring role in the Wizard of Oz as one of the munchkins. Maybe he wasn't that small but his red hair and round belly reminded me of the coroner from the movie. Anyway, when we told him what we wanted, he told Justice that she could pick a wedding dress to wear if she wanted to be in one for the ceremony. Her eyes lit up. He called his assistant out and she took her to the back. They were back there for what seemed like ever. How many wedding dresses did they have back there?

When she finally came back out to the front of the chapel, my mouth dropped. She looked gorgeous in the black dress that I'd picked her up in, but now she looked simply heavenly, like my very own angel. She had chosen a floor length straight lined dress with a plunging neckline that was covered in pearls and a veil that had pearls on it as well. You know where my mind went. We needed to hurry up and get this over with. We had purchased tickets to go home later on the next day. We would plan a real honeymoon later, but tonight, oh tonight.

I took her hand and I said a prayer before the ceremony started. I bet they had never seen that before but I wanted this marriage to be covered and blessed by God. After I finished praying, we said our vows and before I knew it, we were Mr. and Mrs. Jared Shea. It was a done deal. The beautiful woman standing in front of me was now and forever, until death did us part, my wife. I allowed all the passion that I had been holding back for the past few months to be felt when I kissed her.

I pulled back and whispered in her ear, "Let's finish making this night special. I want to make love to my wife."

She took my hand and said, "Let me change back into my dress and we can make that happen." Then she kissed me again, and I could feel myself start to get hot under her touch. Oh yes, this was a time to thank God.

When she walked away from me, I watched her walk and this time didn't hide the fact that I was in fact watching. She was all mine now. I said another prayer and I allowed the emotion I felt to flow. I cried as I thanked God again for bringing this woman into my life. My mother always said that a man who can cry is a man that can handle anything. Mama! Oh shoot. I forgot to call her. Well, I was sure she could wait until tomorrow. She would be upset that Justice didn't have a "proper wedding" but I was sure she would understand why.

Justice was back and we headed out to find a room at a nice hotel. We found a room at the Signature at MGM Grand. We checked in and before we got into the room good, the clothes were coming off. We had both waited a long time for this. I made sure to grab the Do Not Disturb sign and hang it on the door. She was nervous. I assured her that it would be alright. We made sure to take all the necessary precautions, then I made love to my wife for the first time.

ADDISON

I could only think of one place to go after I saw that my building had burned to the ground. That was to Kenyon's place. I figured that he couldn't ignore me if I was in his face. I banged on his door until he opened it. I knew he was home because his car was parked out front and I didn't think there was anyone here with him since he was so dead set on being back with that woman. Finally he answered the door looking like I had awaken him from some good sleep. I didn't care. I broke down when he answered. All I could do was cry. And usually I was a man who didn't show much emotion, but when you lose everything like I'd just lost you can't help but be emotional.

"What are you doing here?" he asked with an edge to his voice. He was looking at me like I was the last person he wanted to see.

I told him what was going on and he actually held me and let me cry. I would take what I could get for now. I needed to be comforted and he was the one I wanted to comfort me. We talked for a long time. I realized just how much I missed this, how much I missed him, how much I needed him. He told me that he had given Genesis her divorce papers, signed. My heart leapt at the news but I was still skeptical. Just because he'd decided to stop fighting for her and give her freedom didn't mean he wanted to work things out with me.

Then he said the words I'd been longing to hear since the night he moved out. "Addison, listen. I know what I said before but I was wrong and if you still want to work this out, well, I'm all for that."

I didn't speak; instead, I took his hand and led him into his bedroom. Right now my actions would speak louder than any words I could say. I closed his bedroom door behind us and took him into my arms. This felt like home. I knew that this was right for me. I allowed myself to forget all of my troubles for a little while and rested in his love.

GENESIS

So much had happened in my life in the past six months. I'd found out that my test results were wrong, gotten my divorce finalized, started a new relationship, and was headed down the aisle once again. That's right. Axton had asked me to marry him the day my divorce was final and I said yes. We had spent every free moment together since we had gone to lunch the day I got my results back. It was all so fairy-tale like. If I hadn't lived it, I wouldn't have believed it myself. I couldn't thank God enough for making life so much better for me.

I was sitting at my desk working on plans for a program we were planning to have at the church on HIV awareness for the youth and young adult ministry. So far, the program had been working well. It wasn't your traditional ministry. There were several people who felt like we were condoning fornication and sex before marriage. It wasn't that we were condoning it; we still gave these young people the word but we also were aware that many of them were still going to do what they were going to do. We felt that if they were still going to choose to participate in it, then they should protect themselves in every way possible. Yes, abstinence was the godly way. It was the preferred way, but the generation of young people we were dealing with didn't do things the way we wanted them to do. They were the generation of YOLO (You Only Live Once) and living once was killing them. There were so many young people walking around uninformed, unprotected, and dying. That was what we were trying to prevent.

As I was working on the program, my phone rang. I was really too busy to talk at the moment, but I answered anyway. It was the hospital. My first thought was that something happened to Axton. I didn't want to sound panicked but I was afraid.

"Is this Genesis Maicott?"

I didn't want to tell them it was me, but I did. "Yes this is Ms. Maicott. How can I help you?"

"This is Dr. Santorelli calling from Mercy West hospital. I was calling because you were listed as the next of kin for one of our patients and we needed you to come right away."

"I don't understand. What patient?"

I was expecting him to say my mother or father, even Axton, instead he said, "Mr. Kenyon Swan."

"There has to be some mistake. He and I are no longer married. We've been divorced now for three months. I'm sure that he has someone else listed as his emergency contact."

"No ma'am. Only your name is listed on all his paperwork."

"What happened to him? Why is he there?"

"Well I can't really tell you much over the phone, only that it's not looking too good and we need someone to come and soon."

Just when I thought things were looking up, here he came back into my life to complicate things . I decided then and there that I would not allow that to happen. I told the doctor that I'd come but I had some business I needed to handle first. I wrapped up the things that I was working on for the program and called Axton.

"Hey, are you busy?"

"I'm not busy, what's up? You sound like something is wrong." We had promised that there would be no secrets between the two of us. That wasn't the way I wanted this marriage to go. I knew from first-hand experience that secrets could and would kill a marriage. Plus, God was the basis and foundation for this relationship. "I just got a call from the hospital about Kenyon. He's in the hospital and has me listed as his next of kin. They want me to come now. Apparently things are not looking too well for him. I'm not sure what's wrong because they wouldn't tell me much over the phone. I just wanted to call and let you know and see if you were too busy to come with me."

He was silent for a minute. "Sure, I'll go with you, but first I think we should pray."

We prayed before and I grabbed my things and headed to the hospital. I really didn't understand why Kenyon had me listed as his next of kin still. Traffic was backed up for it to be mid-afternoon, but I quickly saw why. It seemed they were always doing construction around here for one reason or another. I took out my phone and plugged it into the charger and the auxiliary unit on my car's radio and played a message by Jamal Bryant called, "Here We Go Again." I thought it fitting for the situation and I needed to calm my mind. I didn't want to think the worse but since the doctor had said things weren't looking good, I kept thinking that maybe Kenyon was about to die. I wondered if he had ever decided to accept the fact that there was indeed a God and if he'd confessed his sins before Him. If he was still the man I knew him to be, then the answer to that question was a resounding NO. That made me sad.

I finally made it to the hospital and up to the ICU where he had been admitted. I stopped when I got to the nurses' station and saw a man sitting in the waiting room in front of the nurse's station. I went to the nurse's station and told her that I'd received a call about Kenyon. She said that she would call his doctor and let them know I was there. I found a seat in the waiting area and said a short prayer. While I was praying, I heard someone come into the area I was seated in. I didn't bother to look up. I thought maybe it was Axton or the doctor. I was wrong.

"What are you doing here?" So, it began. I wasn't in the mood. It's not like this was a courtesy visit. I did not want to be here. There was a lot more that I would rather have been doing with my time.

If he was here, what did Kenyon have them call me for? I didn't have time for drama. . The last time this man had said anything to me, he had threatened to kill me. There was nothing for us to say to each other.

"Why is that any of your concern?" If he wanted a confrontation, then that's what he would get. I wouldn't be nasty, but I wouldn't allow him to disrespect me either. I'd had enough of that. It would end here and it would end *now*.

"What do you mean, why is that any of my concern? I'm the one that's been here all night. I'm the one who was there when he wouldn't wake up in the middle of the night. I'm the one who's been taking care of him for the past few months. It's my concern because we are together. So again, I ask why you are here."

I laughed. He was the one who'd been taking care of him? "Aren't you also the reason he's sick? You're standing in my face with this attitude like you're doing him some favor or something by taking care of him. You should be taking care of him. You're the one who infected him. It's because of you that he's in the position he's in. So please don't walk up on me talking to me like I'm intruding."

"Girl, you had better watch yourself. I'm not the one.".

I stood. "Let me make something clear to you Addison. I don't want Kenyon, so you don't have anything to worry about. I wouldn't even know he was in the hospital if his doctor hadn't called me, so I suggest you calm down and get out of my face. We aren't over the phone now and you do not intimidate me."

I needed to let him know that I wasn't afraid of him. There was nothing that he could do to me. Just as I got ready to sit back down, I saw Axton getting off of the elevator. I didn't move. I just watched him watch us. When Addison began to speak again, Axton walked over and said, "Excuse me is there a problem here? Do you need something, sir?" Addison looked like he wanted to run. Axton was at least three inches taller and forty to fifty pounds heavier. He didn't want an altercation with him.

"Who are you?" Addison tried his best to sound tough. It wasn't working.

"Addison, this is my fiancée Axton Kyle." He actually looked a little relaxed. "I told you I don't want Kenyon, so this bull dog act you've got going can stop now. He listed me as his next of kin. I'm here because the doctor said it's not looking good."

"I asked you a question?" Axton wasn't about to let this go. "Is there a problem?"

Addison looked like he could spit fire, instead he said, "Not anymore. I was just wondering what Genesis was doing here since she and Kenyon are no longer married." I laughed inside. You can intimidate a woman but when a real man comes at you, you tuck your tail between your legs and run. Typical.

"Then I suggest you get out of her face." I sat back down. Addison walked away. Axton stood until Addison had taken his seat on the other side of the waiting room, then he sat down beside me. "Are you alright?"

I looked up at him, always my knight in shining armor. I was still trying to figure out why God had chosen to bless me with this second chance. "Yeah, I'm fine. He doesn't intimidate me. I intimidate him because he knows that if I say the word, Kenyon will come back to me so fast it would knock his world off its axis. .He needs to realize that he has nothing to be afraid of because I don't want that man. I have a great man in my life and I'm not risking that for what was."

He leaned in and kissed me. Surprisingly this was the first real kiss that we'd had and I had to pull away. If we wanted to do this the right way and stay saved until we said, "I do," he would have to keep his hands and his lips to himself.

"You know you weren't supposed to do that." I scolded him.

He gave me the puppy dog look. "I'm sorry I don't know what came over me. I..."

Right before he finished his sentence, the doctor came out finally.

I stood to greet him. "Ms. Maicott, thank you for coming. I know I didn't give you much information over the phone but that's because in cases like this it's best to give all information face to face."

I wondered how bad things really were. "I don't mean to be rude, Doctor, but if his lover has been here all night, why not just talk to him about what's going on with Kenyon?"

He turned red in the face and said, "Well, Mr. Swan asked that we contact you. He said that you would know what to do."

I had no idea what this man was talking about. "I'm not sure I understand what you mean. Do about what?"

"Well, his estate and such."

His estate? Was Kenyon going to die? I hated to even consider the thought but the way the doctor was talking, he didn't have very long left here. "Is he dying?" I needed to know.

"Well at this point, we aren't sure. Things could really go either way. He's fighting a severe infection and his body is rejecting the medication we're using now. We are trying to find the right combination of medications to give him but so far we are having no such luck."

"Have you shared any of this with Addison?"

"No, we were not at liberty to discuss his treatment with anyone other than the next of kin. That's why we called you. Mr. Swan has been asking for you, not for him."

I wondered if they were fighting again. I was sure that there had to be some resentment there. You can't not resent someone who virtually ruined your life, even if you were a willing participant in your own downfall.

"Can we see him?"

"Sure you can. Right this way."

We picked up our belongings and followed the doctor out of the waiting room. I walked into Kenyon's room first. There were tubes and machines everywhere. If he wasn't dying, it sure looked like he was. I wasn't sure how I should feel but this made me sad. I took

Axton's hand and walked into the room. I sat down in the chair near-est the bed and just looked at him. This wasn't the man I'd married, once so full of life and laughter, once so bold and confident. No, that man was gone. In his place laid an emaciated shell of a man. It looked like this disease was eating him alive from the inside out. I felt sorry for him. I knew he would never want my pity but I couldn't help it. Seeing what he had become, that's all I could feel for him. There were no emotions of love, no feelings of wanting to take care of him, make him well.

He started to stir. I guess he sensed me here. He turned his head and when he opened his eyes, one tear fell. I don't know if that's be-cause he didn't think I'd come or what. "You came."

I had to sit for a moment before I could respond. He was so fragile now, even his voice sounded small. "Yes Kenyon, I came. I'm not sure why you wanted me here though." I didn't see the point in wasting time or words; it didn't seem like he had much time for either.

"I wanted you here because there are some things I trust only you to handle for me. I know that I don't have the right to expect or even ask you to do anything for me, but please? I believe that somewhere in your heart, there is a still some love towards me. I have a few final wishes that need to be carried out; will you take care of them for me?"

Final wishes. So he was dying. I didn't know if I wanted to be re-sponsible for him again, but he was my first love and I felt as if I owed him that much. There was no one else that would handle his affairs the way he wanted. I didn't trust Addison to do right by his children or anyone else that Kenyon may have wanted to leave something for.

"What do you want me to do?" It was a simple question.

"I need you to make sure that my children are taken care of. I know that you and Justice have formed a friendship. I'm not sure how you could or why you would, but she tells me that you love the girls. I am leaving them trusts. I need you to make sure that it is all executed the way I've specified. Everything else, I've left to you."

"To me? What do you mean you've left it to me? Why would …"

"I left it to you Genesis because you deserve it and so much more. I've made so many mistakes where you're concerned. It's the least that I can do. I may not have done right by you in life but I am determined to do right by you in death."

Axton rubbed my back. I had almost forgotten he was with me until then. This was all about to make me very emotional. I didn't want Kenyon's money, yet I knew better than to fight with him. Once his mind was set on a thing, there was no changing it. "Kenyon, that's not necessary. There is someone I want you to meet. I know this may not be the best time but better now than, well you know. This is my fiancée, Pastor Axton Kyle. I hope you don't mind him being here but I needed him here with me."

He looked at Axton, but I couldn't tell what was going through his mind. I supposed that was a good thing. "Hello Kenyon. It's nice to finally meet you. I've heard a lot about you."

"All bad, right?"

"Well actually no, it hasn't been all bad, but it definitely hasn't been all good either."

"Well, I guess it's nice to meet you, too. So, you're engaged to my wife, huh? How long have you known her?"

I knew that he was going to do that. Strangely, it didn't affect me. "Well, I've known her a little over a year now, but I knew from the first time I laid my eyes on her that she would be my wife."

I wanted to tell him that Axton was the best thing that had ever happened to me but the Holy Ghost quickly checked me. This was not the time or place.

"Do you love him?" That question was directed at me. It caught me off guard and I had to make sure that my response wasn't in anger.

"Yes. Yes, Kenyon. I love him."

"Well, I guess there's nothing more for me to say then, is there? I've always hoped that one day you would come to your senses and realize that you still loved me, that you wanted me back but I guess there is definitely no hope of that now."

Why in the world would I want to go back to being lied to and disrespected? The look on my face must have said it all because Axton cut in and said, "Do you mind if I pray for you?"

"You know, no, I don't mind. I need all the prayers I can get." That was surprising. Kenyon didn't believe in God, he had always been terribly agnostic. Hearing him accept prayer made the sorrow in my heart ease just a bit.

We all bowed our heads and Axton began to pray, "Dear God, we come to You as humbly as we know how. Our hearts are heavy, God, because we are facing uncertainty in the life and health of one of Your children. Fatherf we know that if we are in it, You either ordained it or You allowed it, and so we say thank You. We thank You Father, for the lessons we are learning in the midst of these painful times. We ask You now to send Your healing virtue into this room and into his body God. We believe that there is yet work for this man's hands to do in Your vineyard God and so we ask that You touch like only You can. We also ask Father that you help his unbelief. You know the source of his pain and the beginning of his unbelief in You, God. Heal the broken places. Speak to the dead places in him, Jesus. Give life where it has left in every area of his life, his mind, his finances and most importantly, his health. We ask all these things in Your name, Father. Amen."

I wiped tears from my eyes and noticed that Kenyon had been crying also. At least he was touched. I wouldn't stop praying that he would one day give his life to God and live for Him. I turned as the door open to see Addison coming in. He walked around the other side of the bed and pulled back the curtains. I guess he felt it was too dark in the room.

"Please close them. The light bothers my eyes."

He looked at Kenyon like he wanted to say something to him and thought better of it. I didn't say a word. "How are you feeling?"

Addison asked with an edge to his voice. Obviously he was still upset because I was there. He should really get over it.

"I feel better now actually." I decided that maybe it was time for us to go. I could see that this was getting ready to turn into some drama and I didn't want to be there when it did.

"Kenyon, I've got to get back to work. Call me and give me the details of what you need me to do and I will make sure it gets done. Feel better. I may come back tomorrow when I have some free time but I'm not making any promises." I leaned over and kissed his forehead and we left.

When we got outside of the room, I felt like I could breathe again. I leaned against Axton and let the tears I held fall. It broke my heart to see a man I once loved like that. I didn't know if I'd be able to handle him dying, not now, but for some reason I didn't think that death would be his for the time being.

JEREMIAH

Addison still hadn't been home. It had been almost two weeks since I'd set his building on fire and torn up his house. I was way past pissed. I had taken to sitting outside of Kenyon's apartment and watching them come and go. They didn't leave that apartment much. They'd only come out twice in the two weeks I'd been watching until late last night when the ambulance had come to take Kenyon to the hospital. Apparently, the queen was sick. I started to follow them to the hospital but I thought better of it.

I needed a new plan because the one I had wasn't working. I was just going to call Addison and see if I could convince him to come see me. This was taking much longer than I'd planned for it to take and my time was running out. I would spend my last days with the man I loved or we would die together. I would leave the choice up to him. But there were only two options and those were it. Whichever he chose I was ready. I didn't have anything left to live for if we weren't together. Plus, my time was coming to a close anyway. My mama always said you knew when death was going to come for you and I knew that I'd sown enough bad seeds and karma and whatever else you could sow to guarantee yourself a seat in hell. And if I had my way, he would be sitting right next to me. This was the way it was meant to be. He and I. Him and me. Together we formed a perfect match. We were a set. He had just been distracted but I was going to clear that right on up. If I had to kill his lover to get him to see that I was done playing, like I'd said before, Kenyon didn't stand a snowball's chance in hell, honey.

Loving this man had been all I'd known how to do for the past 15 years. The thought of loving someone else no longer appealed to me. I was too old for the games he wanted to play. I wasn't sure why he felt the need to keep dragging out the inevitable. We would end up together. I was going to be sure of it. Just as I was sitting there thinking that maybe it was time for me to go, who pulls up but Addison. Just the person I needed to see. He got out of the car and so did I. I ran to catch up with him. "Why haven't I heard from you?" He looked at me like I was crazy. I hated that look. I wanted to slap it right off his pretty, chocolate face.

"What are you doing here, Jeremiah? How did you even know where I was??"

Ha. "You'd actually have to go somewhere in order for me to follow you. So technically no, I'm not following you because you don't leave the house." He tried to walk past me but I wasn't having it. I'd waited too long for this. "No, no, no sir. You're going to listen to what I have to say. You've played me off for way to long and I'm tired of it. You know I love you, Addison. All I've ever done is loved you. I catered to you, took care of you, I gave you the world and this is the way you treat me? By falling in love with some man who doesn't know what he wants. How dare you give up on all the years we built together to be someone's second choice. You know he doesn't want you. He wants her. He's just settling for you because she's moved on. Is that what you really want?"

Before I knew it, I was on the ground. I guess I had struck a nerve because he actually put his hands on me. "Don't you ever as long as you live say no mess like that to me." I got up and dusted myself off. I stood there and looked at him, daring him with my eyes to pull that again. I knew he wouldn't though. He wasn't as crazy as he had been acting. Not really.

"You mad? Am I supposed to care? The truth hurts, doesn't it? You know you're just second choice and it pisses you off because I know it too."

"Man, I'm telling you. Watch what you say to me before I…"

I cut him off, he wasn't getting ready to sit here and make threats. "Before you what? What are you going to do Addison? Don't forget I know you. Everyone else might think you're tough, but I know you. You should really watch yourself. Being around that soft little boy of yours has really made you forget who was the man in our relationship. I guess the roles have changed, but I'm not him and I would hate to have to hurt you. Have you been home lately?" He looked at me again with that crazy look. "No. You haven't been home. I know you haven't because I've been there."

"What do you mean you've been there? What were you doing in my house?"

"Oh boy, please. I bought that house I will go there whenever I please. Don't you dare sit here and get high and mighty with me like you've done something. I made you. Everything you are is because of me. Let's not forget who and what you were when we met. I will ruin your life and then I will take it. If you think I'm playing, keep trying me. I'm done being nice. I'm done begging you to come home where you belong. Done. If you want your little lover to die because of you, keep playing me off like I'm some kind of joke. You will regret it. That is a promise I intend to keep."

I walked away before he could respond. I bet that gave him something to think about. If he wanted to go back to his days of being nothing and nobody then he would stay right where he was. He didn't have to love me; I loved him and that was enough for me. I got back in the car and drove off. I believed that what I'd set out to accomplish had just been accomplished with that conversation. He would learn sooner than later that the gloves had come off. This was war.

ADDISON

This day was just not going well. First Genesis showed up at the hospital. Then Kenyon acted like he didn't want me around. He wanted her back; I knew it, but he denied it. If he didn't want her back, then why was she there? He wouldn't tell me what she was doing there or why the doctors wouldn't discuss his care with me. I was the one staying up with him all night while he was in pain. I was the one giving him medication when no one else was there. I was the one running to the store in the middle of the night, but the doctor couldn't discuss his care with me?

We'd gotten into a heated argument after Genesis and her new man left. He was acting all kinds of different and I didn't like it. I made it a point to tell him so. He got pissed when I asked him about allowing them to pray for him. He told me that at this point he had nothing to lose. He just wanted to get better. He wasn't ready to die and if prayer could help him live, then yes, he would pray. I left. I couldn't deal with all of this.

Then I get back to our place only to be met by Jeremiah. He was the last person I wanted to see or be around. I didn't have time for him today. I just didn't. He'd asked me if I'd been to my house. I hadn't but I was getting ready to go there now because I needed to know what he had done. As soon as he pulled off, I turned around and got back in my car.

Once I pulled up to my house, I was afraid to go in. I didn't know what Jeremiah had done and I wasn't so sure I wanted to find out. I sat in the car for a while in front of the house. It had been a while since I'd been here and it felt strange pulling into the driveway, like this was no longer my home. I got out and walked around the house to see if there was anything wrong from the outside. All of the windows had been busted out. That was nothing compared to what he'd done to the inside. I was in no way prepared for what I saw when I entered the house. He had torn up everything and when I say everything, I mean, everything. From the front of the house to the back, my belongings had been broken, shredded, cut, annihilated. This mutha... I needed to calm down. I was seeing red. For the first time I really wanted to hurt Jeremiah. Physically hurt him. I wished I'd never met him, never fallen in love with him. If I hadn't I wouldn't be in this mess. This had to end and it had to end soon. I couldn't go on living my life like this. Something had to give. If he wanted a fight then he would definitely get one.

Who would have thought that when we met fifteen years ago this was where we would end up? I know I hadn't. When I met him I was just a boy, barely eighteen and fresh out of my mother's house. I'd just moved away from home for the first time. A freshman in college, I'd been given a football scholarship. I needed a way to make some extra money and I'd heard some of the other guys on campus talking about this club that hired male dancers so I went to check the place out. After a short audition, I walked away the newest dancer at Sin City. On my third night there, I came out on stage and I started my routine. There was a guy in the front. He was just a bit older than me from what I could tell. He stood up and I could see he was maybe 6'0 tall, caramel colored, dark eyes and long wavy hair. He was gorgeous. He walked closer to the stage, flashed a smile, stuck five $100 bills in my G-string, winked and handed me his card. He told me to call him. I did and it had been me and him ever since. I moved off campus and into his condo. Once I finished school, he gave me the money to start my business. I never doubted that he really loved me until now. I looked at the mess around me and wondered how everything had gotten so out of control. I started to clean up. I was too anal not to. I wanted to go after him but I knew Jeremiah and I knew that he would be counting on my rage to bring me straight to him. I wouldn't give him the satisfaction. I wouldn't let him win. Not this round. As I walked through the damage that used to be my belongings, I wondered if Jeremiah really was behind the fire that had been set at my office. Would he really stoop that low? Something wouldn't allow me to believe that he would. After all, he did love me. Didn't he? He wouldn't be trying so hard to get me back if he didn't, would he?

My mind was full of questions that would never be answered . Sometimes, I wished that my life had taken a different direction. You know, like, I wished that I had been attracted to women and then maybe my life would resemble normal. All this drama that I'd dealt with over the years was starting to take its toll on me. I was tired. I sat down on what used to be my couch and looked around the room. It was in shambles, even after I'd tried to straighten it up, much like my life. I'd gone through life trying to clean up my messes but it never quite fixed things and there was always another mess. I knew that my mother would have been so disappointed in me if she had lived to see who I'd become. I wasn't who she raised me to be. Thinking about my mother made me sad, so I didn't do it too often but for some reason as I sat amidst the wreckage, tears started to fall. It had been a long time since I'd cried. I wasn't sure what I was even crying for. Maybe for myself and all of the karma that was apparently coming back at me. Maybe I was crying because all I'd ever wanted was for someone to love me and no matter what I did to make that a reality it seemed to blow up in my face. Maybe I was crying because I loved Kenyon but knew deep down inside that he loved Genesis still. Maybe I was crying because I knew that my time was running out and I didn't have enough time to right all of my wrongs; there were far too many. I guess when you don't care who gets hurt and you take on a do what I have to do no matter what mentality it always comes back to haunt you. I never imagined that this was where I would end up, but that was where I found myself.

I went to my closet and pulled out the box I kept my gun in. In this moment, I no longer saw the point in living. I took the gun out, put it together, went to the kitchen, took out a bottle of wine, poured myself a glass and went back into the living room. I sat in my favorite chair and laid the gun in my lap. I didn't want to do this anymore. Soon enough it would all be over. First, I'd have a glass of wine.

KENYON

Addison stormed out of here like a mad man. He was actually mad because I'd allowed Genesis and her fiancée to pray for me. Who really gets mad because you accept prayer? I mean, I never said that I was a believer but at this point if the God Genesis had always believed in was real and could heal me or at least make me well enough that I wouldn't die now, then yes, I would allow them to pray for me. It would be stupid for me not to. Truth be told, after he finished praying, something on the inside felt different. I wasn't sure what it was but I knew that I felt something. I didn't expect to cry during his prayer but I did. Maybe God was softening my heart. I had no idea. I didn't know how all that God stuff worked. I wasn't raised in church like Genesis and took no particular interest in it when I met her. I mean, I'd go to church with her on holidays and stuff just to keep the peace but I never really paid much attention and I never prayed on my own. I didn't see the point in praying when I didn't believe in whom or what I was praying to.

Facing death puts things in perspective for some people. It certainly had for me. I didn't know that I would get this sick this fast. It had been a year since I told Genesis that I wanted a divorce. I was so sure then. I was so sure of everything. I had no idea that I was sick. Had no idea that I would lose the love of my life because of my actions. I had no idea that I would cause my wife to lose our baby, a baby that she had wanted so badly for so long. I had no idea that I would impregnate and infect my mistress with the HIV virus. I had no idea that my love would infect me. I had no idea that a year from then I'd be lying in a hospital with an illness that would ravage me from the inside. I had no way of knowing any of those things. If I'd known then what I knew now I would have chosen differently, but isn't that what we all say? Instead of making the right choice in the right moment, we allow our desires to become so great that we give in to them even though we know that they could cost us so much. We never measure the consequences before we act.

I've learned through this whole experience that I can't just use people or hurt them and expect them to be there because they'd always been there. People get tired of being hurt. They get tired of being abused, used, misused, and mistreated. Genesis had. If I could make her see just how sorry I was, I would but I knew I couldn't. I knew that it no longer mattered to her if I was sorry or not. She would never stop praying for me. I didn't believe that she would ever stop loving me. She had proven me wrong. She was happy and she was in love. I could see it in her eyes and hear it in her voice. When she looked at him, there was something there that I'd never seen when she looked at me. She admired him. She respected him. He had her heart. Maybe he was the man God had for her, I didn't know, but I believed that he would take care of her. To me that was all that mattered. He wasn't the kind of man I was. I could tell just by looking at him and watching them together. I was happy for her. I was glad that she had agreed to carry out my wishes just in case God decided that it was indeed time for me to pay the piper.

AXTON

I knew it was hard for Genesis to see her ex lying in that hospital bed. She'd had a pained expression on her face the entire time we were in the room. Almost like she was trying not to let him see how concerned she was. Once we walked out of the room, every tear she'd held back in that room fell. I held her until she released what needed to be released and we stood in silence. There were no words to be spoken in this moment. I knew that. She was glad that he had allowed us to pray for him. I had to admit that he was nothing like I'd expected him to be. Maybe it was the illness that had taken away his strength and made him look so weak lying there. I don't know. What I did know was that he would never again have the chance to cause her pain. I wanted to ask her why she had agreed to help him, but if I knew Genesis, it was because no matter what she would always have love for him in her heart. It was the kind of person she was. It was one of the things I loved about her: her ability to love you beyond the pain that you caused her. She exhibited true forgiveness. It was something that I still struggled with even as a pastor. I had to admit that when I got off that elevator and saw that guy in her face, my flesh rose up. I wasn't thinking about prayer but I definitely gave thought to laying hands. He didn't want it with me. I could tell that he was no more man than Genesis so I politely let him know that if he had a problem with her then we could handle it. After that, he went and had himself a seat. He was a smart fella after all.

I guess I had gotten lost in my own thoughts standing there with

Genesis crying against my chest because I hadn't heard her calling to me. "Axton?"

I looked down. I stood almost an entire foot taller than she did. She was only 5'7. "I'm sorry; I didn't hear you from way down there."

She nudged me and we both laughed. It was good that she could still laugh in a moment like this. I hugged her tighter. I didn't plan to ever let her go. "Are you alright? What's on your mind, seemed like you were thinking really hard about something just a minute ago."

I planted a kiss on her forehead and said, "I was. I was thinking about you and how I'd do anything to keep you safe."

She pulled away, looked up at me, took my hand and led the way out of the hospital. We decided that since we were already together, we'd catch lunch before we headed to the meeting at the church.

JUSTICE

Married life was wonderful so far. I didn't know that love could transform your life the way it had mine. I had never been so happy. I was thankful that in spite of all of my issues and my illness Jared had chosen to love me. He could have had anyone, could have chosen anyone, yet, he chose me. Sometimes I still had to pinch myself to be sure that this was real. The girls and I moved into his house because he owned it and there was just more room. It just seemed like the right move to make. They loved being with him full time too. Everyone was happy.

I'd gotten into event planning years ago just as something to do on the side for extra money and found that I actually loved doing it. So I started Poetic Justice. I did everything from birthday parties to weddings to receptions. You had an event that you wanted to throw and I was your girl. I even wrote a little poetry and made gift baskets, hence the poetic part. Since I'd started doing it full time, business had been great. I was sitting at my desk working on preparations for an event that was coming up for my business when the phone rang. "Poetic Justice, how can I help you?" I always answered the line in the office using my business; name.

"May I please speak with Justice?" The voice sounded familiar but I wasn't sure who it was.

"This is Justice speaking; may I ask who's calling?"

"This is Genesis. Is now a good time to talk? You're not busy, are you?"

I thought I had recognized her voice. We hadn't spoken in a few months but after everything that had happened she and I had gotten to be good friends. It was amazing to me how she could even speak to me let alone befriend me and do things for the girls. I guess she was the better woman because I could not have done it. I was part of the reason she lost her baby and her marriage, yet she never treated me anything less than kindly.

"Oh hey. Now is a good time. I'm not too busy."

"I need to speak with you about Kenyon. Can you meet me for lunch or dinner today?"

Now I was nervous. I hadn't heard from him in almost six months, although his child support payments were never late. Whenever I called, he didn't return my calls so I stopped calling. I figured if he wanted to be in his children's lives then he would without me having to beg him to do so.

"Is everything okay?"

There was a slight pause so I wasn't sure what to think. "No. Things aren't alright, but I don't think it's a conversation for the telephone. Kenyon is very ill. The doctors don't think he's going to be here much longer."

Kenyon? Dying? I sat back in my chair. How was it that we had the same disease and he was on the verge of death? I silently thanked God. I'd had a few sick days but not many. I couldn't imagine. "I don't know what to say. He's in the hospital?"

"Yes. He is. I actually just left there not too long ago. He's asked me to handle some things for him, which is the real reason for my call. I need to speak with you concerning the girls. I have to swing by the bank and get some paperwork but I'm free for the rest of the afternoon if you're available to meet with me."

"Should I go see him? Do you think it would be okay? I mean I haven't seen or heard from him in months. I'd like the girls to see him also if it's not looking too good."

"Oh I'm sure he'd love to see them. Just don't be surprised. He's not the Kenyon you know." Now I was really worried. I wondered how bad he really looked. I also wondered if it would be a good idea to take the girls to see him in this condition but they hadn't seen him in what seemed like forever so they probably wouldn't even remember him. I thanked Genesis for calling and told her that I'd meet her later on that day so that we could discuss things. I called Jared at work to let him know what was going on. The last thing I needed were secrets between us. I was not starting my marriage off that way. I didn't think it was wise to go see Kenyon without Jared knowing. That could totally blow up in my face.

"Hey, how's your day going?" I tried not to sound like something was wrong. "It's going good. What's up?"

I took a deep breath. "Are you in a place where we can talk for a minute? It's kind of important."

It sounded like he was shifting things around. Finally, there was silence. "Okay. What's going on? I'm not so sure I like the tone in your voice. Is everything okay?"

"Well everything is okay with me and the girls. I just got a call about their father. He's in the hospital. They aren't expecting him to make it much longer." I stopped and let that sink in. I wasn't sure what his response would be. I knew that he didn't care for Kenyon.

"He's dying?"

"Well, unless God performs a miracle that's what the doctors are saying. Genesis wants to meet with me later today to talk to me about the girls. I told her that I'd meet her. I wanted to talk to you first, though, because I want to take the girls to see him."

He was silent. I listened to him breathe on the other side of the phone for what seemed like ever. I knew better than to keep talking. We'd had several conversations about Kenyon and he didn't understand how I could not hate him for what he did to me. I told him that hating him didn't keep Kenyon bound. It kept me bound and I chose to live my life free. He would answer for all the things he'd done in this life. Now it looked like his judgment day may come sooner than any of us expected.

"You're not taking my daughters to see him. They don't even know him Justice"

"He's their father. I don't care if they remember him or not. They should see him if he's dying." Was he really about to do this? "I'm taking them. I don't really care if you don't want them to go. If you're feeling insecure you're welcome to meet me there but we are going either way."

I got ready to hang up, when he spoke again. I sighed hard enough for him to hear. I couldn't believe this is what we were fighting over "What time are you picking up the girls? I can meet you at the hospital. I'm not about to let them get hurt because you're feeling some type of way." I told him where to meet me, then he hung up.

I headed to the daycare to pick the girls up. They looked so much like their father it was scary sometimes. They were identical but mirror image, which means that one had a dimple on the right side, the other on the left. Today they were both dressed in pink. I never dressed them exactly alike; they were two different people with the same face. I walked in and they both looked up at the same time.

"Mama." One simple word but it was always music to my ears. I couldn't imagine leaving my girls. They were the reason I fought so hard to make it after all hell broke loose with Kenyon. I promise I'd been blessed. The doctors did not understand how neither of the girls were positive being that both their father and I were. I told them they didn't have to understand the way God worked, but I knew it was nothing short of a miracle. For some reason, He'd chosen to smile on me through them. I was forever thankful. I gathered all their bags and belongings, got them strapped into car seats and headed to the hospital.

When I pulled up, Jared was sitting there waiting for us. He took one of the girls, strapped her into the stroller and I did the same with the other but he didn't say anything to me. He was still mad. We walked in and headed for the floor Genesis said Kenyon was on. I told the nurse why we were there and she told me she would check to see if he was up for having visitors. Usually children under twelve weren't allowed in the ICU but she said they'd make an exception if he was up for it. I silently prayed he was. They needed to see their father. We waited about fifteen minutes and the nurse came back out and said that he could see us now. I told Jared to sit with the girls. I wanted to go in first and see just how bad he looked. He rolled his eyes as I got up to walk away. I wasn't prepared for what I saw when I looked in the room. I wanted to cry. My breath caught in my throat and I had to check myself and my emotions before I walked into the room. This was not the man I'd been in love with. He was so small.

"Hello Justice." I didn't even realize that he was awake. I tried to be quiet just in case he was resting when I came in the room. I guess I failed.

"Hello, Kenyon. You don't look so good." My thoughts were out before I could stop them from leaving my mouth. I know it was probably not the best thing to say but I'd never been good at hospital situations.

"Genesis called you?" I see he was the same old Kenyon even though he looked so much different. Cut right to the chase. No small talk. I guess that's what happens when you're staring death in the face; you realize just how much time you've wasted on insignificant things.

"She did." I really didn't know what to say so I kept my answers short.

"How are you?" I was surprised he'd asked. I wondered if he really wanted to know. His asking made me angry. If he cared why hadn't we heard from him? "Why haven't you called, Kenyon? Why haven't you made any effort to see your children?" I thought I'd made my peace with him not being around but I was wrong. I hadn't made peace with it. I just refused to think about it. "Do you know how much time you've missed? How many milestones? You weren't there for their first birthdays. They're walking now. Did you know that? Or did you think they were still the same little green eyed girls we bought home from the hospital? What in this world could be more important than you having a relationship with those girls, Kenyon? I don't understand. Do you know how many times I've wanted to pick up the phone and call you in the middle of the night when they were sick or cutting teeth? How many times I've wanted to bring them to your door so that you, their father, could see how much they've changed, how much they've grown? Do you know that they look so much like you it makes me angry? Those are all things you should know. But you don't because you haven't been around. You don't know them because you chose to walk away. By this time, he'd sat up in the bed and just looked at me. "Don't just sit there looking at me. Answer me. You owe me that. You owe *them* that."

"J... I.." I cut him off. I wasn't here to be sentimental.

"No. Don't call me that. Kenyon, look, I'm married. The girls have a daddy. They have a man in their lives who loves them and nurtures them and protects them and does all the things that you, their *father,* should be doing but chose not to. I didn't come here to rehash the past. I came here because you're dying and your daughters need to see you, even if it will be their last time." I could tell that my words had hurt him. I wasn't trying to hurt him or maybe I was. I don't know. All I knew was that at this point I didn't want his excuses; I wanted his truth. That's all. Whether I'd like it or not, I needed to hear his reasons for abandoning our children.

"Tell me the truth Kenyon. You've spent your life lying. Haven't you had enough?" I didn't want to cry. He didn't deserve any more of my tears. I wiped my eyes with the back of my hand and said, "You owe me at least that. That's all I want from you, for once, the truth. Are you capable of giving me that?" I saw the tears in his eyes but I didn't feel bad for him. This was what happened when you lived your life doing people wrong.

"Justice, I'm sorry." I didn't speak. I just stood there. Waiting. There had to be more than I'm sorry. "I know that I've been selfish. I know that I've made mistakes and I've wasted so much time, time that I'll never be able to get back, that I'll never be able to redeem. I could sit here and give you a million excuses but I know that it's time out for them. I've made enough excuses."

He took a deep breath. He sounded so weary, so tired, and frail. "The truth is that I wasn't ready to be a father. I still thought, even though I'd been diagnosed with AIDS, that I would have time to live and I could make amends later. I'm still young. I didn't know that this would be how things would end. I thought I had plenty of time for apologies and making things right. I just knew that I'd be able to be a father to them later, after I'd done all that I wanted to do for me. I didn't ever take time to consider that maybe death was really a reality. The doctors kept saying I had nothing to worry about, that things would be okay, that people were living long full lives even with this disease. They kept telling me that the medications had improved so much over the years. For a while, I was fine. I was good. And then all of a sudden, my medication stopped working. They tried another and then another. None of them worked until I found myself lying in this bed being told that it doesn't look like I'm going to leave the hospital alive. That's when it hit me. I'm not invincible. I'm not some superhero that's immune to life. I've got to answer for all the things I've done. But I've done so much there isn't enough time to answer for it. There isn't enough time to make amends, to make things right. I think about the girls all the time. I carry their pictures with me everywhere I go. I just had more important things to do. You know, business, making money and being in love. I never meant to hurt anyone, but how could I not think that someone would get hurt? I was stupid. I know that now. And I'm sorry. You don't have to forgive me. I couldn't be mad at you if you didn't. I am sorry though."

For the first time in a long time, I actually believed him. I had no words right now, so I just kept standing there wiping my eyes. My emotions were betraying me. I didn't want to feel bad for him. He deserved everything that he was getting but how could I think that when I knew he was married and still chose to sleep with him hoping that one day he'd choose me instead of Genesis? I was no better than him. I knew that.

"The girls, are they here?" I wondered if he was going to ask and in all that had been said, I'd forgotten why I'd come.

"Yes." It was all I could manage. I walked out the door to get them. When I reached the hall, I broke down. I cried for Kenyon. I cried for our children. I cried for me. I wondered if one day I'd leave here the same way, from some kind of AIDS related complication. God I hoped not. I got myself together as best I could and went to get the girls. Jared insisted on coming back with me. I didn't have the energy to fight him. I walked back into the room with the girls. I knew he wouldn't be able to tell them apart. I was with them every day and some days I still had trouble. Their eyes were different colors today, but that was something else he wouldn't know. You miss a lot when you choose to be absent. They didn't know him either. Kenyrah was always just a bit more trusting then Keniyah, so she went to him with no hesitation while Keniyah stayed with Jared.

"They've gotten so big," he said as he held her. I wondered if he thought they would stay babies forever. Eventually they would grow up and he wouldn't be there to see any of it.

"You've missed almost a whole year of their lives. What did you think would happen?" I felt myself getting upset again, Jared must have noticed too because he held my hand and shook his head just slightly. I'm not sure that Kenyon noticed any of it.

"So you're their father?" I just looked up. He must have been deep in thought all the time he'd been standing there because up until now he hadn't said a word.

"Yeah, I am." Kenyon was cocky. How he felt he had the right to be was beyond me.

"No. You're not. I am. How can you even fix your mouth to call yourself their father? You don't know them. You can't even tell them apart, can you?" Jared was angry. He had the right to be. He'd been here since the girls were three months old. He was the only father they'd known. When he said he was their father, he was well within his rights. "You haven't been around when they've been sick. You don't know which of them have a dimple on the right or on the left. You don't know who's right handed or who's left handed. You don't know what their cries mean. You're their sperm donor, the reason they are even alive, yes, but I'm their father."

Kenyon looked deflated. I guess he knew that Jared was right. "Keniyah, do you want to go say hi to Kenyon?" I asked her. But she wouldn't let go of Jared. I tried to pull her away from him but she wasn't having it. I knew that we didn't have much time. "In case you haven't guessed it, that's Kenyrah you're holding. She's the more trusting of the two."

"They both look so much like me, like my mother. I wish she could meet them."

His mother? Hadn't he told me that his mother was dead? "What do you mean you want them to meet your mother? The same mother that you told me died in an accident when you were in high school?"

Was everything he told me a lie? "I was ashamed Justice. You have to understand. I'm not proud of my background."

I didn't want to hear any more of his lies, I wasn't interested. He'd fed me enough bull to last a lifetime. "Kenyon, shut up. I brought your children to see you, now I have to go. I will be praying for you."

I took Kenyrah out of his arms and walked out of the room. I stood there for a minute waiting for Jared to step out. I'm not sure what he said; I didn't even really care. Once he finally came out of the room, we left the hospital. Even close to death, he hadn't really changed much. I guess some people were who they were, no matter what. Kenyon was obviously one of them.

I strapped the girls in their seats and kissed Jared. I thanked him for coming because honestly I probably would have snapped if he hadn't been with me. I watched him drive off and head back to work. I got in the car and just sat there, tears falling. I said a prayer for Kenyon. He needed God to touch his heart and it needed to be touched soon.

My phone was vibrating in my purse. I let it vibrate. Whoever it was, I'd call them back in a minute. Right now, I just needed the silence. I gathered my bearings and pulled out of the lot. The phone vibrated again. This time I reached over and pulled it out of my purse. I pushed the button to answer.

"This is Justice." I knew I was being short but my mind just wasn't on it.

"Justice, it's Genesis again. I was calling to see if you had decided on a place where we could meet."

I'd almost forgotten. "Oh, hey, I'm sorry. I just left the hospital. How about we meet at the Stix on Cheshire? I'm close to there now and I can feed the girls."

"That works for me and I'd love to see the babies. It's been a while. I'll meet you in fifteen minutes. Is that good?"

"Sure that works for me. I'll have them seat us and we'll be there when you get there. See you in a few."

"Okay. See you in a few."

We arrived at almost the same time. I hadn't seen Genesis in a while. She looked good. She'd lost some weight and had let her hair grow out even more. From the first time I saw her I had no idea why Kenyon would cheat on her. She was absolutely beautiful. Not only was she nice to look at, she had a beautiful spirit. Sometimes, I wished I could be more like her but I knew that I was who I was intended to be.

"Oh look at them. They're getting so big." She had walked over to the car to help me get the girls out. There was something different about her but I wasn't sure what it was.

"Yes, they are. It seems like they get just a little bigger every day. Can you believe they are about to be two?" I hadn't noticed that she was standing there staring at Keniyah.

"Is something wrong, Genesis?"

"No, nothing's wrong. They just look so much like him. It makes me wonder if my baby would have looked like him too." Just like that, she was back. I had forgot that she had a miscarriage because of Kenyon's confession about our affair. This is what I was talking about. There's no way that I'd be sitting in a restaurant with my ex-husband's mistress *and* his children like we were one big happy family. Forgiveness was a very hard thing to come across, especially when you had committed the kind of infidelity we had committed. I say "we" because I was just as guilty as he was. I didn't know her, but I knew of her and I was self-ish, young and dumb and I thought that maybe he would leave her for me and that we would be one big happy family. I'd gotten pregnant intentionally. I was trying to keep a man that never belonged to me in the first place. I can admit that now. And I had caused this woman more pain than she deserved. She hadn't done anything to deserve what we had done to her. I was sorry. I could never make her under-stand just how sorry I was and when I'd tried, she basically told me it was unnecessary, that all things happen for a reason, and that this was part of God's plan for her life. Every time we spoke, she left me in awe. I always learned something from her.

"So, did you see him?"

Right to the point. "Yes, we saw him. I wasn't expecting him to look so bad. He said a lot of things that sounded good but they say that people always make deathbed confessions when they have been told that they don't have that much longer to live. I wonder if that's what he was doing or if he was really sincere about the things he said. Do you know he told me he wanted the girls to meet his mother? He told me she was dead."

She stopped when I said that, like she wasn't expecting to hear that. "He wants the girls to meet his mother? I thought she was dead too. He told me his family died tragically in a fire when he was in high school two years before we met."

I gave the waitress my order. "He told me she'd died in a car accident." It's sad when a person lies so much they can't keep their lies straight.

"Well, it doesn't matter now. I just pray that he accept the Lord before it's too late. No matter what he's done, I don't want to see him die and go to hell. No one deserves that, especially when they've had the chance and opportunity to make things right. We prayed with him when we were there and I sincerely hope that it touched him in a place that he had never been touched before. He asked for the prayer so there must be some kind of change going on. One can only hope. Anyway, I know I told you that I needed to meet with you to discuss something that Kenyon asked me to do. So, here are some papers for you to have in case he doesn't make it out of the hospital alive. He's started trusts for each of the girls as well as college funds. Both Keniyah and Kenyrah have substantial amounts of money saved for them. He may not have been the best at being present in their lives but he's made sure that his children will never want for anything."

I was speechless. I didn't think that he'd cared enough to do more than make sure his child support payment arrived on time. I looked over the papers that she'd given me. I was shocked. He'd made sure that each girl had a trust in the amount of $2.5 million dollars as well as their college funds. That was not inclusive of any life insurance monies they would receive once he passed. She handed me another envelope.

"What's this?" She didn't speak. She just sat back in her chair with her hands crossed in front of her. I opened the envelope. A letter fell out. I picked it up and began to read:

Justice, I'm sorry for all the pain I've caused you. I could have been honest with you, yet I made a very conscious decision not to be and for that reason, your life has forever been changed. I'm sorry. If you cannot forgive me in life, I hope that you can find the peace and forgiveness you need in my death"

-Kenyon

I hadn't expected that at all. "Look inside the envelope."

I opened the envelope and out fell a check for $2.5 million dollars made out to me. In the memo section was written the word "recompense." I felt the water on my face before I even realized that I was crying. Kenyon was dying and he wanted to make things right.

"Genesis, how long have you known about this?"

"I've only known since yesterday when I went to see him at the hospital. He made me promise that I would handle this last thing for him in case he did not make it. He also said in the event that he does survive, he wants you to keep the money and the paperwork for the girls as that will be theirs no matter what when they turn twenty-five."

I guess this just went to show that people could surprise you when you least expected it. I had pegged him for a selfish man but he had thought far enough in advance to make sure that his daughters would be taken care of once he was gone. I would have to call the hospital and tell him thank you. It was the least I could do after the way I'd talked to him today. I wasn't sure how Jared would feel about the money but I suppose that it wasn't really something I should concern myself with since it was for the girls.

I noticed the ring on Genesis' finger when we were getting ready to leave. "Girl, that is a beautiful ring."

Her face lit up and her smile was so big. I could tell that whoever had given her the ring had made her very happy. That was it. She was genuinely happy. "Thank you. It's my engagement ring. I'm in the middle of planning my wedding now. I never thought I could be so happy but I was so very wrong. This man is everything that Kenyon wasn't. It is amazing how God works. I thought Kenyon was the one for me, but God had other plans and things had to fall apart so that Axton and I could be together. He makes me want to be a better woman."

I had no idea she was engaged. We sat back down at the table. I ordered desserts for the girls. I wanted to know all about this man. I just realized that she didn't know about Jared. I never even thought to call her and tell her that I'd gotten married myself. "Congratulations, I'm happy for you. Looks like we've both found our Prince Charmings." She looked down at my hand.

"Omg! You're married? Why didn't you tell me? I would have come to the wedding."

"Well, it all happened so fast. We've been married for just a little while. I didn't have a big wedding. He asked at dinner one night and I said yes. We flew to Vegas and I am now Mrs. Jared Shea. Genesis, this man makes me so happy. I didn't think I'd live to see love but I guess God had other plans." We high fived each other and laughed.

"So tell me about this man?"

"Well, he's my Pastor. I met him when I joined the new church. The first time we spoke, he told me that he believed I was going to be his wife. He even asked my father for my hand in marriage.. He's been nothing but a gentleman and nothing but up front and honest. He didn't even want a wedding. He just wants us to be together. I don't know, I feel like we were always meant to be.. It's just different. Where Kenyon was weak, Axton is strong. Where Kenyon acted as if I bothered him, Axton makes me feel like everything I say matters to him. It's a wonderful feeling to know that the person you're in love with was hand crafted just for you.. This is truly a love story written by God. I didn't have a hand in it but I've released myself to love this man. My heart is free to accept what he is giving and I'm happy. I love him. He loves me. We are one without being one, if that makes any sense."

I knew exactly what she was talking about. It was the same way I felt about Jared. We were meant to be. I knew it the first time I met him. I wasn't sure he did but apparently, God had spoken the same thing to the both of us.

"I know what you mean. Being happy is a wonderful feeling. I thank God every day that even though I did the things I've done, He still saw fit to send a man like Jared to love me when I thought I was unlovable. Jared is the kindest, gentlest man I've met. He told me that he wasn't sure that I'd be interested in someone like him. I asked him what he meant and he told me about his past. All I could think was how could I judge someone because of their past? I laughed at him and he wanted to know what was so funny. I told him simply that I was the biggest sinner I knew so whatever he'd done, I'm sure it was tame in comparison to the things I've found myself involved in. Sometimes, I want to pinch myself because I still have a hard time believing that this is real. That this is my life."

"I'd felt the same way. There were days that I convinced myself that this had to be a dream. I still don't understand why God loved me enough to work so many miracles in my favor. Axton told me to stop questioning being favored but some days I can't help it. I guess we are both living testimonies that with God any and all things are possible. You should come by the church one Sunday. We would love to have you there and then maybe we can all do dinner."

"I would love that. Have you set a date for the wedding yet?"

"Yes, we have actually. We are planning a wedding for New Year's Day. You know new beginnings and all. We both figured what better way to begin our lives together than the start of a new year."

She was making me wish I'd planned a wedding but I guess we could have a wedding any time. "That sounds beautiful. Don't forget to send my invite!"

I was just kidding and wasn't expecting what came next. "Well, I was going to ask you if you'd like to be my maid of honor. I know a lot of people would probably think me crazy for even asking given our history and all but you've become a great friend and I consider you and the girl's family. I just feel it's right to ask."

I got up and hugged her. She didn't know it because I'd never told her but I felt the same way about her. She was like the big sister I never had. There had been times I'd called her for advice and just to vent and to get prayer. She had definitely been one of the reasons I was able to stay sane through being sick and everything else. "I would love to." I couldn't stop the tears.

Genesis checked her watch. "Oh, I didn't know it was this late. I've got to go. I have a meeting at the church with my girls tonight. You should come by the church; I'd love for you to talk to my group of young women. You know, give your testimony, tell them what the forgiveness and salvation of God can do for a life that's messed up."

No one had ever asked me to do anything like that before. "Call me and we'll talk details, I'd love to help someone avoid the mistakes I've made."

We talked for a few more minutes and then we left. We promised that we would talk in a few days to schedule a time for me to come speak to her young ladies. I was excited. No one needed to travel the path I had if they could avoid it and I hoped that by telling my story, I could help someone do just that.

Once I got home, I talked to Jared about the money that Kenyon had left the girls. For a minute I thought better of telling him about the check he'd given me, but I told him and he told me to take the check to the bank and deposit it. I was surprised but I knew better than to press him about it. First thing tomorrow morning, I was going to the bank.

GENESIS

I was running late for my youth meeting. I knew those young ladies hated to be kept waiting but the time had gotten away from me. I was with Justice and the girls. They had gotten so big. I couldn't believe how much they looked like their father. They both had his green eyes and his dimple. It made me wonder what my child would have looked like. He or she would be the same age as the twins, almost two. I couldn't believe it had been almost two years since this whole mess had started. I'd come a very long way. We were approaching the end of another year and I for one was excited to see what the future held. Axton and I had decided to have our wedding on New Year's Day. I felt like it was the best way to start our lives together. The beginning of a new year would be a new chapter of life for us. I was glad that Justice had agreed to be my maid of honor. I knew that my mother would have an issue with it but I had forgiven her and we had become friends.

I pulled into the lot at the church. Axton had made the deacons put a "First Lady" parking space next to his spot. I was still hesitant about parking in it because I was not yet the First Lady but he told me that soon enough I would be. All of the congregation was in agreement with him, so I stopped fighting and pulled into my space. I went into the room where we normally met and my girls were all there waiting.

"You're late, Ms. Genesis." That was Shakira. She was my mouthy one. I loved her to life. She was full of spunk and personality. She was also a foster child who felt like no one cared so she pushed her limits. I had talked to Axton about her coming to live with us after the wedding. We were both considering it. She had truly grown on us.

"I was handling business, ma'am. I apologize for being late, I know you all hate to be kept waiting." The room burst into laughter. I had come to love these girls. "Where did we leave off in our last meeting?" I couldn't recall but they were so into the conversation we were having they didn't want to stop talking so I knew they would remember.

"Well, I think we were talking about why we should abstain from sex. You were giving us some lame reasons." Again, laughter filled the room.

"Okay, why do you say the reasons I gave were lame?" It was always interesting to see where their minds were, what they thought about.

"I mean, you know? We aren't old like you. This isn't the old days when it was cool to be a virgin. People laugh at you now if you haven't had sex with at least one person." I was amazed at the things these girls shared with me. I cherished the fact that they trusted me enough to talk candidly and openly to me.

"I am not old, first of all. So, since it's not cool to be a virgin, tell me, is the in thing to be a teenage mother? To have an STD? I mean what is it, a badge of honor?"

Shakira's hand was back up. "Yes, Shakira?" I wanted to know her thoughts. She tried to come across as a bad girl but deep down she was just a big teddy bear looking for someone to love her, for someone she could trust.

"It's not cool at all to be a teen mom. Who wants to be chasing snot nosed kids around when you could be having a good time? I want to go to college. I want to be someone. I can't do that with no baby hanging on my hip. And I'm just not ready. I sit back and watch all these girls chasing these niggas that don't care nothing about them and then when they end up pregnant and he's gone, they look stupid like they didn't see it coming. All you have to do is pay attention to other people and you can see if it ain't work for them it ain't gon' work for you. Besides, there are too many birth control methods to end up pregnant by some boy that don't even know what love is."

See? She was smart. "So are you a virgin?" I could tell she wasn't expecting that question. She looked around the room. "Technically, no. I'm not. But that's because I was raped. I'm not having sex because I didn't like the experience and I'm not ready."

I had no idea. I could see the tears well up in her eyes. I didn't want to push so I asked for someone else to explain why they thought my reasons for remaining a virgin were lame. I got a lot of answers. The last response I got was the one that was concerning. Tamika, who always sits in the back and rarely says a word raised her hand.

"Yes, Tamika?"

"I aint no virgin. I don't have a reason to be. Men don't love you unless you sleep with them. You can get anything you want out of a man when you use your body as incentive for them to do what you want. We have the power, so to tell me that it's better to abstain is crazy to me. I take care of myself and my daughter by having sex with dudes. They pay me. I pay my bills. I mean, I ain't got no other skills. I had to drop out of school when I found out I was pregnant. My mother put me out so I have to support us some kind of a way. If I'm not having sex, Ms. Genesis, then how will I take care of my child?"

By this time, she was crying and so was I. It was true you never knew what another person had to do to make it through each day. . She sat down and I closed out the meeting. I asked her to stay after so that we could talk. I hugged each girl, told them as I always did that if they needed me then they could call me anytime. They each had my home and cell numbers as well as my personal email address. I had an office here at the church and they were welcome to come here and talk to me as well.

When the last girl was gone, I gave Tamika my full attention. "Why haven't you said anything before now?"

I had been meeting with these girls for about six months weekly and she had never said more than a few words. I didn't even know she had a baby. "I mean, what would anyone have done if I had said that I had a baby? Or if I'd said that the only way I can take care of her is by having sex with countless, faceless men? It's not something I'm proud of but I do what I have to do to make sure we have what we need."

I wasn't sure what to say. "Would you like to find a job? I know you said you don't have any skills, but if you'd like I can help you get back in school and we can get you some job training. I'll even pay for your daughter to go to day care if you want to go back and finish your education. I can't say I know what it's like having a child and having to do what you can to care for her because I don't. I'm not going to lie and tell you that I understand, because I don't. What I do know is that you have a desire to be better than what you are right now. I see that desire in your eyes every time I look at you. I also know that you're hurting. I want to help you. Please let me."

Maybe no one had ever been kind to her. Maybe she wasn't aware that not everyone wanted to use her. I don't know, but she didn't respond for a long time; she was too busy wiping tears from her eyes.

"Where are you staying?" She looked down at the floor and twisted the fabric of her coat between her fingers.

"Well, we just got evicted. So, I'm looking for somewhere to stay. My daughter is with a friend of mine right now."

"I have a spare room. You and your baby can stay with me if you like. We can discuss details later."

"You'd do that for me? You don't know me like that. Why would you do something like that?"

Because God told me to. "Because I am fortunate enough to be in a position to help you and for that reason, that's what I will do, but only if you want me to. I won't force you into something that you don't want to do. I'm not asking for anything in return. All I want it to let you know that there is someone who genuinely cares about your well-being and wants to see you be the best you can be. Someone took a chance on me. Now let me take a chance on you. I'm sure you won't let me down."

She was still crying. It made me feel good because I knew that no one else had told her that they believed in her. She didn't think she could be anything more than what she was now but with God's help she would be exactly who He created her to be.

"Thank you, Sis. Genesis. I promise I won't let you down. This means the world to me."

She got up and gave me a hug and I held her. I needed her to feel my sincerity. "Let's go get that beautiful baby of yours."

We finished cleaning the room. I stopped by Axton's office to see if he was still here. He was usually here late, especially during the week. He was sitting at his desk studying intently.

"Knock, knock."

He looked up. "Hey, First Lady" He got up and came to the door. I wanted to kiss him but I settled for a hug.. Two more months and it would be official. I was counting the days.

"Hey, Pastor. I see you're studying tonight. I just wanted to let you know that I'm headed home. I'm going to have a house-guest for a while. Tamika and her daughter are going to be staying with me." He had that look on his face. "I know. I'm not trying to save the world, just trying to make sure that she is able to get into position to be effective. I didn't even know she had a child before tonight and she's been sitting in those meetings for six months not saying a word. Well, she told her story tonight and I just felt compelled to help her".

"Another reason I fell in love with you. You have a heart the size of the world. Help her. Have you talked to Shakira yet?"

Now she had grown on him too. He wanted to be a part of her life as much as I did. "I haven't. I want us to do that together after the wedding. I didn't tell Tamika, but once she finishes her diploma, I'm going to pay for her to go to school. What good is having money if you never give back to those less fortunate? I have to run. We're going to pick up her daughter, stop and get her things and then head home. Call me tonight when you leave and let me know you've made it home safely please. Oh, have you eaten today? Looks like you've been in here most of the day and if I know you, then you haven't had a thing to eat."

"You think you know me so well, huh? I've eaten. I made sure of it. I have to keep up my strength for the wedding night."

I pushed him, kissed his cheek and walked out of the office with a smile still dancing on my lips.

JARED

I finally got a chance to meet the infamous Kenyon Swan. He wasn't all he was cracked up to be. I felt nothing but sympathy for him. He was weak. How Justice had ever gotten herself involved with him was something I'd never understand, but that was her past and I promised her I'd let it be. I didn't know which was worse: the fact that he hadn't seen his children in almost a year or that he couldn't even tell them apart. I was thankful that these children were in my life. They made me want to be a better man. When Justice came home from meeting with Genesis and told me about the money, I was not about to encourage my wife to be a fool. Keep the money. It was the least he could do for putting her through what he had put her through. No, she wasn't innocent. She played a part in messing up her life too but we all make mistakes. Who was I to hold that against her? I mean, my stuff just hadn't caught up with me, but I had to remember that it very well could have been me. I was out there before I got saved and met my first wife. As a matter of fact, I wasn't much different from Kenyon, except I'd never mess with a dude like that. It was just... yeah, I'll pass.

He'd written her a check for 2.5 million dollars. Dude was obviously well off. He could afford it. Even if he made it through whatever was wrong with him, he was going to have to pay at some point. I figured she had better cash the check before he made it his business to change his mind. So when we got up this morning, I took Justice to the bank. I knew her. I knew that she had a soft spot for people who were trying to make things right. I wished she would try to give him this money back. Sure, she'd agreed to keep the money for the girls with no problem because it was for them. She felt that he owed them that, felt it his responsibility to take care of his children so she would never give him that money back. But, she didn't feel like he owed her a thing other than an apology and he'd given her that. We had a long conversation about it. She was surprised. She thought I'd tell her to give the money back to him but Mama didn't raise no fool. It was money that we could put to good use.

Once she deposited the check into the bank, I took her back home and I went to work. I called her just to make sure she was alright once I got to the office.

"Hey babe, how are you feeling?"

She was silent for a few minutes. "I'm alright. You know me, I just have to pray. I need to make sure that accepting that money was the right thing to do. I don't want this to come back to haunt me." If she needed to pray that was fine but she was not giving that money back. "I'm going to go back to the hospital to see Kenyon, I need to talk to him without the distraction of the kids being there and without my anger. I'm going to go after I make a few calls about some events that I'm working on."

After the other day I didn't have an issue with her going to talk to him especially since she had told me and didn't feel the need to sneak around to do it. "That's fine. Call me when you're back home. Justice, I love you." I hung up before she responded. I trusted her. I realized that a relationship without trust was nothing. I wouldn't do that to us. No doubts here.

ADDISON

I woke up in a cold sweat. I didn't know if it was the alcohol or the dream that had me feeling like something was terribly wrong. I looked at my watch. It was four o'clock. I didn't even know what day it was. I looked around the room. It was still torn up. There were seven bottles of wine scattered at my feet, all of them empty. I'd never been a drinker for real but I guess I'd taken it to the extreme. I was still trying to remember why I had even come here. I stood up and to the floor fell the gun. The gun. I was starting to remember now. Jeremiah. Kenyon. Suicide. Alcohol. My life. It had fallen apart.

I had to fix this but I wasn't sure how. I didn't know what I needed to do to make things right. I didn't even think I could make things right. I sat back down in the chair, kicked the bottles from around my feet. I picked up my phone and dialed a number I hadn't dialed in a long time. I wouldn't say anything, I just needed to hear the voice. I didn't know if he was still alive, but one could only hope.

"Hello? Hello? Is anyone there?" I didn't breathe. I didn't make a sound. I listened for a few minutes more and I hung up. My father. The reason I was the man I was. I still hated him. I had prayed so many nights for God to help me. He never did. I was subjected night after night to my own father coming into my room and doing things to me that no little boy should ever have to deal with. I hadn't thought about it in years, but my dream reminded me. If it hadn't been for him, maybe, just maybe I could have grown up a normal boy. Instead, I had to deal with being called names like "sissy" and "fag." It didn't help that

I had a girl's name. Addison.

The tears fell, hot against my skin. I let them fall. I'd never cried for the boy I was before. I wasn't even sure that I was crying for him now. Maybe I was crying for the man I'd become. I had learned to silence the boy long ago. I wouldn't allow him to speak now. I sat there for a few minutes longer letting the tears fall. Someone once told me that tears were cleansing, healing. I didn't know if there was any truth to that. I guess now I would begin to find out. I wiped my eyes, went into the bedroom to see if he had left any of my clothes untouched. I found an outfit, took a shower and got dressed. I started to call the hospital to speak with Kenyon but thought better of it. It had been two days since I'd seen him. I still couldn't believe I'd drank enough to knock me out for two days.

I arrived at the hospital and before I walked in the room, I saw there was a woman sitting in the room next to the bed. I didn't bother to go in. From here, it didn't look like Genesis. I decided against going in. I'd wait. I grabbed a seat outside his door. I called into the room from the hallway; I knew he hadn't seen me.

"How are you feeling?" I was trying to keep my tone even. I didn't want to alert him that there was an issue.

"I'm feeling better. Why haven't I heard from you the past few days? Are you still upset?"

Was I still upset? He had no idea. Breathe, Addison. "Upset? No, I just had some stuff I had to take care of the past few days and I must have been really tired because I slept for a long time." I wouldn't tell him about Jeremiah trashing my house. He didn't need to know about that. At least not yet. "So what are you doing right now?" I asked because I wanted to see if he would be honest enough to tell the truth.

"Nothing, laying here watching the game on television. Other than that, it's been a pretty uneventful day. The doctor's been checking my levels and he thinks that I may recover after all." He lied so effortlessly. He didn't stutter nor stumble. I got up and opened the door to his room. I couldn't handle the lies. Not today. My plan was to not say a word but my anger got the best of me.

"Sitting here watching the game huh? I saw her head before I called. You're so full of it. So you're cheating on me? Again?" The woman in the chair still hadn't turned around so I hadn't gotten to see her face. She stood up and faced me.. "Who are you? What are you doing here?" She looked at me like I was something on the bottom of her shoe. Ms. Thang didn't want it with me. "I asked you a question."

"If you must know, I'm here because I needed to talk to the father of my children."

"Justice?" So this was the other woman. He'd finally decided that it was best he wasn't involved in the lives of his children and I was glad. So why was she here now?

"What do you have to talk about? He doesn't want anything to do with you or those babies." She didn't even flinch.

She looked at Kenyon and said, "I'm going to go. I see your little friend doesn't know how to act like an adult." Kenyon shook his head and looked at me as if I were the one who was wrong. He had some nerve. He was the one who lied to me.

"Justice, you don't have to leave. I want to finish our conversation. I need you to understand some things."

He was really telling her to stay in front of me. "Kenyon, she should not be here." I looked at him. If looks could kill…

"Addison, it's time you grew up. Seriously. Justice is married. We are over. Have been for almost two years. You need to stop being so jealous. She doesn't want me. She came here to discuss something between the two of us. I'm so sick of your jealousy. You're the one who has the man trying to kill him. Not me. You think I don't know that you were still sleeping with Jeremiah? A pair and a spare, huh? I'm not as dumb as you'd like to believe. Sad thing is even though I knew you weren't being faithful I've never been as jealous as you. Your jealousy isn't flattering. It's incriminating. You should really stop."

I didn't bother responding. I just walked out of the room. He was right. I didn't think he knew but I wasn't stupid enough to admit to being unfaithful, especially not with Justice there. My mama used to say, "A closed mouth don't get fed." I never really understood the saying until recently. I didn't get it until I got to a place where I let fear of being alone keep me from admitting to what I really wanted. I wanted Kenyon, but I hadn't made that clear to him. I hadn't made it clear to Jeremiah and now it was all slipping through my fingers. I was scared to death because the man I loved with everything in me was lying in the hospital sick. The doctors weren't sure at first if he was going to make it and here he was feeling better and hadn't bothered to pick up the phone and call me. I wondered where his loyalties lied. Could I honestly be mad at him though? Wasn't he just doing what I'd done to him so many times? Something else Mama used to say: "If you can't take it, don't dish it." I should have listened. She told me when I was a kid that one day I would look back on all the things she had said and wished I had listened to her. It would have made life so much easier. I missed her. I wished she was here now so that I could call her, get her advice. I wasn't the man that she had wanted me to be but she never loved me any less. She was always right there in my corner standing tall. She protected me. When she found out what my father had done to me, she left him, pressed charges against him and always made me feel like she loved me more than anything in this world. When she died, my life spun out of control. That was right before I met Jeremiah. I had nothing else to live for. Looking back, I should have gone the other way the day he approached me but I didn't and now, here I was.

I got in the car and pulled my phone out of my pocket. I called Jeremiah but didn't get an answer. I didn't leave a message. There would be time to handle what needed to be handled between the two of us.

KENYON

"It's just my way of saying I'm sorry. I know there's no other way I can ever make any of this right and I know that money doesn't make it right either, but it does make sure that you can live the way you've always wanted to live."

I wasn't trying to buy her forgiveness, I needed to make her understand, but I don't think I was doing such a good job of it. Justice had come back without her husband and our daughters. She wanted to know what kind of game I was playing by having Genesis give her the money. It wasn't a game; it was just me trying to make things right in a way that was beneficial to her. I could never go back and undo what I had done. I'd wished for that so many times, but that wasn't how life worked. Once you did something, you couldn't take it back. I didn't think about that before I acted. I was impulsive and selfish and for that reason, I messed up so many lives.

Now, I was sorry. Yes, I was sorry because I was dying. I wasn't going to lie about it. Death had a way of making you regret even some of the things you did for all the right reasons that turned out wrong. Death also made you realize that you would never have time to right those wrongs. When you were doing it, you felt like you'd have all the time in the world to say I'm sorry or to try to fix what you had broken. Death told you that was not so. I was in my not-so stage right now and money was the only way I knew to make this right. I couldn't give her back her health. I couldn't give Genesis back our child. I wanted to give her nothing more. I knew that was one thing she always wanted.

She had feared that she, like her mother, wouldn't have been able to have children and had been trying since we had gotten married. I had no idea that she was pregnant until they told me she had lost the baby. I think that devastated her more than my indiscretions and I would never forget the look on her face when she heard that she lost the baby. It was like everything inside of her broke.

"Justice, I'm only doing what I know to do. I can't give you back the things I took from you. I can't give you back your innocence. I can't give you back your health. I can't give you back all the things that mattered to you, but I can do what I can do. I have money. More than I'll ever need and it's not like I'll be here that much longer to spend it, so I want the women in my life to be taken care of when I'm gone. Yeah, you're married now. I respect that. I'm happy for you. I hope he takes good care of you and the girls but I needed to do something for you too. It's not a game. There's no catch. I promise."

My phone rang. It was Addison. I hadn't talked to him in two days. I thought he was just that mad at me that he had nothing to say. I didn't really care but part of me wondered if he was okay. He asked what I was doing. I knew better than to tell him that I was sitting here talking to Justice so I told him that I was watching TV. His jealousy had gotten out of hand. It was to the point that if I spoke to a woman he had an attitude. It was really a bit much and I wished he would stop.

All of a sudden, the door to my room pushed open and in came Addison. He was hurling accusations like boomerangs. I wasn't in the mood. Not today. Justice got up to leave. I told her she didn't have to. I wasn't doing this with him. Not anymore. I'd had enough. When I finished what I had to say, he stormed out of the room angry. What was new? It seemed that the more things changed the more they stayed the same. Justice asked me why I stayed with him. She wanted to know if I loved him.

"I love him, you know, like familiar things. I can't say I'm in love with him, at least not anymore, but I do love him. I can't really explain it. I think part of the reason I stay is because I have nowhere else to go. I suppose that in the grand scheme of things we all just want to be loved. In my last days, that's all I want."

She looked at me kind of strangely. "If that's what you want, then why put up with the jealousy? I remember when you were like that but it's because you were guilty yourself. It's funny to me that people can't handle having what they do to others done to them. You need to talk to your man. If you love him at all in anyway and you plan to stay with him, you don't need the stress. You would think he'd want to make life happy, make it comfortable, especially if he didn't think you had that much longer to live."

I knew she was right. I'd call him when she left. We definitely needed to have a heart to heart. I couldn't live like this. I didn't want to live like this, not anymore. I'd left him once. I'd leave again. Maybe that's what I needed to do. Live out my last days in peace and serenity. Go somewhere exotic and enjoy life until it was over.

Justice told me that she had to leave. She kissed me on the cheek, thanked me and wished me well. I told her if I made it out of here alive, I would make a special effort to spend time with my daughters if she would allow me to. She told me that was fine with her. It's what she had wanted anyway.

When she walked out the door, I picked up the phone and dialed Addison's number. When he answered, I didn't give him time to say a word. "What is your problem?" I had a major attitude right now and I wanted him to hear it. I was beyond tired of him embarrassing and accusing me when I had done nothing wrong.

"I don't have a problem, Kenyon. What do you want?"

Really? He had the nerve to try to be mad? "You know, I'm so sick of you. So sick of your nasty attitude and your jealous ways. I'm not putting up with it anymore. Either you get your life together or you can get your things from my home and leave. I'm done. You are the only one I have been faithful to, yet you're accusing me of being unfaithful every time I turn around and I'm tired of it. If that's not going to change let me know now."

He was quiet. I knew he hadn't hung up. "Kenyon, what do you want from me?"

Was he even listening? I think I had made that pretty clear. "Are you listening to anything I've said? I *just* told you what I wanted you to do. Either you can or you can't but I won't live my last days unhappy or miserable. I love you but I will love you from a distance if I need to. Don't believe me? Try me."

I hung up. The conversation wasn't going anywhere and I didn't feel the need to continue. I turned my phone off in case he decided to call back. No sooner than I hung up the phone, the doctor came in and told me that I was doing well enough to be released.

"Must be some kind of miracle because you were sick enough to die and now all of your levels have gotten back to stable positions."

He was right. It was a miracle.

JEREMIAH

I had a missed call from Addison. I wouldn't call him back. I would see him soon enough. I had no more words for him. I was all talked out. I was in full fight mode. If I couldn't have him, no one could. I'd played this game for far too long. Two years too long. I was done playing. We would be together, whether in this life or the next. If he didn't want me here, I'd see him in hell. That's where the both of us would end up anyway and I made my peace with it. I thought about paying his little boyfriend a visit in the hospital but thought better of it. He wasn't even my focus anymore; it wasn't his fault Addison decided to play with my emotions. I was mad at the wrong people. I needed to refocus my anger. Now, it was what fueled me.

I'd been to the doctor myself recently. I didn't have long left. I knew that. It was partially my own fault. I'd stopped taking my medication. I was tired. When people got tired they did crazy things. I didn't think what I was planning was crazy though. For me, it was necessary. I'd taken away everything that meant something to him just like he'd done to me. Except one thing and I planned to take that next. I didn't know when, I didn't know where, but I knew for certain that I was going to kill him. In my mind, it was the only logical thing to do.

I sipped my glass of wine and looked around my room. So many things here reminded me of him. The leather chair in the corner, he picked it. The African artwork on the wall, he picked it. The statues that graced the bedside tables and the dresser, you guessed it. My bed still smelled of him. He was all around me, consuming my every thought, my every desire. I went to the dresser and retrieved my gun from its case, something else he'd given me. I bet this was one gift he would regret giving. I had no fear. I was actually anticipating firing the bullet that would make him mine for all of eternity. Oh yes, if I couldn't have Addison Limon,' I guarantee you know one else would.

AXTON

We met for lunch and talked. I didn't bring up Kenyon and neither did she. Instead, we talked about our wedding and where we wanted to honeymoon. We settled on going to Ocho Rios, Jamaica. Our wedding date was set for two months. I kept trying to convince her to go to the courthouse. What did we need a big wedding for? She kept telling me that this was my first wedding and that I needed to have the ceremony as much as she did. I didn't agree but I'd give her the world if I could, so against my will, I'd wait two more months to make this woman my wife.

It was getting harder and harder each day to restrain myself. She just did something to me. She stopped wearing her hair down because it turned me on and she didn't want to do anything to make this any harder for either of us. I'd switched my cologne because it turned her on. We were compromising. We only spent time together in public when it got late because we both wanted to make love but we knew that we needed to wait and remain in the will of God. I had many nights where cold showers were my best friends. There were nights I couldn't even talk to her when it got too late. She would call to let me know she had gotten home or I'd call to let her know, especially when we were out late. I couldn't wait to introduce her as my wife. In my mind she already was. She had always been.

"What are you eating? I'm starving."

She laughed. "When aren't you? I'm not sure. I'm thinking maybe a steak and some potatoes. I'm hungry too."

We had just come off a fast so I was ready to get my eat on. "You're going to eat steak and potatoes?" I played shocked. She usually had something healthy. I guess the fast had made her miss good food.

"Oh hush. I eat all the time. I'm just not in the mood for salad today. I want some real food."

We ordered and ate. She was telling me about her dress. I was picturing her without it. I had to catch myself. I was a saved man but I was a man and this woman made me feel and think things that no other had ever made me feel or think.

"So when am I to report for tuxedo tailoring?" I was following directions. She said be there, I was there. I didn't want to be involved in the dirty work it took to plan a wedding. She had recently gotten the chance to meet my parents and they both loved her. They knew her mother and father and Mrs. Maicott, or Mom as she insisted I call her, had invited us all over for dinner. She hadn't told me that my parents would be there. As a matter of fact, I didn't even know that my parents were in town. They hadn't called me and said a word. I was just as surprised as Genesis when we walked in and my mom met me at the door. She asked Genesis if she remembered her. Genesis said that she hadn't. Apparently, we've known each other for a long time. We fellowshipped together until my father got called overseas in the military.

According to my mother, I'd always had a crush on Genesis. She said, "You would always say, 'She's so pretty with her long hair. Mama, is she a real life doll?'" I blushed. I remembered that. I just didn't remember it was Genesis.

My mother asked her a million questions about the wedding, about the girls group at the church, and about whether or not she was prepared to be a First Lady. Genesis told her she'd had an excellent example to follow and thought she was equipped for the job and should anything arise she couldn't handle, she would go to God. That answer seemed to satisfy my mother. It looked like they'd get along just fine.

My mother pulled me to the side when the evening was over. "You did good, son," she had said. I smiled. Inside I felt proud.

We finished lunch. I headed back to the church and Genesis headed to a meeting she had with a client and then to do what she had promised Kenyon she would do.

"You know you don't have to do this right away. You have time."

She shook her head. "Did you see him? I may not have time. I told him I would get it done and I want to do it now. As soon as possible. I know God can heal him. I know God can bring him through but I also know that sometimes, healing doesn't happen this side of heaven. I just want to keep my promise while I can tell him it's been done."

I understood that. "Do what you need to do. Let me know if you need my help. I'm going to head to the church. I have a meeting with the deacons and I'm sitting in on the young men's group tonight. Bro. Jerman asked me to and I told him if I was free this evening, I would. I'll see you at the church this evening."

"Oh okay. Yes, I'll be there. I'll see you tonight. Do you want me to bring you dinner?"

She was always trying to feed me. "No. I'll get something between meetings." I kissed her cheek and headed out. Every time I walked away from her, I thanked God.

GENESIS

I could not believe that two months had passed so quickly. So much had happened in that time. Tamika and her daughter had come to live with me. She was doing so well. It made me proud every time she came home and told me about something that she had learned or a new skill that she had gained. Axton had agreed that she as well as Shakira could live with us after we were married. Tamika had agreed. Shakira said she would think about it. I may never have children of my own but I definitely would be a parent. I had grown to love these girls like they were my own. I'd do anything to help either of them.

I was getting ready to meet with the wedding planner again. We were finalizing details. Both Tamika and Shakira had agreed to be bridesmaids and Tahari, Tamika's daughter was a flower girl along with the twins. Two more days and I would be Mrs. Genesis Kyle. I couldn't wait. There was so much to do and so little time to get it done. I had hired amazing people to handle everything for me. My mother was here and she had completely taken over. She was happier than I was. My father, always stoic no matter what, would be down the day of the wedding. He had made it clear that we had better not start without him being there. He was at a conference. I promised him we would wait if he was running late. I wouldn't get married without my father being there.

I finally arrive at my meeting with the planner. The lady with my dress was there. It was beautiful. When she took it out of the bag, I cried. When I tried it on and saw myself in it for the first time, I cried again. I was sure that Axton would do the same when he saw me walk down the aisle.

"You look beautiful," my wedding planner said.

I hadn't told my mother that I was coming to try on the dress. I wanted to be sure it fit and fit it did. I felt like a princess. I couldn't stop looking at myself. I hadn't looked this happy in my first wedding gown and I was sure that man was the love of my life. It just went to show that when you got out of God's will, even while being saved you made a mess of things. I believed that Kenyon was the one God had chosen for me. I'd since learned to distinguish between God's voice and all the others that we so often hear. Satan sometimes speaks quietly too. There's only one way to tell if God is speaking and that's to pay very close attention to everything around you. He will send you signs. Good ones. I had finally found God's true will for my life and I couldn't have been happier. It had taken a while, but I'd learned to forgive Kenyon. Once I started praying for his salvation, for his soul, God started releasing infinite blessings into my life.

I was getting ready to marry my biggest blessing. Our rehearsal dinner was tomorrow. I had found someone to sing my favorite song at the wedding. I couldn't wait. It was a surprise for Axton. I had thought about singing it myself and everyone was trying to talk me into it. I still had time to decide. He was truly an answer to prayer. He kept me sane. I kept him balanced. We kept each other happy. That's how it should be.

AURELIA

My daughter's wedding date had finally come. Two more days and she would become Mrs. Axton Kyle. We had known their family for what seemed like ever and his mother and I had always thought that Genesis and Axton would make a great couple. Genesis, however, had other plans and married that boy. I was so glad it was over between them. He'd hurt my daughter in so many ways. I hoped she'd never have to worry about being hurt like that ever again. For that, I was thankful.

She didn't want me to help with the plans for the wedding but I had news for her. I hadn't gotten to plan the first one so I was helping with this wedding whether she wanted me to or not. Besides, who was going to tell Mrs. Judah Maicott no? No one in their right mind would do something like that, not even Genesis' wedding planner.

She had called to tell me that Genesis was trying on her dress today. I wasn't going to miss that for anything. I opened the door to the shop just as she came out of the dressing room. I stopped speechless. She looked amazingly beautiful. I was supposed to be quiet. She wasn't supposed to know I was there but I couldn't help myself.

"Oh my, you look so pretty. I can't believe my baby is getting married."

She turned around. "Mama! What are you doing here?" She couldn't wait to let me have it.

"Well, you didn't tell me that you were coming to try on the dress and someone thought I should be here for that. So here I am." Her planner was looking down at the floor. A dead giveaway that it was her who had given the information.

"Colette, I'll deal with you later," Genesis said to her planner with laughter in her voice.

"Really baby, you look beautiful. I don't think you were this pretty the first time around."

She nodded. "I know, Mama. I was just thinking the same thing."

I pulled out my phone. I wanted a picture before the wedding. "Stand still, child. I want to take a picture."

She looked mortified. "Mama, you can't take a picture of me in the dress before the wedding."

I laughed. "Girl, what will it hurt? We both know you and that boy are getting married whether I take a picture or not. Now stand still and let me take the picture. I want one with the veil and one without it."

She knew better than to argue with me. "Yes, ma'am." She stood still and I snapped the pictures. I sent one to her father since he wasn't in town yet.

He called immediately. "My baby girl is really getting married again. She looks so beautiful. Why is it every time I see her I still see her as a five year old climbing up in my lap?" He was sentimental. The first time around, he was angry because he knew that Kenyon was not the man for our daughter. This time though, he was excited and sentimental. He gave Axton his full support. I didn't know if it was because of something God had shown him but I knew that once my husband was in your corner, even if you fell, he was still in your corner. He told me he was trying to cut his meetings short so that he could surprise Genesis at the rehearsal dinner tomorrow. I told him he should just reschedule them all. I knew he wouldn't do that. He took church business very seriously. We said our goodbyes and I told my daughter I'd see her at home. I was taking those lovely girls she had staying with her to lunch.

AXTON

Two days. There were just two days before I made the love of my life my wife. Two days before two became one and I was ecstatic and nervous all at the same time. I had cold feet, hot hands, butterflies, you name it, I had it. I'd never been married before. She had. I had no experience but I knew that my desire was only to love and protect this woman like she had never been loved and protected before. That was the charge God had given me and I intended to uphold it until my very last breath. This, for the both of us, would be 'til death do us part. We had chosen to write our own vows. She didn't want to have another traditional wedding so we weren't. We were doing a salt covenant and jumping the broom. What she wanted, she got. I told her I didn't need all the fanfare but she insisted that this wedding was as much for me as it was for her. I wasn't so sure.

My groomsmen and I had to try on our tuxes. I had to admit, I looked good. She had chosen our colors of course. They were lilac, silver, and crème. I had a crème tux with a lilac cummerbund and pocket square. I had yet to see her dress. She was adamant that it was something I was not supposed to see until the wedding. I missed her. I'd talked to her this morning but I hadn't seen her in a few days because she was so busy trying to make sure everything was perfect. I had had meetings and our schedules just conflicted but I guess it was for the best. It would make seeing her in her dress at the wedding about to become Mrs. Axton Kyle so much more exciting.

She asked her father to give her away. He, of course, gladly said yes. Apparently, he had refused to give her away the first time. I was thankful I had his blessing. I wasn't sure that I could marry a woman if I didn't have her father's blessing; I was just old fashioned like that. Bishop Maicott also agreed to perform the ceremony so we'd asked one of the associate ministers to ask who would give her away and then he would take over from there. It was a different way of doing things. I thought about performing my own ceremony but that would be virtually impossible. I could dream though, right? I laughed to myself. This new chapter was exciting. Not only would I be getting a wife, but we had agreed to let two of the young women in our congregation come live with us after the wedding. I wanted children of my own and I knew Genesis did too. She was scared she wouldn't be able to have children after having the miscarriage but if it was God's will, we would have a few little ones running around in no time.

My phone rang. I didn't know who would be calling me now but I'd get to it later. I had important business to handle now. I turned the phone off without looking to see who it was. I looked around my office to make sure I wasn't forgetting anything and headed out to my meeting.

JUSTICE

Genesis' wedding was in two days. I couldn't believe that the New Year was almost here. So much had happened in the past few months. I had gotten married, Kenyon had almost died, and he'd given me money and made sure the girls would be taken care of. He was in the hospital for a while but he had been released and was doing so much better. He made good on his promise to spend more time with the girls. They spent every weekend with him now. Jared made him painfully aware that he was not going to be a part of their lives if he only felt it would be part time. He told him that either he was serious or he need not waste his time or ours. He would not allow him to hurt the girls. He agreed that they needed all the memories of their father they could have since we never knew what would happen.

Things were good. I was happy and I was getting ready to help my best friend celebrate her new beginning. Like I said, so much had happened in the past few months. Getting ready for this wedding, we had spent a lot more time together. I'd gotten the chance to go and speak to her girls group and had started attending regularly. Jared and I visited on a few Sunday mornings and were considering joining their church. It was a wonderful congregation with lots of wonderful young people. And I was getting back in to the swing of being who God called me to be. I hadn't realized how much I missed ministry and speaking until the night I talked to those girls. They were so attentive; all of their eyes on me, hearing every word I said, wanting to know how to avoid ending up where I had ended up. They wanted to know if

God would have the same mercy on them that He had on me. I assured them that He would. It was just the kind of God He was.

I was at peace. Something I hadn't felt in a very long time. Everyone I loved was healthy. I had all that I wanted but more than that, I had all that I needed. My health hadn't failed me when it very well could have. I guess when you made God a priority He made taking care of you His. I loved Him for all that He had done for me but I praised Him for giving me another chance to get this right. I knew that He could have very well allowed me to die in my mess.

I was headed to get my dress for the wedding. Genesis had called and said they were ready. I was so glad that she hadn't picked those old ugly dresses that most people picked for their bridesmaids and maids of honor. My dress was beautiful and it was flattering. She wanted everyone to be beautiful in their own ways. Tomorrow was pamper day. We decided that we would get our hair and nails and feet done tomorrow, as well as full body massages. She didn't want a bachelorette party. She was saved so I understood why she didn't want the traditional party but we had planned a nice night for her. She wanted to invite Kenyon to her wedding. I told her I didn't think it was such a good idea so she didn't. I never would have invited him to mine had I had one. It was a good thing we had decided to get married in Vegas. It just made things so much easier.

I called the planner and asked if there were any last minute things she needed help with. She asked if I could help her pick up the flowers that were to go to the church so that's where I was headed.

KENYON

It had been five weeks since I was released from the hospital. I was grateful to be alive. I just knew that I was going to die there. I guess the prayers that they had prayed for me had actually worked. Maybe there really was a God. My heart started to feel like it was actually beating again. I had started spending time with my daughters like I promised Justice I would. I was actually having a good time being a father. I had no idea that spending time with them would make me feel like I was actually doing something with my life. More than all of the accomplishments I'd made and all of my education, taking care of my daughters was the best thing I'd ever done with my life. I had missed out on so much but I was redeeming the time or at least I was trying to. I couldn't begin to explain the feeling I got when they were with me so I didn't try. I apologized as best I could to Justice and to Genesis. I tried to make things right. I didn't want to leave here and not say I was sorry for being selfish and causing them unnecessary pain. I called my mother for the first time in years. She told me she missed me. I took my daughters to meet her. She instantly fell in love. I was making things right with everyone in my life. I told my mother that I was sorry for being ashamed of them, ashamed of her, of where I came from. I always sent her money; I just didn't have anything to do with her. I made sure she was taken care of and I thought that was enough. I didn't realize how much pain I caused her too and I didn't realized how much I missed her.

The only relationship I couldn't seem to make right was the one between Addison and me. I still loved him and I missed him but he was still mad I guess. He would call me at least twice a week but things hadn't been the same as before I'd gotten sick. I tried to convince him that there was nothing going on between me and either of them, but he wanted to believe what he wanted to believe and I was tired of trying to change his mind. The last time he'd come over, I had the girls. It was just something else for him to be upset about.

"Why are they here?" he had asked.

I tried to keep my voice calm. "What do you mean why are they here? *They* are my children."

He looked exasperated. "I know that, but what are they doing here? They've never been here before, so why are they here *now*?"

Did he really feel like I needed to answer that? He looked at me like he was waiting for me to answer his question. I reached over and picked Keniyah up and sat her in my lap for effect. "I am getting to know them. I've missed almost two years of their life. I don't want to miss any more time. I get them on the weekends. If this will be a problem, then you should tell me now because until I leave here I will never neglect my daughters again." I could see the tears in his eyes. "What is wrong with you? Why is it that every female you know is part of my life you have an issue with? These are my children, Addison; they can't take me from you."

He didn't say anything, just sat there staring out the window. Maybe he was thinking about what used to be. How he had me to himself and how that was changing. I never thought he would be jealous of my children. I didn't know how to feel about it.

"Maybe you should go and we should discuss this when the girls aren't here," I said to him as I was putting the girls in their high chairs to feed them. When I turned back around from strapping Kenyrah in, he was gone. He hadn't even said goodbye.

ADDISON

I was losing him. I didn't know how to handle it. If it had been the illness that was taking him from me, I think I would have handled that better, but it wasn't. It was all those women in his life. It was Genesis. It was Justice. It was his daughters. He was so focused on them that he had no time for me. I couldn't deal with that. Yes, I knew it was crazy to be jealous of his children but I couldn't help it. I felt like I was on the outside of his life looking in now and I didn't like being in this place. I couldn't explain it to him, not in any way that he would understand, so I didn't say anything. Even when he told me that he wasn't going to neglect his children anymore, I had no words. I didn't know what to say to him. When he suggested that we talk about it when the girls weren't around, that was fine with me. I simply left, didn't even say goodbye. I hadn't wanted him to watch me walk out because I wasn't sure that when I left this time I'd be able to go back. I was in love with this man. He had become my reason for living, he was everything to me and I'd already lost everything else. In my mind, it only made sense that I lost him next. No more goodbyes. I had said goodbye to so many people in my life I was tired of saying goodbye. I didn't this time. I just left. Who knew what would happen?

JUDAH

My baby girl was about to get married. I made it into town a day early and had been able to surprise her at the rehearsal dinner. The look on her face was priceless. I was happy for her in ways that I wouldn't even try to put into words. I prayed that God send her the man that He had always had for her and I believed that He answered that prayer when He sent Axton back into her life. The two of them had grown up together until Axton's father had been transferred over-seas to pastor a church in Germany. They had been gone for years. Axton and Genesis didn't even realize that they'd known each other before until Axton's mother reminded them at the dinner Aurelia had surprised them with.

I was getting ready to give my baby girl away. I had to get all of my emotions out before it was time. I wasn't afraid to cry in public but I was performing the ceremony and couldn't be crying like a father when I did that. I remembered when she was a little girl, how she would always say that one day she would find her Prince Charming and live happily ever after. I didn't believe in fairy tales but I think baby girl had done just that.

GENESIS

Last night had been amazing. It was just what I needed, spending time with the girls before my wedding. Time was moving so fast. Just a little while longer and the wedding would be getting started. I still hated that I hadn't invited Kenyon, but I knew that Justice was right. There was no need for my past to watch me step into my future. He would find out soon enough that I had remarried. I was rereading the vows that I wrote for Axton. I had decided not to have the traditional vows this time around because he was a different kind of man. I wanted this to be nothing like the first time. My father was giving me away today. I was so happy. Every time I thought about it, I wanted to cry. He refused to do so at my first wedding. He was adamant that Kenyon was not the man for me. I wished I'd listened but I had to go through that to get to this. I realized that now. I was thankful for the pain that Kenyon had caused me because it had grown me up spiritually. It made me realize that pain had purpose and for that reason I was thankful to him.

Justice was getting ready to do my makeup. I told her to give me a few minutes. I had a feeling that this makeup job wasn't going to last through the wedding. I was already emotional just thinking about where God had brought me from. In two years I had been spared from having an illness that could have very well taken my life, I'd met the man I would spend the rest of my life with, I'd fallen in line where I was supposed to be ministry wise, my career had taken off and I was better than ever. I owed all of the glory to God. I knew that. I sat in the room and I prayed a prayer of thanksgiving for all of the blessings God had given and would give to me. If no one knew what a miracle looked like, all they had to do was look at me. I was indeed favored.

When Justice came in the room, she hugged me. "It's going to be alright. You're about to become Mrs. Pastor Axton Kyle, honey. Dry those tears. Today is a good day."

She was right. Today was a good day. She helped me with my make-up, my dress and my veil and then went to get dressed herself. Now I was just waiting for someone to come and tell me it was time. My hands were sweaty and I was nervous like I hadn't done this before. Colette knocked on the door and told me it was time to begin. I took a deep breath, thanked God one more time and walked out of the room. This was it.

I met my father at the entrance to the church looking dapper in his tuxedo. "Baby girl, you look beautiful." I felt the tears well in my eyes. I couldn't cry yet. We hadn't even started. I heard the music begin playing and my body was on autopilot. I looked around at all the faces and they all blended into each other. There were so many people there. The church, which seated three thousand people, looked to be full. I didn't remember inviting that many people but when you're marrying a prominent pastor, people would flock to see, I guess. The reception was only for our closest family and friends.

I looked up to the front. There was only one face I cared about seeing and there he was standing there waiting for me. He looked so handsome, better than he'd ever looked to me. I wanted to take off and run to him. I held my composure and followed my father's lead. We reached the front of the church and Axton was crying.

"Who gives this woman to be wed?" asked Elder Fontleroy.

"I do," said my father. He released his hold on me and traded places with Elder Fontleroy. He started the ceremony. It was time to say our vows. We had decided that I'd go first. "The couple has chosen to prepare their own vows. Genesis, whenever you're ready."

I took another look around the sanctuary and then I focused my attention on Axton. "I'm standing here today to become your wife. I suppose that to those on the outside looking in, we make an attractive couple but it's not about that. It's about so much more than that. You make me better. I believe that you are the answer to so many unspoken prayers. It is because of you that I learned to believe in love again. You are everything he wasn't. You are kind. You are love. You are sun. You are light. You are God's goodness in human form. You are a gift, especially for me. And this, this love that we share was orchestrated in the heavens. You are the reason I smile. You are the reason I sing. You are one of the reasons I know there is a God. And you solidify everything that is shaky in my life. You are the other half to my whole. We fit. Together. Puzzle pieces. You made my world brighter and I look forward to every day here after with you. You aren't my first love but you are the only love that matters. You will be my last love. I give you my heart. I give you my hand. I give you my life. I promise you eternity. I am yours now and always."

It took everything in me to get through that without crying. When I was writing them, I had to think of all he meant to me. I had written and rewritten until finally this felt right.

"Axton."

He took my hand, "Genesis, I've never been in love like this before. I've never been in love before. I supposed that maybe I was waiting for you all this time. The first time I saw you, I knew you were the one. I'd dreamed of you. God had given me clear vision of you. I always saw you as an angel and I never realized just how much of an angel you are to me until this very moment. Your beauty surpasses anything I've ever seen. You make me look at God's love in a whole new light. You taught me what grace was. You've shown me what true love looks like. You've shown me what true forgiveness is. You've shown me what the love of God can do for a heart that is willing to let go. I prayed for you, before I ever knew who you were. You are music. My heart sings your song. You are melody, covering me in my sad times. You are finite; I know you'll always be by my side. You are everything I never knew I needed until you were here. You have given me tremendous happiness. You have shown me all the things my eyes had been closed to before. You are mine. I am yours. We belong to each other. Our souls were bound together by God. No matter where you were before, you were destined to be here, with me, on this day, to become one. Together, we are love. We will be love. I promise to protect your heart. I promise to guard you at all times. I will cover you. I promise to be the man that you need me to be always. And I promise to seek God for the directions of our lives. I love you."

We exchanged rings. I sang to him. I had decided that it would mean more if I did and it was a surprise because no one knew I could sing. My father performed the salt covenant and we jumped the broom. When he said that Axton could kiss me, I thought I would melt for sure. This man's lips felt so good. Oh my! We had decided to not so much as kiss because we knew that could lead us down a path we agreed we would not take, but tonight, the gloves were coming off. We left the church and headed to the reception. I was finally Mrs. Axton Kyle.

AXTON

The day had finally arrived. I was getting married to the woman I loved today. No words could express what I was feeling. I was sitting in my suite looking out on the water. It was a beautiful day. It was the start of a new year, the start of a new chapter in my life. Excitement and anticipation filled me. I felt the adrenaline coursing through my veins. I wanted to spend some time alone with God. Quiet reflection was always good my father had taught me. I was thinking of all the things that had happened in the past few years, all of the changes that had taken place. I was thankful to God for where I was in my life, my ministry, my faith and my relationship with a wonderful woman. God had truly been good to me. The boy I used to be hadn't sabotaged the man I was destined to become and for that, I praised God.

I had set the alarm on my phone to go off when it was time to start getting ready and it was going off now. I got up and went over to the closet to get my tux. There was a knock on the door. It was my dad. I was glad to see him. "Are your feet cold yet son?" he asked with laughter in his voice.

"Actually Pops, they've been cold a while but I'm not missing the chance to make this woman my wife. Is this how you felt when you married Mom?" I couldn't recall ever hearing a story of their courtship.

"Well son, I don't think we've ever talked about your mother and I. I didn't actually court your mother. Ours is a different story. I was running a revival and your mother was attending the church where the revival was being held. I saw her and heard God say she was going to be my wife. I told her what the Lord had said and that I'd be back to marry her in one year. I left. We never so much as spoke on the phone A year later, I came back and we were married."

I had no idea. "You're kidding me right? You never even took her out to dinner?"

He looked at me like I was the crazy one. "Son, we lived in a different time. She trusted God and by extension, trusted me. I made sure she never had reason to regret her decision to marry a virtual stranger. I've always loved your mother and I've spent my life making her happy. My point here is that you do the same. That young lady has already been hurt. You show her what the opposite is."

He was right. It was going to be my job to make sure that Genesis stayed happy. I thought about what he said all the way to the altar. Genesis was breathtaking. Literally, when I saw her it was hard for me to breathe. I hadn't realized that I wasn't breathing until Elder Fontleroy whispered in my ear, "Breathe, Pastor." He chuckled. She looked angelic coming down the aisle in her white dress. The top of it was covered in pearls and the bottom was flowing, it followed her down the aisle. She came to a stop standing next to her father. It was like there were just the two of us in the room. No one else mattered. It had been that way any time she was in the room with me; that's how I knew she was the one. I wondered if I'd make it through the whole ceremony without losing it. When she read her vows to me, I didn't try to stop the tears from falling. I had no idea that she felt the way she did but I was glad to know that she willingly gave of herself to me. I was glad to know that she trusted me to be different than what she had previously. Who was I kidding? I was just glad that she had chosen me.

We made it through the ceremony and I was now a married man. I don't know if anyone else ever felt different after they were married, but I sure did. I felt connected to Genesis in ways that I hadn't before. I couldn't wait to *connect* with her later. We partied at the reception. I was glad that we had chosen to have a small reception. We left for our honeymoon in the morning.

As we did our first dance as husband and wife, I whispered in her ear, "Thank you."

"What are you thanking me for?"

I pulled her closer. "Thank you for trusting me enough to become my wife." I kissed her before she could respond. I'd waited so long to be able to do that. I pulled away from her, "Let's get out of here. They can enjoy the party without us."

She looked at me like I was crazy. "You can wait. We've waited this long. Let's finish celebrating. I promise that tonight will be worth every second of the wait. Trust me. You won't regret it." She had that look in her eyes.

"Fine, but I'm holding you to that." I couldn't wait to make love to my wife. I loved the sound of that, "my wife." This was only the beginning.

ADDISON

I missed Kenyon. Ignoring my gut, I called him and asked him to come over so that we could talk. I needed to see him. It was a Tuesday, so I knew that he didn't have the twins. There was no reason he shouldn't be able to come over.

"Hey, what are you doing?" I asked when he picked up the phone.

I didn't want to sound too anxious though so I tried to keep my voice level. I twirled the cord to the phone around my finger absently as I waited for him to respond.

"I'm not doing anything. What's up?" He didn't sound too annoyed with me yet. Hopefully, that could be avoided this time around.

"I want to see you. We need to talk. Can you come over here please?"

I held my breath. I knew that things between us were really on bad terms and I knew that it was my fault. I had to make him understand. I had to make sure that he knew exactly how I felt before he made his final decision concerning the two of us.

"Addison, I'm not so sure that's a good idea."

I figured he would be hesitant after the way the last conversation went. I hadn't talked to him since that day. "Kenyon, please just come talk to me. I want to explain some things to you and then you can make your decision. I just need the air to be clear. I can't leave things like this. I know I've messed up and I'm sorry. Please just hear what I have to say."

I knew that I was pushing it, but I was desperate. I needed to see him. I had already decided that if he wouldn't come to me, I would go to him. Either way, we were going to talk or I was going to talk and he was going to listen. Someone said that desperate times called for desperate measures and I was indeed desperate.

"I will give you one hour and if things get to be too much I'm leaving. I need you to tell me what's going on with you because I'm tired of this back and forth. I'm tired of the drama. I'm just tired. I cannot continue to live like this. I refuse to do that. So, make sure that you're serious about whatever it is you have to say to me, Addison."

That was good enough for me. I'd take whatever he was willing to give at this point. "I'll see you in an hour. Thank you."

I hung up. I got up to straighten up. I didn't know exactly what I'd say when he got there but I knew that it would be the truth and nothing but. I made a pot of coffee and waited for him to get there. I needed to be completely sober for this conversation so I chose to forgo my usual glass of wine. . He was about ten minutes early but I expected that. If he was nothing else, he was punctual.

I went to the door. He looked good standing there. He actually looked better than I'd seen him look in a long time. My first thought was to take him into my arms but that's not what he was here for. I let him stand there for a minute so I could take him in. He had on a slate gray sweater and black jeans. His locs were pulled back into a ponytail and his emerald green eyes sparkled. God, how I loved him.

"Come in." It was all I could manage. He stepped inside and hung his coat on the rack in the corner. He went into the kitchen and poured himself a cup of coffee. I guess in a way this was still home for him.

"Your hour begins now," he said as he took a seat at the table in the kitchen. I guess he wasn't in the mood to waste time. Neither was I. Enough time had already been wasted so I couldn't say that I blamed him. I didn't. I got my coffee and sat down across from him at the table. I needed him to look me in the eye.

"I asked you to come here because there is so much wrong in this relationship. I want to make things right but I'm not sure how to do that. Somewhere along the way, our lines got crossed and we stopped communicating. For that, I want to say I'm sorry. I know it doesn't make things better but I am. There are so many things I want to say to you, so many things that I should have already said and I'm not sure where to start." I stopped talking and looked at him. This was going to be harder than I thought, especially because I was used to moving as I talked. I wasn't the kind of person that did face to face conversations per se. I just talked. I looked out the window and I talked, I walked around the room and I talked, but today I was doing something differ-ent. I was sitting. I was sitting across from him so that he could see that I was serious. So that he could see the truth in my eyes. I needed that.

"So start with the truth, Addison. What has been going on with you lately? I don't even know who you are anymore. I don't like the person that you've become but more than that, I don't like the person that I am when I'm with you. We used to be good together. Tell me what happened."

Hearing him say that he didn't like the person he was when he was with me made me feel some kind of way. I couldn't put my finger on it exactly but it wasn't a good feeling. I wanted to stand up. I wanted to move. I forced myself to stay seated. I took his hand. He started to pull away, but I held him tighter. "I don't know. I feel like I'm losing you. It's like you're fading away from me and I don't know how I'm sup-posed to feel about that. For the longest time it was just you and me. You told me that you were done trying to get Genesis back. I thought that when you signed the divorce papers that it was done for you, but then you started talking to her. And then I come to the hospital and Justice was there and I didn't know what to think. I can't lose you. I've lost everything else that mattered to me and now I'm losing the only thing I have left. I'm losing you." I didn't try to stop the tears that had fallen. I just let them fall. I sat back still holding his hand.

"Where do you think I'm going, Addison? With Genesis? With

Justice? Genesis is engaged and Justice is married. I was trying to make things right. I don't know if you've been sick enough where the doctors thought you were going to die before, but death has a way of putting life into perspective. It has a way of making you realize that you are not immortal, that at some point you are going to die and that you'll be leaving behind unfinished business. I didn't want to die like that. I don't want to die like that. I needed to attempt to make things right. I called Genesis because I needed her to do something for me. I didn't think that Justice would come if I called her but I knew that in all I had done to her, Genesis would be there when I needed her; it's the kind of woman she is. Both of them have moved on. I have been faithful to you since we decided to be together. You can't say the same, can you?"

There it was. I would have to tell him the truth about Jeremiah sooner or later. I thought I'd have more time. I guessed not. "I haven't been. It's something else I'm sorry for. I just didn't know if you were being faithful to me and I wasn't going to be left completely alone. I don't know how to be alone. I don't want to be alone but somewhere along the line, I realized that you were all I wanted. You were all I needed and I cut it off with him. He's pissed about it too. He's burned down my business. He came here and destroyed my home. He's taken away everything that meant anything to me. He's even threatened to take you."

He pulled his hand away from me and sat back. He was clearly upset. "What do you mean he's threatened to take me? Take me where? Addison, what aren't you telling me?"

I sighed. "He said that he would kill me and kill you too. That if I won't be with him, then no one could have me. He said that he would kill you because then I'd have no choice but to be with him."

He stood up. So did I. "Have you called the police? I mean, he's obviously crazy. I don't understand what's going on here. How did you get involved with this guy?"

I asked him to sit back down. I recounted the story of my meeting Jeremiah up until now. When I finished, Kenyon asked me, "Do you still love him?"

I told him, "No." I meant that. I had no love for Jeremiah. We had history and they say history always repeats itself. I was hoping that this would soon come to a close. I didn't know then that's exactly what would happen.

JEREMIAH

They were together. I'd been sitting outside of Addison's house for the past five hours waiting for him to come out. He never did but Kenyon had gone in about forty-five minutes ago. I was tired of playing games with him. Today was the day. I had to end this once and for all. It was driving me crazy, literally. Everywhere I looked, there were reminders of him, reminders of the fact that he'd chosen someone else. I couldn't handle it. I called his phone. I'd call three times and wait for him to answer. If he didn't, then I'd go to the door and I'd knock. If he didn't answer the door, I'd use my key. I still had it. He hadn't been smart enough to change the locks. I wonder if he'd wished he had today. His lover was going to watch him die and there would be nothing that he could do about it. The more I thought about it, the more it felt like the right thing to do.

I dialed his number. I watched him pick up his phone, look at it and put it back down. Strike one. I waited a few more minutes. I called again. It was a beautiful day out, especially for January. Again, he looked at the phone and put it back down. I sent a text: "Don't ignore the next call or I promise you'll regret it." He didn't think that I had it in me to kill him. He was counting on the fact that I loved him. He hoped that I loved him enough to let him go. My love for him only made me want to hold on more. I smoked a cigarette before calling again. I sat there and I watched them talking to each other. They looked like two men in love who were having trouble in paradise. They were brainstorming, trying to figure out what to do to make things better. They had no idea that in a matter of minutes, none of it would matter anymore. I took one last drag on the cigarette and flicked it out the window. I called the third time. I knew he wasn't going to answer. This time he didn't even bother picking up the phone. I pulled out another cigarette, lit it, put it in my mouth. I reached into my glove compartment, took out the gun, opened it and loaded the bullets into the barrel. Five bullets. I'd only need two. One for me. One for him. This was it. I got out of the car and walked to the door.

KENYON

Addison called me and asked me to come over. I was hesitant at first. I didn't have time for more of his games. He sounded sincere, so I agreed to meet him. I told him that he had one hour. That's all I was going to give him. I didn't want to fuss or argue. But, I agreed that we did indeed need to talk. What he had to say would determine where we went from here or if there would even still be a relationship so to speak. I had reached my breaking point with things. I wasn't happy anymore.

I was shocked to hear some of the things he was telling me. I had no idea that this other guy was threatening to kill me. He had kept that a secret. I felt like it was something that he should have told me. I told him to call the police and he basically told me that the cops weren't interested in protecting a gay man involved in what they referred to as a lovers' quarrel. He told me the history between the two of them and I understood things better now. While we were sitting there talking, his phone started to ring. He picked it up and looked at it. But he never answered it. It rang three different times.

"Do you need to take that call?" I asked him. Whoever was on the line seemed to be very persistent. They wanted to talk with him badly or so it seemed. I looked at my watch and told him that I needed to go; his hour was up. I didn't know if I could continue this relationship knowing that he had put us both in danger by being with this other guy. He begged me to give him another chance. He said that he handled Jeremiah. That he was harmless, he just talked a good game. He told me it was nothing to worry about.

That was the last thing he would ever say to me.

GENESIS

Ocho Rios was beautiful. Being Mrs. Axton Kyle was even more beautiful. I was enjoying my honeymoon and my new husband. We'd been here for a few days. It was almost time to go home. Making love to him for the first time was magical. If I said that I hadn't missed the way a man felt, I'd be lying. Now, it wasn't something I'd have to miss ever again. Just thinking about the things he did to me made me blush. I was supposed to be a good Christian girl.

I got up and walked down to the beach. I missed things at home. I was always going so I didn't know how to relax. I was learning though.

"Baby, aren't you ready to go home?" I asked Axton when I found him lounging on a beach bed.

He pulled me down next to him and kissed me. "I am. I thought it was just me. I'm having a great time and all, but I keep wondering what's going on at the church. I keep thinking of all the meetings I could be having or something."

We'd booked opened ended tickets so we decided that we would go home tomorrow. After all, we planned to make our marriage one long lasting honeymoon. I called the airline and they confirmed our flight times. We started packing. I called home. My mother had stayed with Tamika and Shakira.

"Mom, hey, we're having a marvelous time. Yes. Well I called to tell you that we're coming home tomorrow. Our flight gets in at four pm; someone needs to be there to get us."

My mother was going to start. I knew it. "Girl, what do you mean you're coming home tomorrow? You're supposed to be gone another seven days. You really need to learn to relax. These girls are fine. Things are under control."

I laughed. "No Mama, it's not that. We just miss being home. We're both home sick. He's anxious to get home and back to the church and I have a million things I could be doing." She finally gave up when she realized that this was one battle she was going to lose.

My cell had been off the entire time we'd been gone. I retrieved it from the suitcase and listened to my messages. There were a few business related messages, but there was one that concerned me. It was from Kenyon. He was asking me where my church was, said that he wanted, no that he needed to come to church immediately. That was from three days ago. He would be the first call I'd return when I got back to the states. I wondered what was wrong. I had only heard him sound so scared one other time before and that's when he thought he was going to die. Maybe he was really ready to give his heart to God. I said a prayer of protection and comfort for him and went to find my husband.

ADDISON

Jeremiah was calling. I didn't know what he wanted but I knew that this was not a good time. I pushed ignore. He called again. Again, I hit ignore. He sent a text; "Answer the next call or you'll regret it." When he called a third time, I just turned the phone off. I didn't even bother to press ignore. I was on the verge of losing Kenyon because of him. I was definitely not about to answer and talk to him in front of Kenyon.

There was a knock on the door. I didn't answer. I didn't know who could be at my door now of all times, but whoever it was would have to wait. I was busy trying to save my relationship with the man I loved.

I didn't realize that the door had been opened until Kenyon said, "Who are you and how did you get in here?"

I turned around already knowing who would stand there. Jeremiah said "Don't worry, lover boy. I didn't come to see you."

Kenyon looked at me. "Is there something you want to tell me? You've got me over here talking about how you want things to work out and in he walks like he's supposed to be here. You've got to be kidding me, Addison. Do I look stupid to you?"

Sh… This was going all wrong. "Jeremiah, why are you here?" I was pissed. I couldn't figure out how he had gotten in here. "How did you get in my…"

I didn't get to finish. "Shut up, Addison." That was Jeremiah. "I had a key remember? You never changed the locks. Thank you."

He was right. I hadn't bothered to change the locks after we'd broken up. "Why are you here?"

He looked at Kenyon and said, "I was just about to ask the same thing about him. Why is he here, Addison? Did you have him come here so you could let him down easy? So that you could tell him that you were choosing me?"

What kind of game was he playing? He knew that I didn't want to be with him. "Choosing you? Jeremiah, you're delusional. I'm not choosing you. He's here because he's who I'm choosing. I love him. I want to be with him. I told you that before. Get out of my house."

He pulled a gun out of his waistband. Kenyon backed into a corner. He didn't say a word though.

"Oh, that's right. You *did* tell me that, didn't you? And what did I tell *you*? I believe it was something like if I can't have you *no one* can. I meant that."

He was serious. I didn't think he'd had it in him to try to kill Kenyon. "Jeremiah, you don't have to do this. It's not his fault. He didn't know."

He laughed this wicked laugh. I had never heard anything sound quite so evil in my life. "Oh him? I'm not here to kill him. I'm here to kill you. See, the way I figure it, you're right. It's not his fault. It's yours. You played the game. You lost the game. Having him here is just a bonus because there's nothing he can do to save you. He gets to watch you die."

He pointed the gun at me.

JEREMIAH

He looked so afraid. I loved it. They were both cowering in corners like the little girls they were. Addison was begging me to hear him out, saying something about us coming to an agreement, if that agreement was he and I being together there was nothing we needed to talk about.

"Kenyon? That's your name, isn't it? Do you think you can save him?"

I wanted to see if lover boy had any guts. He didn't say anything, just continued to stand there in the corner. I knew he was a punk. I tried to tell Addison he was choosing the wrong man.

"If you don't want to be with me, and you clearly don't, there's nothing left for us to say to each other. Tell your little boy toy that you love him." I was going to enjoy watching them say their goodbyes.

"You're not serious. You're just. You're just mad right now. Calm down, we can all sit down and talk about this like adults."

I laughed. "Shut up. Shut up. Shut up. I'm beyond talking. I've been trying to talk to you for so long, but you couldn't hear me because the only thing that mattered to you was him." I spat with as much venom as I could. "Now, tell him you love him. Tell him you love him and you'll see him in hell. I'm counting to three. If you haven't said it by the time I reach three, you'll never again have the chance. Try me."

I felt like death was standing next to me. I knew that this was it and I didn't care. All the mistakes I'd ever made made perfect sense in this moment. All I wanted to do in life was love him and he wouldn't let me. Now, he had to die. I started counting.

"Kenyon, I, I love you and I'm sorry." He started to move to where Kenyon was.

"You better not move."

They were both crying by now. I was all cried out. All of my tears had his name on them and I didn't have any more left. "Now you tell him you love him too."

Kenyon looked at me. He was unsure so he did as he was told. "Addison, I love you."

I smiled. "Wasn't that just sweet?" Sweet hell; it was sickening. I was ready to get this over with. "Even if you said you were sorry today, I'd kill you. Do you know why?" He shook his head. "I'll tell you why. I'd kill you because that's what you did to me, in every sense of the word. We were supposed to be together forever. I made sure of that when I gave you the disease but no, you went and fell in love with someone else. And every time the two of you were together a part of me died, so that there is nothing left. I thought I'd be satisfied taking everything you cared about from you, but I wasn't. I won't be satisfied until I've taken the one thing you refused to ever give me."

I walked up to him and put the gun right to his heart and I pulled the trigger. He collapsed. I didn't have to look to know that he was dead. I saw Kenyon move to him. I put the gun to my head and I pulled the trigger.

This was how we would end.

KENYON

I couldn't believe what was going on. He had a gun. They were yelling. Addison was begging. Accusations were being hurled like rocks across the room. How did I get caught in the middle of this? I was afraid. He asked me if I thought I could save him. I didn't so I didn't answer. Next thing I knew, Addison was in a bloody heap on the floor. Before I made it to him, there was another shot and there he lie. Lifeless. I went to Addison; I picked up his head and laid it in my lap. I cried and rocked him back and forth. I couldn't think straight, nothing made sense. I looked around for his phone; I needed to call the police.

I found the phone and dialed 911. "There's been a shooting. There are two people dead."

I hung up. I didn't want to talk. How do you tell someone that you'd just watched your lover's lover kill him? How do you form the words to make that make sense? You didn't. I couldn't. When the police arrived, I was still holding Addison. They wanted me to let him go; I couldn't. I didn't realize until it was too late that I wanted to make things work with him. I loved him. This wasn't supposed to happen. This had to be a bad dream.

"Sir, you have to let go." It was one of the officers. He was still trying to get me to let go.

"I want to go where ever you're taking him."

He felt pity for me. I could tell by the look he gave me. "I think you should come with us instead. Were you here when this happened?

Did you see it all?"

I didn't want to tell him that I'd seen any of it. So I told him "No, no, I... I didn't see it. They were like this when I got here. He'd called me to come over. We were supposed to...we were supposed to talk."

That was all the lie I could manage before I broke down. I couldn't believe it. I finally let go of him. I kissed his head before letting go. I felt hollow. I needed to get out of here before I got sick. Suddenly the smell of blood was overpowering. It was such a sweet sickening smell. I got up and ran out the door.

GENESIS

We made it safely back into the states. My mother was waiting for us when we got off the plane. It felt good to be home. I couldn't wait to get back into the swing of things. I scheduled meetings for first thing tomorrow morning. It was Friday. Saturday was my day to do business. I would return Kenyon's call as soon I made it home.

Once we reached the house, I spent some time catching up with the girls. They both had things they wanted tell me. Axton headed straight for the church. He was definitely a pastor at heart. And now, I was officially the First Lady. I went to my bedroom and took out my phone. I called Kenyon's home number first and there was no answer. I left a message for him. I called his cell next. Maybe he was with Addison. I left a message on his cell too.

I turned on the television and the news was on. I turned up the sound because of the caption. It read: Local Business Owner Dies in Murder-Suicide. They flashed Addison's picture on the screen. Immediately I got knots in my stomach. I listened intently waiting to see if they made mention of Kenyon's name. When the story went off and they hadn't mentioned his name. I thanked God.

My phone beeped. It was a text: "Addison is dead. I'm alright. I'll call soon."

I felt relieved. I couldn't imagine coming home to that kind of news. No one deserved to die like that. I didn't care what kind of person they were. They didn't deserve to die like that. I knew that Kenyon would call again when he felt up to it. I picked up my phone and texted him back. "Are you sure you're okay?" It took a few minutes but he finally responded.

"I was there when it happened. I watched him die." I hurt for him. I couldn't imagine watching the person I loved gunned down. How do you get over something like that?

"I'm so sorry. Please let me know when the services will be."

"I will. I just don't want to be around anyone right now. Say a prayer for me. Ttyl." I guess that was the end of the conversation so I didn't bother to text back.

I guess I needed to be trying to figure out what I'd wear on my first day as the new First Lady of St. Luke Memorial. I called Kenyon's cell one more time so I could leave him the address and phone number of our church. I knew a man that could take the most broken person and make them whole again. My ex-husband was indeed broken. I wanted to introduce him to the man that could make everything wrong in his life right again.

I sent a text: "Come to church. Let God heal all your broken pieces."

I waited for him to respond. He, of course, never did.

KENYON

I listened to Genesis' message on my voicemail. I didn't feel like talking. I'd been sitting in my room in the dark since the other day except the day I went to identify his body. It was all still very unreal. The news had been running the story non-stop and the police kept trying to get me to talk to them. I didn't want to. I had nothing to say. I wished they would leave me alone. I told them I hadn't seen anything. They obviously didn't believe me. I knew that my fingerprints were all over that house. I also knew they weren't on the gun. I had nothing to worry about. I'd had the body moved to the local funeral home and would have to decide what to do soon since he had no family left. I was thinking it may just be easier to have him cremated and have a memorial service for him. He was, after all, a respected businessman in the community and it would only be right to give people the chance to say goodbye. I called the funeral home and made them aware of what I wanted to do.

No one could ever make me believe that when a person you loved was gone, part of you didn't go too. I felt like a part of me was gone now and I'd never get it back. Like I'd told him, death had a way of putting life into perspective. The past few days I couldn't help thinking that if I could, I would try to get Genesis back. She was my last hope. I'd tell her how I felt and I prayed that she would listen to me. I prayed that she would find it in her heart to give me another chance.

That was something else I'd been doing lately. I'd been praying. I knew that as sick as I had been it must have been nothing but their prayers that had made the difference and I wanted to get to know their God for myself. I didn't understand how a God who I had always denied still loved me enough to heal me. I was in awe of Him. I'd been reading the Bible too. I took Genesis' inviting me to church as a sure sign that God wanted us to be together again. Maybe He would indeed work things out in my favor, even though I didn't deserve it. I'd go to her church tomorrow. It was Sunday. And my mama always said, "When Sunday comes all your troubles would be gone." I was about to find out if there was any truth to that.

AXTON

It was our first Sunday back. It was our first Sunday as Pastor and wife. We decided to dress alike. She wore a beautiful lavender St. John suit and a matching hat and I wore a coal black Cole Haan suit with lavender tie and pocket hanky. We looked good. She stepped into church looking like every bit of the First Lady. She took her seat at the front where she had always sat. The congregation exploded in applause. I stood up to the podium and I thanked them for welcoming us back with such a rousing applause.

When it came time for me to bring the message, I was nervous. I didn't know why. I stood up to pray like I usually did. I felt the urgent need to pray. As I was getting ready to start, I noticed a man that looked like Genesis' ex-husband walking down the aisle toward the altar. I stopped. I waited for him to make his way to the altar before saying, "Good morning brother. We're glad that you could be with us today. What is it that you need from God on this morning?"

Now I understood the feeling. This service was not going to be your regular Sunday morning service. Satan was going to test me my first Sunday back in the pulpit. He wouldn't win. I had no issue with this brother. After all, I was married to his ex-wife. I wasn't sure that he was aware of that. As a matter of fact, I don't think he noticed that Genesis was the woman in the hat. He looked much better than he did at our first meeting. This was the man she had described to me.

He reached out his hand when I came out of the pulpit to stand in front of him. I took it. "I don't know, I just know that I need God to make some serious changes in my life. I've lost everything that mattered to me. I know it was my fault. I also know that God saved my life for a reason. You prayed for me. Do you remember that?"

"Yes, I remember. We're glad that you've decided to give your heart to God. Now, I can lead you in the sinner's prayer now or we can do it privately. I'll leave that choice to you."

I didn't usually leave the choice to the person on the altar but I felt maybe in this case it was best. "What's the sinner's prayer?" he asked. It was a valid question. Genesis had told me that he was an agnostic when they were married. He flat out refused to believe that there was a God. For him to be here now acknowledging that God had saved his life was a miracle in and of its self. I looked over at Genesis to be sure she was okay. She nodded to me to let me know she was.

"The sinner's prayer is a prayer you say when you are ready to acknowledge that you are a sinner and that you cannot live this life without God's grace and mercy guiding you. It's a prayer you pray when you are ready to acknowledge and accept that Jesus Christ died for your sins on a hill called Calvary. It's a prayer you pray when you're ready to seek forgiveness for the wrongs that you've done in this life, when you're ready to turn away from living a life of sin."

He seemed to understand what I was saying. "Yeah, I'd like to do that now. I'm tired of living my life this way. I lost my wife. I lost my lovers. I lost everything I cared about. I want to get those things back. I believe God could help me with that."

He wanted to get those things back? Well there wouldn't be any chance of him getting Genesis back but I didn't say anything about that to him. "Good. I'm glad to hear that." Again, the congregation applauded. "Repeat after me, Lord Jesus, today, I come before you admitting that I am a sinner. I ask you today to forgive me for all of the wrongs I've done. I'm sorry, Lord. I realize the error of my ways and I acknowledge that I cannot live my life without you another day. I ask you right now to come in and make my heart your home, Jesus. I ask you to show me the way that you would have me to go. I accept your gift of salvation although I know that I am unworthy to receive it. And I thank you, Jesus, for loving me enough to die for me. I acknowledge now that I am saved by grace and covered by your blood. In Jesus' name, I pray. Amen."

When he finished repeating the sinner's prayer, I had the prayer team take him in the back and get his information. It was standard procedure for new converts to have a special prayer after receiving salvation. The Holy Ghost swept the room and we praised God like we hadn't praised God in a long time. I truly enjoyed service.

I stood by the door when service was over, but this time I had my wife standing there with me. Kenyon came through the line and when he got where he could shake hands, he looked almost like he'd seen a ghost. I don't think he had expected to find Genesis standing there. She told me that she was going to talk to him for a few minutes and she would meet me in my office when they were done. I told her that was okay. I watched them walk off together and then I turned my attention back to my members. I had nothing to worry about.

GENESIS

I could not believe that Kenyon had not only come to church but had walked to the front of the church and got saved. I was rejoicing. This was a very good day. I was so happy for him. I was standing with Axton greeting the members when he walked up. We had been congratulated what seemed like a million times. Kenyon looked from Axton to me standing there in our matching outfits and he looked deflated. I couldn't be happy at his distress. I knew that he had just lost the person he loved and I knew that this time was hard for him. I leaned over and told Axton that I'd meet him in his office but I wanted to talk to Kenyon. He had so many questions in his eyes. I'd never gotten the chance to tell him I was married now.

I led him to my office, which now had a plaque on the door that read First Lady. He walked in and looked around. He was unsure of himself. "I'm still the same woman, so why the uncertainty?" He took a seat in one of the wing chairs that sat in front of the desk. I pulled off my hat and laid it on the table in the corner. I sat down behind the desk. "I'm glad you came today." I wasn't sure what to say to him right now. I'd let him lead the conversation.

He looked like there were so many things he wanted to say. "Genesis, look, there's no sense in beating around the bush. I came here today for two reasons: to give my life to God and to tell you that I'm still in love with you and I want you back. I can see now that the second thing won't happen. You could have told me before I came here and made a fool of myself."

He was upset with me? I took a deep breath. "Kenyon, you knew that I was engaged. I did tell you that much. I just didn't tell you when the wedding was. We got married on New Year's Day. You had to know that I was over you. You've known me since we were teenagers. I've never been dishonest with you, even when you were being dishonest with me. I never had a reason to because unlike you, I had nothing to hide. Yes, I'm married. I'm sorry if that hurts you but you did this and I'm thankful that you did."

I knew that would throw him off. I watched the pained expression on his face change. "What do you mean you thank me? Are you being funny?"

I didn't think he would ever truly understand what his indiscretion had done to me, but I'd do my best to explain it to him because he deserved at least that much from me. "I've been praying for you this whole time, that God would touch your heart. That He would make all those hard places in you soft again. I prayed that He would save your life because I didn't want you to die and go to hell, not because I wanted us to work. I've moved on. I had to. You hurt me badly. You took things from me that I never thought that you, as my husband, would take from me. You lied to me, betrayed my trust and you didn't take our vows seriously. I didn't understand it at first and I was angry. I was mad at you, but more than that, I was mad at God. I started to doubt Him. Then one day, my daddy sat me down and he told me that I needed to accept my responsibility in this. He told me that it wasn't all your fault, said that I wanted you to be the one so badly that I ignored all the red flags and I married you anyway, when everyone who loved me told me not to. And you know what, he was right. I'm so happy that God answered my prayers about you. I'm so happy that He did indeed touch your heart, so much so that you came here today and gave it to Him. I'm sorry for all of your losses, but Kenyon, you have to accept your responsibility in all of this too."

I wiped my eyes just as Axton came in the door. I got up and went to where he was. I took his hand and I continued talking. "You see Kenyon; it's not that I don't love you because I do. I always have. It's just that my heart no longer beats your name. I could have continued loving you. I could have stayed and forgiven you. We could have worked on us. We could have moved past your infidelity, past the pain that you caused, past all of the damage. I could have. I know I could have. I also know that if I had, I would have given up everything that God had for me. I could never have become who God wanted me to be all along if I'd continued living in the house your lies built."

He looked at me and then he turned his attention to Axton. "Don't make the same mistakes I did. Take care of her. She deserves the world."

He kissed me on the cheek and shook Axton's hand again and then he left. It was the last time I'd see him. I'd think about him through the years, wonder if everything was okay. I'd get updates every now and then from Justice who had joined our congregation and was leading the Christian women's meetings now. He kept his promise to spend time with the kids. Axton and I would continue to grow the congregation as well as our family. I was expecting our first child in a few months, but that was a story for another day. I had learned to be grateful for all that God had done for me. It just went to show that God's love could indeed bring about redemption, love, and peace.

I looked out the window and thanked God one more time for all that he had done.

CPSIA information can be obtained
at www.ICGtesting.com
Printed in the USA
JSHW020228170623
43396JS00001B/26